firefly

THE GHOST MACHINE

THE GHOST MACHINE

firefly

BY JAMES LOVEGROVE

TITAN BOOKS

Firefly: The Ghost Machine
Hardback edition ISBN: 9781789092240
E-book edition ISBN: 9781789092257

Published by Titan Books
A division of Titan Publishing Group Ltd
144 Southwark Street, London, SE1 0UP.

First edition: April 2020
1 3 5 7 9 10 8 6 4 2

This is a work of fiction. Names, characters, places, and incidents either are the product
of the author's imagination or are used fictitiously, and any resemblance to actual persons,
living or dead, business establishments, events, or locales is entirely coincidental.
The publisher does not have any control over and does not assume any responsibility
for author or third-party websites or their content.

A CIP catalogue record for this title is available from the British Library.

Printed and bound in the United States.

Did you enjoy this book?
We love to hear from our readers. Please email us at readerfeedback@titanemail.com
or write to us at Reader Feedback at the above address.

To receive advance information, news, competitions, and exclusive offers online,
please sign up for the Titan newsletter on our website
TITANBOOKS.COM

DEDICATION

For Lou

the Zoë to my Wash
the Kaylee to my Simon
the Vera to my Jayne

We are such stuff
As dreams are made on; and our little life
Is rounded with a sleep.

– Prospero
The Tempest, Act IV, Scene 1

AUTHOR'S NOTE

The events in this novel take place between the
Firefly TV series and the movie *Serenity*.

1

Hoyt Koestler shaded his eyes and stared westward. Where the gorramn hell was Mal Reynolds?

Fella was supposed to have shown up a whole half-hour ago. Would it kill him to be punctual? Hoyt had better things to do than stand out here in the blazing midday sun waiting for some low-rent Firefly captain to arrive and pick up a package.

For Hoyt, "better things" meant, well, nothing useful. Hoyt Koestler was the kind of guy that devoted as little time as possible to work so he could have as much free time as possible to do as he pleased.

But somebody turning up late to a meet? It was disrespectful, was what it was.

Truth be told, it wasn't Reynolds's tardiness that was bothering Hoyt so much. It was his reputation.

Badger, the broker behind this particular deal, had warned Hoyt about Reynolds. "*Slipperier than a greased eel, 'e is,*" he had said via wave. "You need to watch out for the bloke. Sit down to barter with Mal Reynolds, you'd best count the platinum in your pocket when you stand up."

The description slipperier than a greased eel could equally have applied to the Persephone-based black marketeer himself. It was funny, Hoyt thought, how people tended to deplore in others the behaviors they themselves were guiltiest of. It was even possible Reynolds wasn't as bad as Badger claimed. Maybe a crook like Badger saw only crookedness wherever he looked.

Reynolds was still late, though.

Hoyt continued to scan the horizon, his horse shifting its hooves restlessly beneath him.

The six men he had brought along with him were getting restless too.

"How much longer are we gonna be sittin' fryin' our asses out here?" grumbled one of them, Callum Trinder Jr. He spat a wad of used-up chewing tobacco onto the dusty ground and thumbed a fresh chunk of the stuff into his mouth out of a leather pouch. Trinder's fingers, lips, mustache, and teeth were stained deep yellow. His father had encouraged him to take up the tobacco habit when he was barely five years old, saying it was the mark of a real man. Callum Trinder Sr. had died of mouth cancer at the age of forty, almost certainly as a result of inserting plugs of tobacco between cheek and gum and masticating on them all day long—but that didn't seem to have deterred the younger Trinder any.

"We'll be sittin' here until he comes," Hoyt replied firmly.

"What if he don't come?" said another of Hoyt's posse, Cicero "Nine Toes" O'Malley. Given his fondness for the booze, Nine Toes had come by his nickname in a perhaps predictable way: shooting off part of his foot in a drunken sidearm-discharge incident.

"He'll come," Hoyt said, thinking, *He darned well better.*

All six of the men with Hoyt were heavily armed, as was Hoyt himself. That was in accordance with another piece of advice Badger had given. "Mal Reynolds can be free and easy wiv the gunplay," he had said. "Fings don't go 'is way, 'im and 'is crew are apt to shoot first and ask questions never. Make sure you 'ave backup when you meet 'im, plenty of it, and they're loaded for bear and willing to get stuck in if the bullets start flying. I bloomin' well do."

Now Hoyt heard a faint hiss-whine—the sound of a distant jet engine.

"About *gòu cào de* time," he muttered under his breath. To his men, louder, he said, "Look sharp, boys. We have company. Let's do this, let's do it right, and we'll be back in town and hoisting whiskies at Mama Rosebud's within the hour."

2

The Flying Mule sped across arid plains towards the prearranged rendezvous point.

Zoë was piloting, with Mal up front beside her and Jayne in the backseat. All three were wearing goggles against the dust-heavy air blasting into their faces. Mal could feel the dust crusting up inside his nostrils and fought the urge to insert a forefinger and pick.

"What do we know about this Hoyt Koestler guy anyway?" Zoë asked.

"Badger vouches for him," Mal replied.

"Minds me to dislike the fella already," Jayne said.

"Aside from that, he's spent his whole life here on Canterbury. Fancies himself a wheeler-dealer, but really he's just a middleman. Doesn't greatly care who he works for, but no Alliance ties as anyone knows of."

"Not much to go on." Whereas Mal was resisting the temptation to pick his nose, Jayne had given in to it shamelessly and enthusiastically. "And the cargo?"

"Badger was pretty cagey when we spoke. 'Technical apparatus' is all he'd tell me."

Zoë said, "When Badger's cagey about something, it fair sets my—"

"Nutsack to shrivelin'?" Jayne cut in.

"I was going to say nape hairs to prickling, but each to their own."

"Mine too," Mal agreed. "Nutsack *and* nape hairs. And when I pressed him about it, you should have seen his grin. Sort of grin that means 'You're better off stayin' ignorant, old chum.'"

"Other than 'technical apparatus' he didn't give you a clue?" said Zoë.

"None. But you could tell a lot from how excited he was sounding. Whatever the item is, it's valuable, it's hot, and Badger can't believe his luck that he's going to get his grubby paws on it. Reckon people are making a fortune out of this deal all along the line."

"Yeah," said Jayne. "Shame none of those people are us."

"We'll be gettin' paid the going rate," Mal said. "It's enough."

His tone was faintly forlorn, however. Mal had pushed Badger as hard as he could to increase the transportation fee, but no dice. Badger had simply said that there were any number of other ship's captains he could go to who'd be glad of the employ. He'd come to Mal first because the two of them had history and he felt they had developed a solid working relationship, albeit one that wasn't without its ups and downs.

"Of course," Badger had added, "if you don't want the job, Captain Reynolds, you only 'ave to say. But I imagine that flying rustbucket of yours could do with a few replacement engine parts. Then there's fuel, and your crew can't survive on thin air, can they? Even if you're down to seven, now that the Companion and the priest 'ave buggered off, everybody's still got to eat."

How Badger knew that Inara and Shepherd Book had both quit *Serenity*, Mal had no idea. The man had connections, that was for sure. Lines of communication reaching everywhere, and they fed back news to him from all across the 'verse, information he used to further his own ends and, where possible, feather his nest.

A month ago Book had departed for Haven, Deadwood's moon,

where he was now bringing enlightenment and holy succor to a small settler community. His reasons for leaving were many but boiled down to a desire to keep a lower profile. "I could tell you that, since I am but a humble, honest preacher, I want no part of the violence and criminality which we on this ship seem to encounter at every turn," he had said to Mal. "However, as you should have gathered by now, I am no stranger to violence and criminality, and to pretend otherwise would be specious. I have a checkered past and I have been doing my best to run away from it. Unfortunately, the longer I spend in your company, the more my past is in danger of catching up with me. Therefore for my sake, yours, and everyone else's, it's better if I am elsewhere."

As for Inara, in the wake of events at the Heart of Gold bordello she had decided to return to House Madrassa and take up a position training Companions there. As far as Mal could tell, she desperately missed the closeness she had felt with her fellow Companions, the mutual understanding they had all shared. The death of Nandi, her one-time protégée, had instilled in her a need to be among her own kind again. Or at least, that was her excuse.

"The residents of House Madrassa," she had said, "they're like family to me."

Mal had thought he and the rest of *Serenity*'s crew were also like family to her. Maybe not the happiest of families, but they all rubbed along together and had one another's backs. Obviously that wasn't enough for Inara. Not anymore.

Could he have made her stay? He wondered what it would have taken. There were things he had wanted to tell her, had been meaning to tell her for some while. And he *had* tried to say them, but he hadn't said them well enough, or soon enough, or directly enough.

She'd given him a fair few chances afterwards to change her mind, and maybe he could have.

Trouble was, it had hurt when Inara had told him she was going

3

*Z*oë took her eyes off the terrain ahead to glance over her shoulder at Jayne.

He had finished with the nose picking and had started in on gnawing at a hangnail, gazing out absently at the landscape all the while. The distracted look on his face told her that he had drifted off into his own thoughts. What those might be, Zoë neither knew nor cared to speculate. He was, however, not paying attention to her or Mal, and this gave her the opportunity for a quick heart-to-heart with her captain.

"Penny for 'em?" she said, lowering her voice so that Mal could still just hear her above the thunder of the Mule's turbines.

"Doubt they're worth even that much," he replied.

"You're looking wistful. Like you're missing someone."

"Book? Yep, sayin' Grace before meals, gettin' chided for cussing, always being reminded how the Lord is looking out for me—miss it like crazy."

"I'm not talking about the Shepherd, and you know it."

Mal pondered. "Can't miss someone who doesn't miss you."

"You honestly believe that?" Zoë said. "That she's there on Sihnon not thinking about you every gorramn day? Woman was

15

crazy about you, Mal. Anyone with eyes could see it. Even him."

She jerked a thumb behind her at Jayne, who was still oblivious to their conversation. He was really getting stuck into that hangnail, his brow furrowed like he was working out some complicated math equation.

"And you," Zoë continued, "were crazy about her. Don't even try to deny it. You've been moping around like a dog with a broken tail ever since she left. Know how Wash described you to me the other day? 'The dictionary definition of miserable.' And this is coming from a man who's so bad at reading people he can't even tell when I'm mad at him."

"To be fair, you're mad at him quite a lot of the time," Mal pointed out.

"But there's mad and there's really, genuinely, with-good-cause mad, and Wash can't tell the difference. Anyways, this ain't about us. It's about you and Inara."

"Inara did what was right for her," Mal said, tight-lipped. "Ain't our place to judge. All's we can do is accept the choice she made and move on."

"You first."

"'Sides, I don't recall as it's any of your business, my feelings about Inara. So I'd thank you, corporal, to keep your views to yourself."

"Pulling rank now, huh? War's over, in case you've forgotten."

"I'm still your captain, if nothing else. And as such, I'm inviting you to drop the subject."

"Inviting or ordering?"

"Same difference."

"Then yessir, consider the subject dropped," Zoë drawled, firing a sardonic salute at him.

Mal folded his arms and stared ahead.

Moments later, a bunch of people on horseback appeared in the near distance, shimmering into view through the heat haze. They were stationed beside a dried-up arroyo, near a large limestone outcrop that wind and weathering had sculpted into a rough facsimile of a human skull.

"That's them," Mal said. "Gotta be."

Zoë glanced at a screen on the Mule's dashboard and nodded. "These are the coordinates Badger gave us, more or less."

"Plus, big hunk of rock that looks like a skull. Badger said that'd be our landmark."

Jayne had finished with the hangnail, a hard-won victory, and was on the alert now. "Why do so many of these meets have to happen in the middle of ruttin' nowhere?" he groused. "Why can't we arrange to get together at a titty bar or something?"

"'Cause when you're doing a trade that ain't wholly legit, it's best to conduct your business well away from the public," said Mal. "And from titties."

"I know that. I'm just saying, it'd be nice if we did this stuff somewhere civilized for a change. Maybe even a nice restaurant."

"Nice restaurant?" said Zoë. "You've been spendin' too much time around Simon, Jayne. Next, you'll be drinking tea with your pinkie finger raised."

"You saying the Doc's rubbin' off on me?" Jayne shook his head, aghast. "Uh-uh. No way."

As if to prove his point, he resumed his nose picking once more.

Zoë decelerated, the Mule's engine roar gradually diminishing. She coasted to a halt some twenty yards from the gathering of a half-dozen riders. The Mule settled to the ground, its turbines kicking up a last billow of dust, which drifted sideways in the light breeze.

She braced herself.

Here we go. Showtime.

4

"Now, which one of you fine gents is Hoyt Koestler?" Mal said, clambering out of the Mule and pushing up his goggles. With his dust-caked face and the pale silhouette left around his eyes by the goggles, he looked like a reverse raccoon.

"That's me," said a man astride a pinto gelding. He had a long-distance squint and wore a wide-brimmed leather hat and a striped poncho. "You Reynolds?"

"None other."

"You're late," Koestler said accusingly.

Mal gave a slow blink. "Yeah, well, we'd have made planetfall sooner, only there's a distressingly high incidence of Alliance spacecraft in this neck of the 'verse, and us and the Feds, we ain't on what you'd call speaking terms. Our pilot had to do all manner of fancy ziggin' and zaggin' to keep 'em from detecting us. Frankly, you're lucky we even made it."

At the periphery of his vision Mal saw Zoë clamber out of the Mule and sidle over to stand about a dozen yards away at his three o'clock. She moved casually. It looked like she was almost sauntering. Any soldier worth his salt could have told you, though, that she was now well placed to outflank Koestler and his posse if for some reason they got it into their heads to launch an attack. Her hand hung within easy reach of the sawn-off lever-action carbine strapped to her thigh, the type of customized weapon known informally as a Mare's Leg.

Jayne, for his part, had got out too but remained with the Mule. He was leaning against the side of the vehicle, legs crossed, elbow planted casually on the bodywork. But just out of sight, down in the passenger-seat footwell, was the Callahan full-bore auto-lock rifle he liked to refer to as Vera. If need be, he could snatch up the weapon and start firing in less than a second.

Neither Zoë nor Jayne had been told to assume a combat-ready position. They hadn't *had* to be told. They'd been in enough situations like this that it had become almost second nature. Every precaution had to be taken when there was a decent likelihood of things going awry.

"Where's your ship now?" Koestler demanded.

"Holed up in a canyon about ten miles yonder." Mal gestured back the way they had come. "Seemed sensible to park up there and travel the rest of the way by Mule. If anyone's monitorin' activity on the planet's surface from orbit, no need to go giving them a big, fat, juicy target to home in on. Kinda thought you might appreciate the gesture."

Koestler acknowledged this with a small nod. "Just the three of you?"

"These two's all I need for company. I see you've brought friends too. And none of them short on artillery, at that. You expectin' trouble?"

"Put it this way, Mr. Reynolds. Your reputation precedes you."

"Hey now, I'm a friendly type of guy," Mal said, putting on his most easygoing smile. "I see no reason why we can't conduct our transaction and all of us walk away calm and contented and free from bullet holes."

Whether it was the sheer quantity of firearms Koestler and his sidekicks were toting or the antsiness evident in more than one of them, Mal couldn't say. But he was getting the impression that if he wasn't careful, the handover of the cargo might easily turn sour. A badly chosen word, a misconstrued look, the merest twitch of a trigger finger, and guns would start blazing.

Why, oh why, couldn't life ever be straightforward?

Keeping his expression amiable and his gestures slow and controlled, he said, "So perhaps you could show me the goods?"

Koestler motioned to one of his cronies. "Nine Toes?"

The man named Nine Toes slid out of his saddle and went back to the float-sled that was harnessed to his horse. He detached the sled and activated its low-power antigravity generator. The unit rose with a whirr, to hover wobblingly just a few inches above the ground. He grasped its guidance bar and drew it over towards Mal as easily as if it weighed nothing.

Perched on the float-sled's bed was a brushed-steel flightcase. It was roughly three feet by two feet by one foot, with a carrying handle at either end, and was stenciled all over with the Blue Sun logo.

The logo gave Mal no clue as to what might lie inside the flightcase. The 'verse-spanning corporation manufactured just about every product imaginable. You name it, foodstuffs, liquor, underwear, washing powder, pharmaceuticals, sourceboxes, even weaponry.

Of course, the flightcase's contents might have nothing to do with Blue Sun. Koestler could simply have found an old empty flightcase lying around and used it to store Badger's "technical apparatus."

"Don't suppose you'd mind tellin' me about what's in there?" he said to Koestler. "Thing is, I'm a mite wary when it comes to loading cargo aboard my ship I don't know a whole heap about."

"Well now, there's the difference between us," said Koestler. "Me, I tend not to ask questions. Long as I'm gettin' my coin at the end of the day, anything else is surplus to requirements."

"You must at least have some idea where it's from."

"I'll tell you this much. It was part of a consignment came out of the Blue Sun research and development facility that lies on the outskirts of Riverbend, about a hundred-fifty miles north. A couple dozen boxes just like this one were being shipped off-planet. Through a chain of circumstances about which I do not feel prompted to inquire, one less flightcase made it onto the transport vessel than was listed on the manifest. My guess is a security guard was bribed to look the other way."

Mal tutted. "Whatever happened to company loyalty? Seems like you can't depend on anyone these days."

"At any rate, said flightcase has made its way into my custody, and now I am entrusting it to yours. Anymore'n that, I truly do not know nor want to."

"Figure Badger must've had it stolen to order."

"Again, not my concern, but that seems plausible. Now, Mr. Reynolds, enough of the chitchat. Are you gonna take the thing off my hands or are we gonna stand around yakkin' until doomsday?"

Mal deliberated. There was still time to walk away from the deal. Over the years, he had developed a gut instinct, a kind of smuggler's sixth sense. Sometimes the risk was simply not worth the reward, and he had a strong hunch that this was one of those occasions.

It wasn't as if he hadn't expected he would be handling hot property. A deal brokered by Badger? On a tiny, no-account planet on the Border? The whole setup practically screamed "iffy."

What Mal knew now, however, was that the flightcase's contents had been appropriated from a Blue Sun science lab. That was bad. Worse still was the lab's location. You didn't establish a research and development facility somewhere way, way out on the fringes of the 'verse unless you were carrying out work there that you didn't want decent, ordinary folk knowing about. Why else choose a world like Canterbury if not because it was sparsely populated and there was ample room to conduct experiments and trials well away from prying eyes?

That implied the facility was some kind of black site, home to off-the-books projects, which even Blue Sun shareholders—the vast majority of them, at least—were unaware of. That in turn implied that the Alliance had fingers in this particular pie. Blue Sun and the Feds often colluded on military-related endeavors. Billions in funding went from the Alliance to the corporation's armaments and biotech divisions, and the results bolstered the Alliance's dominance over the 'verse and at the same time swelled Blue Sun's coffers.

The presence of so many Alliance ships in proximity to Canterbury now made sense. Whatever was in that flightcase, the Feds wanted it back and they were going to do their damnedest to ensure it did not slip through their fingers a second time.

"Mal?" said Jayne.

"Yeah?"

"We gonna do this or what?"

Hoyt Koestler and his men were growing impatient too. Mal knew he could not ponder a moment longer. It was poop-or-get-off-the-pot time.

"No," he said finally.

Jayne did a double take. "Come again?"

"No," Mal repeated.

"That's what I thought you said. Only I couldn't believe you actually said it."

"Sir?" said Zoë, frowning.

"It's been a pleasure making your acquaintance, Mr. Koestler," Mal said, "but I've decided we won't be taking that flightcase after all. Badger'll just have to find someone else to fly it to Persephone for him."

Koestler looked peeved. His squint deepened. "That is most inconsiderate of you, if I may say so, Mr. Reynolds. See, I am a man of my word, and if I say I am going to deliver a certain item to a certain person at a certain time, I aim to do precisely that. If I do not hold to my word, then that makes me a liar. Would you have me be considered a liar, Mr. Reynolds?"

"No, and neither would I have myself be considered a reckless fool," Mal said. "The more you've told me about that there cargo, the less I want to be associated with it. If it helps any, you can explain to Badger that I'm the one who failed to meet their end of the bargain. No blame will attach to you."

"We're operatin' on a tight deadline here," Koestler retorted. "Badger wants his item by the end of the week. He's got a buyer all lined up and keen to be in receipt of said item. We have to arrange for another ship to fly all the way out to Canterbury to pick it up, that's gonna cause delays, and the kind of people who buy from Badger don't like delays."

"That's his tough *gǒu shǐ*. My involvement in this matter ends here. All's I see when I look at that box is trouble, and I may not have much in this life but trouble is one area in which I sorely do not lack."

Mal spun on his heel and started walking back to the Mule and the crestfallen-looking Jayne beside it.

From behind him he heard Koestler say, "I'd never have pegged you as a coward."

Mal's step faltered. Then he carried on.

Koestler raised his voice. "I said, Reynolds, I'd never have pegged you as a coward. You deaf or somethin'?"

With a shrug, Mal said, "I call it common sense myself, but if you wish to call it cowardice, that's your prerogative."

There was the loud cocking of a pistol. It was followed by the sound of various other guns being readied. Mal looked over his shoulder to see Koestler pointing a six-shooter at him. Koestler's men were doing likewise, some of them with both hands filled. A bristling array of ordnance confronted him.

"The flightcase," Koestler said menacingly. "Take it, or else."

5

Zoë and Jayne reacted instantaneously to the threat presented by Koestler and his pals.

Zoë dropped into a crouch, unholstering her Mare's Leg at the same time, all in a single, fluid motion.

Jayne, meanwhile, lunged for Vera. Hunkering down behind the Mule, he lodged the rifle's butt against his shoulder and brought his eye to the sight.

Mal turned slowly back around to face the posse. His expression was resigned, even weary.

"And there I was thinkin' we'd get through this without anybody resorting to aggression," he said. "Kinda underscores my point about there being no lack of trouble in my life."

"You're taking the cargo, Reynolds," Koestler intoned. "No ifs or buts. It's your duty. Much as it's *my* duty to see that that flightcase gets spaceborne, pronto. So how's about you just load it onto the back of that Mule of yours, like a good boy, and we'll forget this little altercation ever happened. What do you say?"

"I say you had my attention right up until you called me 'a good boy' and then you lost it again. I'll tell you what's going to happen now, Koestler. You are going to let the three of us get back aboard our Mule and depart, without that flightcase and, more importantly, without so much as a single round being discharged. Otherwise, you and your buddies are going to get into a shooting match which, I grant you, you may win, given your superior numbers, but which not all of you will emerge from unscathed. The lady over there is a trained soldier and, believe you me, no one in their right mind wants to be on the wrong end of her gun. As for the big, goateed fella next to the Mule, I know from experience that he can crack off three shots faster than it takes the average person to loose just one. Added to that he's in a strong defensive position, and you, sitting up on your horses there in a nice, neat row like coconuts at a shy, ain't. In other words, you start this firefight, and I guarantee that this fast"—Mal snapped his fingers—"'most every one of you is going to be lyin' on the ground, minus a goodly-sized chunk of flesh. You really want that?"

Koestler sneered. "I've heard some bluffs in my time, but that one just about beats 'em all. I'll say this for you, Reynolds. You have a solid pair of brass *cojones* on you."

"Thank you. I keep them well polished."

"Takes some gall, to stand there with all these guns aimed at you and tell the fellas holding them that they're the ones're gonna come off worst from the exchange."

"I like to think I'm just stating how it is."

Koestler sighed. "I don't got a hankerin' to shoot no one today. I thought we might do this all amicable like."

"I thought so too. And it strikes me it'd be a mite counterproductive for you to start blastin' away at the folk you want to take that flightcase off of you. We're dead, who you gonna get to do the job in our stead, in the time available?"

"Is this about money?" said Koestler. "Huh? Some kinda attempt at extortion?"

Jayne looked at Mal hopefully. He was clearly thinking the same thing, now that Koestler had mentioned it. Trying to screw a little extra platinum out of the other guy—that was the kind of tactic Jayne Cobb wholeheartedly approved of.

"Nuh-uh," said Mal. "It's about self-preservation."

"Well, if self-preservation's the issue," said Koestler, "how 'bout this? I'm gonna count to three, and by the time I get to three, I want to see those two puttin' down their weapons and you pullin' that float-sled over to that Mule. Otherwise... Well, you know what the 'otherwise' is. One. Two."

He never got to three, because that was when the shooting began.

Who actually started it, was unclear. It was one of Koestler's men, that was all Mal knew. One of them must have got itchy-fingered. Maybe he hadn't even meant to fire. He'd had his trigger on first pressure, and the count of three had made him nervous, and he'd tightened his finger a little further without realizing, and *blam*!

The fact that it was an accidental discharge would account, too, for the shot going wild. The round hurtled in the general direction of Jayne but was off-target by a fair few degrees.

Jayne, however, did not hesitate to retaliate. You couldn't send a bullet at Jayne Cobb and not expect to get one in return.

Or two.

Or more.

In fact, Vera boomed three times in swift succession.

In the same swift succession, three of Koestler's men were hurled from their saddles one after another by bullet impacts. The 12-gauge rounds blew an enormous cavity in each man, blood and gore spraying out behind them and spattering the ground for at least ten feet away.

Startled by the extraordinarily loud gun reports and the deaths that followed, all of the horses bucked and reared, whinnying in distress. Koestler and his two remaining accomplices were too busy staying mounted to return fire, and by the time they'd got their steeds under control, Zoë had already put a bullet in the man nearest her. He slumped forward over his horse's neck, and the frightened creature, feeling the reins go slack, wheeled around and galloped away. Its dead rider flopped up and down on its back as it ran.

That left just Koestler himself and one other, a man who showed signs of liberal chewing-tobacco use.

Koestler drew a bead on Mal with his six-shooter. It didn't matter to him why the bullets were flying or that he hadn't given the order to fire. Bullets *were* flying, that was all that mattered, and in those circumstances you were wise to join in.

Mal, however, had his own gun in his hand now, the long-barreled Moses Brothers Self-Defense Engine Frontier Model B, which he dubbed the Liberty Hammer.

Before Koestler was able to get off a shot, Mal fired.

A neat crimson hole appeared in the center of Koestler's forehead, just below the brim of his hat. His squinty eyes widened for perhaps the first and certainly the last time in his life. He rolled sideways off his pinto, one foot still hooked into a stirrup. The horse, following the example of its comrade, took off at speed, dragging Koestler's limp body behind it. The other riderless horses followed suit.

Now Tobacco Stains was the last of the posse still alive. Sensibly, he dropped his firearm and raised his hands.

"Peace," he said. "I know when I'm outgunned. My pappy didn't raise no—"

Bang!

Jayne shot him through the heart.

Mal spun around. "Jayne? Really? Man was surrendering."

The big mercenary straightened up, slinging Vera over his shoulder by its strap. "Never know, do you? Could've just been a ploy to get us to drop our guard. Anyways, it's tidier like this. What'd we do with him if we'd had to take him prisoner? We'd've had to tie him up, get him back to the ship, feed him, water him..."

"Or," Mal said, "we could have just let him go."

"Hmph," said Jayne, shrugging, as if he hadn't thought of that. "Still, doesn't alter the situation any. We got us our cargo, just as before, and I'm presumin' you've abandoned that addle-brained notion you had of leavin' it here."

Mal shook his head with finality. "Then you'd be presumin' wrong."

"C'mon, Mal!" Jayne protested. "Don't tell me you're worried on account of it's stolen goods. We've moved plenty of that type of thing before now, and you ain't so much as turned a hair. What's different this time?"

"I knew the cargo was gonna be hot. Just didn't know *how* hot."

"What about Badger?" Zoë said.

"What about him?" said Mal.

"He doesn't get his goods, he's going to be less than happy. You willin' to burn bridges with him?"

"Badger'll be sore about it, but his hurt feelings don't bother me none. 'Sides, he'll get over it soon enough. Couple of weeks, a month maybe, and he'll be ready to do business with us again."

"You sure about that?"

"No, I ain't. Could be he'll hold a grudge against us until the end of days. But Badger ain't the only game in town. There's plenty others out there we can work with. Some of 'em might even possess a sense of honor."

"Sense of honor!" Jayne echoed with a snort. "That's what this is, isn't it? After all we've just been through, you're stickin' to some whole dumb I-got-principles thing."

"If by 'all we've just been through' you mean a brief exchange of gunfire that went in our favor," said Mal, "then yes, after all that, nothing's changed. Not my mind, not the situation. That thing in the flightcase, whatsoever it might be, is only going to bring us woe. Being as it was stolen from a Blue Sun black site, the Feds'll be scouring the 'verse from end to end to get it back. Remember all those Alliance ships we had to dodge on the way in? Odds are they're on high alert, with orders to stop and search anyone leaving Canterbury, especially cargo vessels."

"We'll stash the box in one of *Serenity*'s hidey-holes so's they won't find it. Not as if we ain't done that before."

"Can't risk it. All it takes is a Fed inspector who's an ounce smarter than average, and we're sunk."

"Maybe that Koestler guy was right. Maybe you are a coward."

"Or maybe some jobs are just more trouble than they're worth." Mal gestured at the dead bodies lying nearby. "If the evidence in front of you doesn't illustrate my point, I don't know what will."

"Admittedly, this carnage was our doing," Zoë said.

"I'll thank you not to point out defects in my argument, Zoë," said Mal.

"Felt it had to be said."

"Gorramn it, Mal!" Jayne thundered. "You're forever bangin' on about how little coin we have and how much it costs to keep a heap of junk like *Serenity* spaceworthy."

"Don't speak about my ship like that, even if she ain't around to hear."

"Right here"—Jayne gesticulated at the flightcase—"is the answer to our problems. All we gotta do is take it to Persephone, drop it off at Badger's, and we're golden. Money in pocket. A spot of R and R at Eavesdown. Maybe a visit to this joint I know where the booze is cheap and the women cheaper. Is that so bad?"

"It stays and that's that, Jayne."

Mal holstered his Liberty Hammer and vaulted aboard the Mule. He beckoned to Zoë, who traipsed over and climbed into the driving seat. There was a resigned, reluctant set to her jaw. The good soldier, obeying orders even if she disagreed with them.

Mal looked at Jayne. "Coming?"

Jayne bared his teeth and clutched at the air, as though he had his hands around an invisible throat and was strangling it. "No, I ain't comin'! Leastways, not without that flightcase."

He strode over to the float-sled and started pulling it towards the Mule.

All at once he found himself staring down the business end of Mal's Liberty Hammer. He halted.

"You wouldn't dare," he rumbled.

"Try me," said Mal. "I nearly dumped you out *Serenity*'s airlock once, didn't I?"

"Sir?" said Zoë, frowning. "Is this true?"

"Back when we hit that hospital on Ariel. He was askin' for it."

"Why? What'd he do?"

"Another time. My point is, Jayne, I came within a gnat's crotch hair of killing you once. Could be I'm that close again."

"Nah," said Jayne. "You were tryin' to scare me that time, is all. Just like you're tryin' to now." He pulled the float-sled closer to the Mule.

Mal fired.

6

Jayne let out a high-pitched yelp. He patted himself all over with both hands, searching for the bullet hole. Then he glared at Mal.

"Warning shot," he muttered.

"Wrong," said Mal. "Look."

Jayne directed his gaze to where Mal was indicating.

Mal had shot the float-sled's antigravity generator. The small, cylindrical unit now had a charred perforation in it from which sparks and a wisp of smoke issued. The float-sled remained aloft but it was juddering and shimmying from side to side. All at once, with a grinding mechanical moan, it dropped to the ground. The impact jolted the flightcase hard, almost dislodging it from the float-sled's bed.

"Don't go thinking that'll stop me." Jayne bent down, grasped the flightcase by its carrying handles and hauled it up off the float-sled. Judging by his grunt of effort and the way his legs bowed, the thing must have weighed north of a hundred pounds. He began staggering towards the Mule with his burden.

"Zoë," Mal said, "start her up."

"You mean that, sir?"

"I sure as hell do. Jayne ain't loading that thing on, not if I have any say about it."

Zoë hit the Mule's ignition switch, and the hovercraft, with a sudden blare of its turbines, leaped into life.

Jayne quickened his pace.

"Let's go," Mal said.

Zoë engaged reverse and started backing the Mule away as Jayne approached. Jayne broke into a clumsy, tottering run. Zoë increased speed. In no time the Mule was outpacing him, and Jayne, realizing any attempt to keep up would be futile, slowed to a stop. Grimacing in frustration and anger, he stood with the flightcase hanging from his arms.

"Mal!" he called out. "Hey, Mal! I get it. Okay. Come back. Let's you and me talk this over some more."

"No," Mal shouted back. "You want that thing aboard *Serenity* so badly, you get it there yourself. We'll be waiting." He turned to Zoë. "Bring us about and get us back to the ship."

"You absolutely sure about this, sir?" Zoë said as she spun the Mule in a neat one-eighty and pushed the throttle forward. "You're just going to leave him here?"

"Jayne can walk ten miles."

"Of course he can. But what if he insists on taking that flightcase with him?"

"He won't. He'll see sense."

"This is Jayne Cobb we're talking about," Zoë said. "When has he ever seen sense?"

"When it's in his best interests to, and now is surely one of those occasions."

"He can always strap the flightcase to one of those horses. Then he won't have to carry it at all."

"What horses?" Mal said with a glance over his shoulder. "Ain't none around anymore that I can see. They've skedaddled, every last one. Jayne's on his own out here. Nobody's liable to come by he can thumb a lift from. It's hot as hell, and that flightcase ain't no sack of feathers. I reckon he'll last a mile at most, then give up on the whole idea and carry on without it."

"And if he doesn't? If he makes it back to the ship with the flightcase?"

Mal took one last look at Jayne, who was rapidly diminishing to a dot on the horizon, the skull rock looming at his back.

"Ain't gonna happen. But in the unlikely event that it does, there's not a gorramn chance the cargo is comin' with us on *Serenity*. Over my dead body."

"You didn't mean a word you said to him just now, did you? About allowin' him to bring it aboard."

"Not one itty bit."

"So much for a sense of honor."

"What did I tell you, Zoë, about not pointing out defects in my argument?"

7

Jayne Cobb walked.

Carrying the flightcase, he walked. And he fumed.

Gorramn Mal Reynolds. Lousy *qīng wā cāo de liú máng*. Who did he think he was? First of all turning down a perfectly good payday, then stranding a crewmate out in the boondocks, in temperatures hot enough to fry the stripes off a coral snake, and expecting him to cross ten miles of desert terrain lugging a box as heavy as a small man.

When Jayne got back to *Serenity*, there'd be a reckoning, that was for damn certain. Mal would be under no illusion what happened to folks who treated Jayne like that.

The honking great big question was not whether Jayne would reach the ship, but would he get there with or without the flightcase? So far he'd gone ten minutes, he estimated, and already his arms and lower back were aching. Twice he'd had to stop to put the flightcase down and take a breather. He'd probably traveled half a mile, which meant, at present rate, he had at least another three hours' walking in front of him.

That was assuming he didn't get lost, which was more than possible. He was following the furrows left by the downdraft of the Flying Mule's turbines, but this method of navigation would only work as long as the ground was dusty soil. He knew from the inbound journey that the territory ahead got rugged and rocky, and then traces of the Mule would be all but undetectable.

If only Koestler's and his men's horses had hung around. He wished the damn nags hadn't got spooked by the shooting and hightailed it out of there. One of them was all he would have needed. Just one. Was it too much to ask?

On he walked, and sweat stung his eyes and his hands began to cramp from holding the flightcase's thin metal handles. He thought he could hear a weird, pulsing hum coming from the steel container, but this was doubtless the exertion of carrying it making his ears buzz. He began to feel dizzy and so paused once more to catch his breath and recover, shaking out his hands to ease the stiffness in his fingers.

He resumed his progress. Now the muscular strain was spreading from his arms to his shoulders and even up into his neck. His feet were dragging. The lower edge of the flightcase kept bumping into his thighs, impeding his gait. Vera, slung on his back, dug its stock into his spine.

He refused to allow any of these discomforts to get the better of him. He distracted himself with a mental image of himself giving Mal a good licking. He knew that in real life he wasn't going to beat up *Serenity*'s captain. The deed, though satisfying, would be unwise. At best, it would get him booted off the ship. At worst, the other crewmembers would gang up and retaliate; they were that loyal to the man. Zoë, in particular, would see to it that such an act of insubordination did not go unpunished, and if there was anyone in his life who scared Jayne—physically frightened him, to the point where he would go out of his way to avoid riling that person—it was Zoë Alleyne Washburne.

Still, the fantasy of punching Mal repeatedly in the face and delivering the odd kick to his nethers was a pleasant one and sustained Jayne for the next mile or so of his arduous trek.

Thereafter, his various accumulated aches and pains drowned out all thought of violent payback. To add to his sufferings, he was getting mighty thirsty. His throat had started to rasp with dryness. His breathing was becoming labored. Each step took more effort than the last. His head swam, and the flightcase seemed to be getting heavier and heavier. What was in it anyway? The lid was code-locked, so you couldn't open it without either knowing the password or using a crowbar. The contents felt substantial. Maybe too substantial to be simply "technical apparatus." Could Badger have been lying? Could it be bars of platinum instead?

Even if it was, Jayne was sorely tempted to set the flightcase down and carry on unencumbered.

But Jayne Cobb was nothing if not determined. "Pigheaded" his mother used to say. As in "That boy is so pigheaded, he could give obstinacy lessons to a hog." Whether she meant it as praise or insult was unclear. Radiant Cobb, though she doted on her two sons, was known to chide them as much as encourage them. Nevertheless, Jayne always chose to take the remark as a compliment. Pigs were pretty smart animals, after all. Smarter than a fair few humans he'd met.

After a further half-hour, Jayne was close to admitting defeat. His upper body was screaming with pain, every muscle a tortured knot. His legs could barely move. His lungs felt red raw. He could scarcely feel his hands.

To add to all that, there were no visible Flying Mule tracks anymore. He was still heading in what he thought was the right direction, westward, but the sun kept dancing around in the sky, refusing to stay still so that he could take a bearing.

Now and then he became aware of that strange throbbing hum again. It appeared to originate from inside the flightcase, but he wasn't sure about that. This only served to increase his disorientation. Possibly the sound didn't exist anywhere outside of his own head.

Then a voice spoke to him.

"Goin' somewhere, son?"

Puzzled, Jayne halted and looked around.

Whoever had just addressed him, they were close by. Yet there was nobody in sight. Nor was there anywhere that a person could be hiding. No shelter, no vegetation, just barren, craggy landscape undulating in all directions.

To make matters worse, the voice had been familiar. Intimately familiar. A woman's voice. It had sounded just like…

Jayne shook his head. *Nah. Couldn't be.*

A hallucination, that was all. His mind playing tricks. Not surprising, under the circumstances. The strength-sapping heat. The brainpan-pounding sun. The weight of the flightcase.

With a supreme effort of will, Jayne trudged onwards. He was going to do this. He was going to get to *Serenity*. He couldn't wait to see Mal's face when he showed up at the ship, flightcase and all. How astonished and ticked-off the man would be. That alone would make the ordeal worthwhile. Mal could be so darned smug. It was time somebody reminded him that others in the crew deserved their say. It wasn't all about Captain Reynolds. Maybe if he wasn't such a stuck-up, arrogant son of a bitch, Inara Serra would have stayed on. If Mal loved the woman as much as he seemed to, how come he'd let her go? And she a Companion and all. Couldn't he have just *paid* her and she'd have hung around? That was what Jayne would have done.

"Jayne, boy, I said where you goin'?"

This time, the voice was so loud and clear that Jayne couldn't help but give a startled cry. He let the flightcase fall to the ground. It narrowly missed landing on his toes.

"Momma?" he asked, looking around. "That you?"

"Course it's me," said Radiant Cobb. She was standing to his left, her head cocked to one side. "Who else would it be?"

Jayne gaped. It was his mother all right, in the flesh. A tall, angular woman, she looked like she had been assembled out of parts, like a scarecrow. Her head was too big for her neck, her shoulders too narrow for her hips, and her legs too spindly for the large feet attached to their ends. Her broad-bridged nose made it seem as though her eyes were set too close together, while her mouth was pinched and narrow, with a faint, downy wisp of a mustache on the upper lip. Nobody would ever call her beautiful but she was, without doubt, arresting-looking.

"But... *zěn me le*," Jayne said. "What are you doing on Canterbury? Whyn't you tell me you were comin' out here?"

"Canterbury? You all right in the head, Jayne? Why would I be on Canterbury? Ain't never left Sycorax, not once in my life."

"Yeah, but this is..." Jayne blinked as a second figure emerged into view. "Matty? You're here as well?"

His younger brother nodded shyly. "Hey, Jayne. Long time, no see. How're you doin'?"

"Never mind me," said Jayne, "how are *you*?"

Matty spread out his hands. "Pretty good, actually. Damplung's cleared up, would you believe. Doctor's given me a clean bill of health."

Matty certainly looked chipper. Jayne couldn't recall a time in recent memory when his brother's complexion hadn't been sallow or his eyes saddled with dark gray bags or his features gaunt and haunted. Ever since the pernicious respiratory disease got him in its clutches, Matty had gradually, steadily, been eaten away by it like a sandcastle eroded by the incoming tide.

Now, though, he had color in his cheeks and he appeared to have put on several pounds. More to the point, he wasn't wheezing or coughing. On the last occasion Jayne had visited home, Matty had been bedridden and barely able to talk, his condition had got so bad. Every breath had been a wet, sticky rattle, and all around him there had been heaps of tissues sodden with bloody phlegm and sputum.

This Matty, the one in front of him, was a whole different proposition. His breathing was normal, unimpaired. He was standing ramrod straight, positively exuding vigor.

Ordinarily damplung was a death sentence. This? This was like some kind of miracle.

Jayne moved to embrace his brother. As he did so, his foot hit a rock and he stumbled, collapsing to his knees.

When he looked up, both Matty and Radiant Cobb were gone. Vanished without a trace.

"Gorramn it!" Jayne growled.

Of course they were gone. They had never been there in the first place. It had just been an illusion brought on by dehydration, exhaustion, and pain, like one of those whatchemcalls, those visions you saw that weren't real. A mirage.

Jayne staggered to his feet.

"You're in danger of losing it," he said to himself out loud. "Don't. Keep your head together. You're almost halfway there. Got another six, maybe only five miles to go. Ain't far. Pick up that box and start walking again. One foot in front of the other: that's how it's done."

He hoisted up the flightcase again, ignoring the protests from the muscles in his arms and back. He set his gaze towards the horizon and urged his legs into motion.

The sun glared pitilessly down.

The landscape stretched before him, bleak and bare.

Jayne Cobb walked.

8

"Been best part of five hours now," Zoë said. "Don't you reckon we should be sending out a search party?"

Standing beside her on *Serenity*'s cargo ramp, Mal gazed across the vista of scrubland. The sky was just starting to purple in the east. Not a thing moved out there apart from a couple of stunted ironwoods shivering in the late-afternoon breeze and a few bundles of tumbleweed rolling from hither to yon.

"I'm not worried," he said. "Come nightfall, then maybe we should start looking. Meantime, we'll give Jayne the benefit of the doubt."

"What's this all about, sir? If I might ask. You aren't intending to take the cargo aboard even if Jayne can get it back here. So what's the point of the exercise?"

"Just remindin' him how things work around here. Man's a loose cannon at the best of times and I don't know as I can always count on him."

"Like after Ariel." During the trip back in the Mule, Mal had explained to Zoë how Jayne had betrayed them on that Ariel job, how he'd attempted to sell out Simon and River Tam to the Alliance. The bounty on the two fugitives' heads had got the better of him.

"Exactly," he said. "Thing about Jayne is he's greedy. If there's money to be had, he'll grab it, not caring where it comes from or who he has to hurt to get it."

"So this is to teach him a lesson."

"That's the general idea. He doesn't get the flightcase here, maybe he'll learn not to question my decisions next time. Same goes if he does but still has to leave the flightcase behind on Canterbury. Call it a rap on the snout, like when you're housetraining a puppy."

"He'll resent you."

"But he'll also know who's boss," Mal said. "That's the main thing. We're down by two crew. Now more than ever we need Jayne Cobb. We need our strongarm guy, but we need to know we can trust him too. Whatever the outcome of this little episode, I've ensured Jayne Cobb remembers his place in the pecking order. It's a win-win."

"Kind of a risk, though, don't you think? Pissing Jayne off means he might up and quit. Then you've lost another crewmember."

Mal made a seesawing motion with his hand. "It's a gamble but I reckon the odds are in my favor. Jayne's got a simple outlook on life. There's some as even call it basic. His kind like to do as they're told, they like a hierarchy; they just don't like admitting it."

"You're playing him."

Mal nodded. "And he doesn't even realize."

"Please don't take this the wrong way, sir, but you are one devious *gè zhēn de hún dàn*."

"I know, right?" said Mal with a grin.

As Zoë returned her gaze to the landscape outside, Kaylee breezed across the cargo bay from the engine room.

"This a private staring competition, or can anyone join in?" she said brightly.

Mal made a be-my-guest gesture.

"Still no sign, huh?" Kaylee said, looking out. "Poor Jayne. Gotta be forty degrees in the shade. He'll be a cinder by the time he gets in. Don't you think it was a bit mean, Captain, leaving him to make his own way back?"

"Mal was just telling me it's for Jayne's own good," said Zoë.

"How do you figure that?"

"Beats me, but the captain has his own twisted logic for it."

"Someday, Kaylee, if you're ever in charge of a ship, you'll understand," Mal said.

"I know that if I'm ever in charge of a ship, I wouldn't abandon a crewmember on a whim."

"Weren't no whim."

"And," Kaylee added with a slight curl to her lip, "I wouldn't allow other crewmembers to go their own way neither."

"Allow?" said Mal. "If you're referrin' to Inara—and I don't doubt that you are—she was never officially part of the crew. She was free to come and go as she pleased. All of you are."

"Still and all, ain't it a captain's duty to keep his or her people together?"

Mal sighed. "You ever going to stop bugging me about Inara?"

"Not just Inara," Kaylee said. "Book too. But yeah, mostly Inara. It don't feel right without her aboard. I'm sure I'm not the only one who's of that opinion. Inara was the soul of this crew. She kept us on the straight and narrow, or at least as close to the straight and narrow as we're ever likely to get. Since she went, life's all been a bit wayward and rudderless, us driftin' from one job to the next without much rhyme or reason, and without much financial gain either. I apologize if I'm speaking out of turn. I'm just expressing how I feel."

"No, you go right ahead and vent, Kaylee."

Mal's remark was sarcastic but Kaylee chose to view it as an invitation.

"I'm not telling you what to do, Mal, but if I was you, I'd be making Sihnon my next port of call. I'd go direct to House Madrassa and I'd throw myself at Inara's feet and beg her to come back. Then things'd be the way they used to be again."

"You ain't me, and besides, you must know me well enough by now to know that I'm not the begging type."

"More's the pity."

"Don't get me wrong, Kaylee." Mal's attitude softened just a fraction. "I realize you and Inara were close. Not having her around anymore is hard on you. It's just, there's some situations that work and some that don't, and for Inara, being on this ship had clearly become one of those that don't."

"You could have made it work," Kaylee said accusingly.

"Me? How? Leaving was Inara's call."

"Keep tellin' yourself that, Mal. Maybe someday you'll start believing it."

Mal was set to deliver a sharp rebuke when all at once Wash's voice sounded over the ship's intercom system.

"You guys keeping lookout for Jayne from the stern," Wash said from up on the bridge, "you may want to turn your attention bow-wards. I've just spotted a big, weary-looking fella out that-a-way, staggering towards us. Description matches that of one Cobb, J., known thug and reprobate."

Mal hit the intercom switch and spoke into the mic grille. "He carryin' anything? Can you see?"

"Apart from a sourpuss look on his face, nothing," came the reply.

"Huh," Mal said, mostly to himself. "Knew it."

He started down the ramp, Zoë and Kaylee following.

"He's coming from totally the wrong direction," Zoë observed. "The meet was due east of here, and the ship's facing west."

"Must've lost his way and gotten all turned around," Mal said.

They skirted around *Serenity*'s flank, heading for her bow end. Ahead, descending from the crest of a low rise, Jayne was visible, silhouetted against the sinking sun. He moved ploddingly, clumsily, like a zombie, seeming not to be aware or care where he was placing his feet. As he drew nearer, the others could see that his face was sunburned and that his T-shirt bore crusty white rings of dried perspiration.

All of a sudden he tripped and fell flat on his face. Mal, Zoë, and Kaylee rushed to his side. Zoë reached him first and turned him over onto his back.

"Jayne? Jayne? Talk to me. Jayne!"

Jayne's eyes rolled. His parched, cracked lips moved to form words. "Whozzat?" he mumbled. "Zoë?"

"And me, Jayne," Kaylee said. "And Mal. You're back at *Serenity*. You made it, no thanks to *someone*." She shot a reproachful look at Mal, who at least had the decency to drop his gaze.

"Kaylee, go fetch the Doc," Zoë said.

"Sure thing." Turning back to Jayne, Kaylee said, "Simon's going to take care of you. You're going to be fine. You'll be in good hands." Then she hurried off.

Jayne lapsed back into unconsciousness.

"Proud of yourself?" Zoë said to Mal. "Look at the state of him."

"Like Kaylee said, he's going to be fine."

Kaylee returned moments later with both Wash and Simon in tow, the latter toting his medical bag.

Simon gave Jayne a quick but expert examination. "Heatstroke. Doesn't look too severe. Man of Jayne's stamina can withstand a lot. Still, we need to get him indoors pronto. Everyone, grab a limb."

Mal, Zoë, Wash, and Simon hauled Jayne to the ship. Kaylee led the way, carrying Vera. She held the rifle away from her body, stiffly, like it might come alive at any moment and bite her.

In the infirmary, they laid Jayne out on the med couch with his feet raised on a pillow. Simon then got to work inserting a saline drip to rehydrate Jayne and raise his electrolyte levels.

"Well, ain't no point us hangin' around on Canterbury much longer," Mal said. "Wash? Get *Serenity* prepped for dustoff. We leave in ten."

Briefly Jayne's eyes opened again. He moaned as if in agony.

"Doc," he said to Simon, "I feel like seven sackloads of goat crap."

"It's okay, Jayne," Simon said. "Just relax. Give the saline time to work its magic."

Jayne turned to Mal, blinking as if trying to bring his captain's face into focus. "Mal, hate to ask, but can we leave gettin' spaceborne till morning? Way I'm feeling, I don't know as I can handle the gees right now."

"Wash can make takeoff nice and gentle," said Mal. "Can't you, Wash?"

"A feather on a breeze," Wash said, then frowned. "Something like that, at any rate. There may be a better analogy."

"Actually, Jayne has a point," Simon said. "In his current condition, the ship's acceleration won't do him any favors. He should be well enough by morning to handle it."

"I'm with Simon," said Kaylee.

"There's a surprise," Mal muttered under his breath.

"When it comes to medical matters, the Doc knows best," Kaylee went on, oblivious. "I vote we wait till morning."

Zoë chimed in. "Can't see the harm, Mal. Can you? Jayne's due some consideration, I feel."

Mal looked around the room. A captain had to pick which battles to fight and which to retreat from. Losing this one wouldn't be such a bad thing, tactically speaking. You couldn't win them all, and people were apt to resent it if you tried. Sometimes compromise was a victory.

"Okay," he said. "Morning it is."

Jayne sank back onto the med couch with a sigh of relief. His eyelids fluttered shut.

"And now," said Simon, "if I could have some elbow room to work…"

The others took the not-very-subtle hint and left.

9

"Jayne better make a full recovery, Mal," Zoë said as they re-entered the cargo bay. "That's all I'm going to say."

"Yeah," Kaylee said.

"He will," Mal insisted. "Man's harder to kill than a cockroach. Since when has there been all this love for Jayne Cobb anyway? He's the one we all make jokes about. The one we bitch to each other about."

"That's beside the point," said Zoë. "He's one of us. Part of the team."

"Many's the time I've wished Jayne hadn't said something he'd just said, or would even lose the power of speech altogether," said Wash. "But still, I wouldn't want him dead."

Mal rolled his eyes. "*Et tu*, Wash? For the record, I don't want Jayne dead any more'n you or anybody else does. In this case, I also didn't want him to get away with disobeying me. Sets a bad precedent. We got him back, at least, and Simon seems to think the prognosis is good. So all's well that ends well."

"Still don't have a cargo, do we?" said Wash. "So this entire trip has been for nothing."

"I tell you what," Mal retorted hotly, "you're so keen to be the fella who gets to make the decisions, go find yourself a ship of your own."

Wash recoiled a little. He was uncomfortable with conflict and hostility. He left that sort of thing to his wife.

"Yeah, well," he said, "maybe I'll do just that."

"And maybe I will too," said Kaylee.

Both of them marched off in different directions, Kaylee still carrying Vera in that gingerly fashion.

"Congratulations, sir," Zoë said dryly. "You're managing to alienate practically everyone around you. Quite the achievement."

"You're going to flounce out too, Zoë? Feel free. Go right ahead."

"As a matter of fact, I will." Zoë performed a smart about-turn and disappeared off after Wash.

Mal's stance—pursed lips, clenched fists, jaw jutting—said, *Good riddance to the lot of you.*

But his eyes told a different story. A sorrier one.

Even when you lost a battle on purpose, you still lost.

10

Sundown came, and darkness draped itself across the landscape of Canterbury like a funeral shroud. Cicadas began to chirrup and bats to flit. Scorpions and prairie dogs crawled from their lairs and set about their nocturnal hunting.

Serenity sat, her hull plates ticking softly as they cooled, the heat they had absorbed during the day dispersing into the air.

Around midnight, all the crew were asleep. The plan was to take off at first light. Where they would be traveling to next was anyone's guess. It certainly wasn't Persephone. What would be the point going there when they didn't have Badger's item on board?

Simon had left Jayne in the infirmary. In his view, all Jayne needed was a good night's rest. By the morning, the big man ought to be up and about, or at the very least conscious.

As the hour ticked past twelve, Jayne's eyelids snapped open.

He took a cautious look around. Listened out.

Then he heaved himself up off the med couch. Rather than detach himself from the intravenous drip, he instead unhooked the bag of saline solution from its stand and lodged it down the front of his T-shirt, along with most of the connecting tube. Moving stealthily through the ship on stockinged feet, he let himself out through one of the personnel doors. Outside, he pulled his boots on. A bright full moon—and a secondary, lesser moon—gave him plenty of light to see by as he retraced his steps towards the low rise from which he had descended earlier in the day.

He soon found the spot where he had deposited the flightcase. He had wedged it in a crevice between two rocks.

It had been a hell of a gamble, leaving the flightcase out here so that he could retrieve it later. If *Serenity* had got spaceborne straight away as Mal had originally intended, then all that walking, all that effort, would have been for nothing.

Jayne's shamming had done the trick, however. He *had* had heatstroke, that was for damn sure, but not nearly as bad as he'd made out. Enough to worry the Doc, and the rest of the crew, but most of it had been him putting on a whole weak-and-feeble act, right down to that little "accidental" stumble of his. The whole thing had been a pretty decent piece of fakery, even if he did say so himself. He could've had a career on the stage.

Lifting up the flightcase—which was just as gorramn heavy as he remembered—he made his way back to the ship.

On board again, Jayne headed straight for his bunk. It was no mean feat manhandling the flightcase down the ladder without causing a disturbance, but he succeeded.

He then set about secreting the thing.

Jayne kept a small arsenal of hand weapons in his bunk. They were cached in a wall recess concealed by a length of cloth.

This, however, was not the only hiding place in the cabin. He undid the screws on a deck plate and pried it up to reveal a crawlspace below. He slid the flightcase in at an angle. There was just enough room for it.

Replacing the deck plate, he smiled to himself.

Neatly done, he thought. Mal didn't want the flightcase on the ship. Jayne did. Simple solution: sneak it aboard when no one was looking. Then, later, Jayne would send Badger a private wave, telling him he had his precious piece of "technical apparatus" and he'd get it to him at the soonest opportunity. A grateful Badger would pay the full transportation fee, and Jayne wouldn't even have to share the money with anyone. He'd consider it ample reimbursement for the hell he had gone through during the afternoon.

His eyes fell on Vera, propped up in one corner. Must've been Kaylee who'd placed her there. Girl didn't know how to treat a weapon right. You didn't leave a rifle leaning against a wall like that. Wasn't good for it, nor respectful.

Jayne couldn't put Vera back in her proper place in the recess, however. If he did, someone might cotton on that he'd visited the bunk during the night, and that might give the whole game away. Though it pained him, he would just have to leave Vera where she was.

He made his way back to the infirmary. There he rehung the bag of saline solution on its hook before lowering himself down onto the med couch.

Feeling very pleased with himself, Jayne closed his eyes.

Soon he had sunk into slumber and was sleeping the sleep of the righteous.

Meanwhile, up in his bunk, the flightcase continued to emanate the low, subtle hum that Jayne had detected earlier and dismissed as a figment of the imagination. The sound waxed and waned, coming in waves. Little by little it began to penetrate the ship, spreading to all corners like an insidious, monotone song, just at the threshold of audibility, droning, droning, droning...

11

The shuttle that Inara had once rented from Mal was empty. Gone were the swags of silk drapery, the curved couches, the ornate hanging lamps, the assortment of exotic furniture, the richly patterned rugs. She had taken all of that with her, and what remained was just the plain, utilitarian interior: bulkheads, metal floor, control console. It could have been any shuttle, attached to any ship. Nothing special about it.

Yet she had left something behind nevertheless.

Mal raised his nose and inhaled.

Yes, there it was. A whiff of incense. So faint it was barely there, but still just detectable. A hint of roses to it, and something richer, headier. Patchouli, maybe.

The scent lingered like the echo in a concert hall after the orchestra has played the final notes of a symphony. Mal stood there, reveling in it.

This had become something of a morning ritual for him. Before anybody else was up, he would rise and go to the shuttle and take a few moments to breathe in the smell he had come to associate inextricably with Inara Serra.

It made him happy. It made him sad.

It made him, above all else, mad.

Mad at her.

Mad at himself.

Kaylee had been right yesterday when she'd said the crew were wayward and rudderless at present, drifting. They were. Mal wasn't actively pursuing work. He was taking only whatever happened to come his way: there wasn't any long-term plan. Maybe there never had been, but all the same, before now there'd always been a certain level of consistency. Not great consistency but consistency nonetheless. One job had usually led to another.

Having a Companion on board had helped. A Shepherd likewise. They had brought some much-needed respectability to *Serenity*'s crew, as well as some much-needed cover for Mal's shadier dealings.

Both of those people were gone now, however, and with them, it seemed, his work ethic.

There were the Tam siblings, of course. Simon Tam, with his private education and his cultured manners, was definitely classy.

But Simon came with a problem attached. His sister.

If Simon was an asset, River was the opposite, a liability. The Feds wanted her badly. Having conducted secret medical experimentation on her before Simon was able to free her from their clutches, they were keen to find their lost sheep and bring her back into the fold. They were after a return on their investment, and if they ever located River, it would doubtless not go well for the crew of the ship that had been harboring her.

In other words, for all the help having a doctor aboard was, having his sister aboard too was a hindrance.

But she might not be. Mal had plans for River. With her superhuman skill set—in particular her ability to read minds and her extraordinary combat prowess, which was only just starting to reveal itself—she could well become his ace in the hole. Maybe *she* was his way out of the doldrums. If he could only figure out a way of getting her to pitch in with the rest of the crew, find some suitable role for her aboard *Serenity*, it could turn things right around. Of course, he'd have to do that somehow without exposing them to further unwanted Alliance scrutiny…

"Or you could just leave her be to get on with her life," said Inara.

Mal nearly jumped out of his skin.

He whirled around.

There she was, sitting on one of the curved, scarlet-upholstered couches.

No. Inara never just *sat*. She was *poised* on the couch, straight-backed, her hands folded in her lap. A study in elegance and self-possession, like a noblewoman in an Earth-That-Was oil portrait.

"River's just a teenage girl," Inara continued. "A troubled one, to be sure, but the Alliance scientists made her a victim. If you use her—take advantage of her—you'll be making her a victim all over again, Mal. You'll be as bad as the Alliance."

"Inara…" Mal breathed. "What are you…? I mean, how…?"

"Come. Sit." Inara patted the couch beside her.

Numb, unable to fathom what was happening, Mal did as he was told.

Inara took his hand in hers. Her touch was soft. Mal's own hand seemed as coarse as sandpaper in comparison.

He noted a ring on her left fourth finger. A gold band. That was new. Hadn't seen that one before. Inara wore rings aplenty but never on that finger.

"Look at me," she told him.

Mal raised his head and looked. Those dark brown eyes, so wise, so full of compassion. *Wǒ de tiān a*, how he'd missed those eyes. How he'd longed to see them again.

"Inara, have you come back?" he said, hardly daring to believe it. "For good?"

"What do you mean? I haven't gone anywhere, Mal."

"Sure you have. Sihnon. House Madrassa. Remember?"

"Silly! I haven't visited House Madrassa in years. We're here. You know where this is."

She swept her arm in a semicircle, bidding Mal to take in their surroundings.

It was a spacious living room in a house perched on a hillside overlooking a broad, verdant valley. Large picture windows offered uninterrupted, panoramic views of treetops, a river, and the snow-capped peaks of a mountain range in the far distance. Out on the balcony, a pair of small, exotic birds twittered in a cage, while from the forest below came a massed chorus of wild birds, singing their joy to the sky.

The furnishings were familiar, some of them. They were Inara's from the shuttle. But there were additions: some gauzy lilac-colored curtains that billowed in a soft breeze, a host of Buddha statues all cross-legged and plumply smiling, an indoor fountain that trickled merrily, a dining table with beaten-copper dishes and slender glass stemware.

"We expectin' guests?" Mal said, noting that the table was laid for four.

"Guests?" Inara laughed her delicate, musical laugh. "Oh Mal, sweetheart, you're such a kidder. These 'guests' of yours are right outside, playing. It's nearly lunchtime. I'll call them in."

She rose and glided over to the windows. Somewhere close by, just outdoors, Mal could hear two piping voices. Children's voices. They were giggling together, sharing some joke.

As Inara opened her mouth to speak, Zoë strode in.

"Sir? There you are. I've been looking all over."

Mal peered up at her blankly.

"Sir, are you okay? What are you doing in here anyway?"

Mal took stock. He was in the shuttle, squatting on the floor. The room with the view had vanished. So had Inara.

What had happened to that house? That glorious, heavenly *home*?

"I'm… I was just carrying out an inspection," he said, getting up. "Checking everything was shipshape."

"Looked to me like you were sitting on your ass daydreaming."

"To the untrained eye, maybe. What's up? Why d'you need me?"

As if in answer, a piercing shriek resounded through the ship. It appeared to originate from the sleeping quarters, and it was full of panic and terror.

"That," Zoë said. "That's what's up."

"River?" There was only one person on board who made a caterwaul like that.

"The same."

"Well, let's go see what's troublin' the girl *this* time."

Zoë headed out through the exit.

Mal made to follow, but then hung back for a moment. He glanced around him at the shuttle's interior. Bare and untenanted, exactly as it had been for several weeks now, and exactly as one would expect it to be.

What the hell had he just experienced? That thing with Inara and the house and the gold band on her ring finger and… and *kids*? Was it some kind of vision? A fantasy?

Maybe Zoë was right and he'd been daydreaming.

It had seemed so real, though. And not just real but something he wished *could* be real. Wished it so hard, it was like an ache inside.

Mal twitched his head to and fro as though trying to shake back into place a component that had come loose in his brain, some vital cog or flywheel.

He had slept fitfully last night, waking up several times from strange, feverish dreams he couldn't recall. He was tired. He was out of sorts. He'd had a kind of mental aberration, that was all. He had wanted to see Inara again, and so he had seen her again. An imaginary version of her, at any rate. It was nothing a bit of extra shuteye and maybe a tot or two of whiskey couldn't cure.

River shrieked again, and Mal hurried off to find out what the matter was. Knowing River, it'd be something crazy and incomprehensible, as per usual.

12

"It's crazy," Wash told Mal. "Incomprehensible."

He motioned at River, who was lying slumped on the floor in the fore passage, outside Jayne's bunk. Her hands twitched convulsively while her eyes were fixed in a glazed, faraway stare.

"I found her like this a few minutes ago," Wash went on. "Tried asking her to explain what's upsetting her, but apart from the occasional loud scream—I mean really loud, like 'I'm going to be deaf in that ear from now on' loud—no response. There's no getting through to her."

Mal turned to Simon, who was kneeling beside River. He had her head in his lap and was stroking her hair soothingly. "Doc? Any notion what's gotten your sis so distraught?"

Simon shook his head. His face was taut with concern. "It's possible she's had a seizure of some kind."

"You don't sound convinced."

"I'm not. It could be any number of things. I'm still not clear what they did to River at the Academy. If this *is* a seizure, then it's a new symptom of her condition, but it wouldn't be all that surprising. Given how those *tiān shā de è mó* messed with her brain when they operated on her, they could easily have caused damage, the effects of which haven't manifested before now. Another possibility is that something's spooked her and she's gone into a kind of catatonic shutdown."

"I've seen spooked," Zoë said. "That's not spooked. That's terrified."

"River," Simon said gently. "River, I don't know if you can hear me. It's Simon. Tell me what's happened. What's got you so upset?"

In answer, River let out another of those short, shrill shrieks. Wash hadn't been lying. Mal felt as though an eardrum had burst.

"Everything's okay, *mèi mèi*," Simon said. "You're safe. I have to know what the problem is, though. I can't help you otherwise."

Mal braced himself, his hands beside his ears, ready to plug each with a forefinger if necessary.

This time, however, River did not shriek. Instead, she swiveled her gaze up towards her older brother. She peered at him, seeming to recognize dimly who he was. Her mouth moved in a gulping fashion, as though there were words within her but somehow she could not get them out.

"Take your time," Simon said. "There's no hurry."

But whatever it was that River had to say, she could not articulate it. All she could do was cast a plaintive look towards the door to Jayne's bunk.

"Is it Jayne? Are you worried about Jayne?"

River's head lolled in a way that could have been *yes* but could equally have been *no*.

"Jayne's fine," Simon reassured her. "I looked in on him just a short while ago. He's sleeping like a baby. He's going to be right as rain, you can count on it. To flatten a man like Jayne Cobb, it'd take a lot more than heatstroke. Now, we're going to get up, River, and I'm going to help you to your bunk. Okay? Then I'm going to give you a shot of something that'll calm you. I know you don't like needles, but it's the best thing for you right now."

Simon rose, then brought River to her feet, with assistance

from Zoë. The girl sagged between the two of them as though every muscle in her body had gone slack. Without protest, she allowed them to escort her to her bunk.

Just as Simon was opening the door to the room, River abruptly stiffened. She twisted around. Her eyes locked on to Mal's.

They were wide and full of fear, as before.

But now full of something else, too.

A kind of dreadful sympathy.

She raised a trembling hand and pointed at Mal. Then slowly, as if they two shared a secret, she nodded.

The way she did this, it fair gave Mal goosebumps. He felt he had been singled out by her for a specific reason. He just couldn't work out what it might be.

13

Can't they hear it? Why can't they hear it?

It was difficult for River to form even this simple thought. There was bedlam in her brain. She was being besieged by a vast mob of people—thousands of faces and voices swirling around her, assaulting her consciousness. Some of them she knew, some she didn't. Some stemmed from memories, some from fancy. All were jostling, howling, clutching at her, clamoring for attention.

It was like trying to concentrate while a fire alarm was going off. The phrase "I can barely hear myself think" had never felt truer.

A siren. That's what's causing this. Putting these people into my head. An enormous siren. Rising and falling. Wailing. Surely the others can hear it. Why can't they hear it?

Out in the corridor, River had managed to focus sufficiently that she could direct her gaze towards the source of the siren. It was coming from Jayne's bunk. That was why she'd been there in the fore passage. She had been tracing the source of the noise but had got too close and been swamped by a tsunami of mental impressions. It had overwhelmed her, and she had collapsed. In spite of that, she had done her best to alert the others to her discovery.

Siren: an alarm signal.

She'd also tried to convey a message directly to Mal using looks and gestures. The siren was inside him. She could see it there. It was inside all of the crew, but with most of them it hadn't taken a firm hold yet. With Mal it had. The siren's tendrils were busy unfurling through his cerebral cortex, spreading from neuron to neuron, making subtle changes as they went, transforming.

Siren: a mythical creature in classical literature whose beautiful song would lure passing sailors to their deaths.

River had hoped Mal would grasp what she was trying to tell him, so that he could act upon it. She didn't think he'd understood, unfortunately. He wasn't as sensitive as she was. None of the crew were. Sometimes it felt to River as though everyone else was blind and only she could see.

Now, in River's bunk, Zoë was drawing back the bedcovers and plumping up the pillow for her. Simon, meanwhile, was preparing an injection. He was drawing some kind of clear liquid from a phial into a syringe.

Something that'll calm you, he had said. *I know you don't like needles, but it's the best thing for you right now.*

River didn't simply dislike needles. She hated them. At the Academy, needles had meant scientists with cold hands and colder hearts doing things to her that left her nerve endings raw and her mind whirling like cotton candy in the spinner.

It was different with Simon, of course. He wasn't one of those stony-faced sadists. But still, the glint of reflected light on a thin sliver of surgical steel never failed to fill River with horror.

She did want to be calm, though. Anything to stop the siren's wail, which was making her brain throb so hard it felt fit to burst.

Some peace and quiet. Just for a while.

Simon rolled up her sleeve. River let him. Zoë put a comforting arm around her shoulders. Simon slid the needle into the crook of her elbow. Did it well, because he was a good doctor. Nearly no pain.

Simon. Zoë.

River trusted them both implicitly. Simon because he was her big brother. Only a dummy didn't trust their big brother. And Zoë because she was a warrior, with a warrior's code, a warrior's loyalty. They wouldn't do anything to harm her, she knew that. Both had protected her in the past and would protect her again any time they had to.

Neither was aware that the siren was working its insidious way through them, like billows of ink in water. They wouldn't have a clue it was there until it made its presence known.

A sudden flash of clarity amid the maelstrom of River's thoughts: *I should help them. Someone has to.*

But too late. Simon had depressed the syringe plunger. The injection suffused River with warmth. The liquid coursed through her, a tide of tranquility racing along her veins. It seemed to have a color, a serenely glowing turquoise.

Rapidly the din of the siren began to subside. River felt herself being lowered onto the bed by Zoë's strong arms. Zoë drew the bedcovers over her and tucked her in. What few people realized was that, beneath her tough exterior, Zoë was all about love. It was love that made her fight. Love that made her fierce.

River looked up at Simon's handsome, compassionate face.

He smiled at her. He, too, was all about love. His love for her, his *mèi mèi*, was so powerful it sometimes frightened River.

He doesn't know. He doesn't know what's coming. None of them do. They have no idea of the hell that lies ahead.

The siren was no more than a muted murmur now, a sludgy undertow of sound. The throng of faces and voices was drifting further and further away, receding into the distance.

River closed her eyes, and soon was floating blissfully in a sea of silent nothingness.

14

As Simon emerged from River's bunk, Mal asked, "How is she?"
"Settled and sedated," Simon said.

"Good. Good."

Mal waited as Zoë clambered out of the bunk. He nodded to her. She returned the nod and headed forward to the bridge.

Then, lowering his voice and leaning close to Simon, Mal said, "Listen, Doc. I know your sister is… *special* and all. I know she can do stuff, sense stuff, the rest of us can't. Is it possible, do you think, that she can…?"

"Can what, Mal?"

"I don't know. This is going to sound more'n a mite screwy, but do you think maybe she can make others do the same?"

"As in imbue other people with her—for want of a better word—powers?"

"Something like that."

"Why do you ask?"

"No real reason," Mal said evasively. "It's just…"

He hesitated. How could he even begin to describe the episode in the shuttle? Looking back, it was as though he had briefly fallen through a hole in space and time, ending up in a situation that never had been and never could be. Everything he had experienced during that weird trance he'd gone into—the house, talking with Inara, the sound of children outside—was hard to believe. Yet at the same time, while it was happening, it had made a kind of sense. Had felt *right*.

One possible means of accounting for the phenomenon was River Tam. If ever strange things were afoot on *Serenity*, odds were River was at the center of it. In this instance, that look she had given him a few minutes ago, and the pointing gesture accompanying it, suggested she somehow knew. Knew that he had had that vision, hallucination, brain fart, whatever you cared to call it.

All the same, Mal couldn't bring himself to elaborate any further on the subject with Simon. For one thing, he didn't want Simon thinking him in any way prey to fancies or delusions. He was like that with all of his crew. For Mal, it was important always to appear cool and in control. The carefree, buccaneering captain who never had a moment's doubt—this was the image he liked to project.

For another thing, the vision of Inara was so intensely personal that telling someone else about it would be like confessing some dark, terrible secret. It had been a picture of domestic bliss: himself, Inara, the wedding band, the dream home in the countryside, the couple of kids who he had no doubt were their offspring, his and Inara's. It was something Mal craved, something he deep down yearned for. It was also something he could scarcely admit, not even to himself—let alone think might one day become a reality. Now, more than ever, the likelihood of a future together for him and Inara was a pipe dream.

"No," he said finally. "Forget it. Ain't nothing."

"It doesn't sound like nothing."

"Really it is. I'm tired, is the long and the short of it. Didn't sleep well."

"Me either," Simon said, stifling a yawn. "Don't know why, but I kept tossing and turning all night. Got up to check on Jayne at one point during the small hours, round about three, just because I happened to be awake. He was sleeping like a baby. I guess maybe my conscience was bothering me, wouldn't let me be until I'd done the doctorly thing with my patient."

"Maybe mine was bothering me too. And before you say it, yes, I do have a conscience."

"Never occurred to me it'd be otherwise," said Simon with the tiniest of smiles.

"I think I'm kinda aggrieved how the whole Badger cargo thing has turned out to be a gorramn bust and we've wasted our time. Maybe it's that has got me making connections where there are no connections."

"Connections? Is that why you're asking me about River?"

"Nope."

"Mal, please, if you have information you think might have a bearing on what's just happened with her…"

"I don't, Doc."

"You're sure about that?"

Mal put on his sternest, brook-no-nonsense voice. "I am, and I'd take it as a courtesy if you'd stop pressing me on the matter. I brought up something that didn't need bringing up, it's not important, and there's an end to it."

He spun on his heel and walked away. He didn't need to look around to know that Simon was staring after him with curiosity and perhaps a touch of disquiet.

He strode onto the bridge, where Zoë and Wash had been busy canoodling. They were actually standing a good couple of yards apart when Mal entered, but he could tell by their faces that not five seconds earlier they'd been locked in a big old hug and a smooch. They must have heard his approaching footsteps, whereupon they'd separated and were now acting all casual and innocent-like, as though nothing had happened. Wash, in particular, was bad at hiding the truth. His cheeks were flushed and his eyes were darting this way and that. Zoë, by contrast, was coolly impassive, but this in itself told a story.

It wasn't that their married-couple displays of affection were anything to be ashamed of. Lately, however, Zoë and Wash had become reluctant about showing their love for each other in Mal's presence. He knew this was out of sensitivity over the situation between him and the absent Inara. The Washburnes didn't want to remind him what they had and he had not. They were unwilling to rub his nose in it.

It was yet another indication of how Inara's departure, and to a lesser extent Book's, had changed the dynamic on board *Serenity*, and not for the better.

Mal said, "Wash?"

Wash snapped to attention like a soldier on parade. "Captain. What can I do for you? Anything you like. I'm ready. Haven't been fooling around with my wife or nothing, no sir, none of that. Been waiting here like a tiger, poised to spring into pilot-type action." He mimed a tiger crouching, about to pounce. "Just give the word. What's your pleasure?"

"Wash, honey," said Zoë. "You need to stop talking now."

"Stopping talking, dear."

"Get us out of here," Mal said. "That's what you can do for me, Wash. I want *Serenity* off-planet ASAP."

"Your wish is my command," Wash said, slipping into the pilot seat. He began pushing buttons on the console, his fingers dancing over his instruments like a piano virtuoso's over the keys.

"Sooner I shake off the dust of this *zhēng qì de gǒu shǐ duī* world from my shoes, the better," Mal muttered.

"Amen to that," said Zoë.

15

Passing Jayne's bunk on his way back through the ship, Mal halted. He recalled the look River had aimed at the door. It had been meaningful. Just like the way she'd pointed at him had been meaningful.

What if...?

"Ah, the hell with it."

Mal hauled the door open and shinned down the ladder.

Jayne's bunk smelled of Jayne. This, though unsurprising, was not a good thing, certainly not in the way that Inara's shuttle still smelling of Inara was a good thing. Incense trumped stale masculine musk any day of the week.

Mal peered around. Nothing looked out of place. Which is to say, the room was a mess, but the messiness was in no way untoward. Bed not made. A procession of empty beer bottles on the table. Items of clothing strewn on the floor, including several socks that looked stiff and in need of a good laundering.

The only anomaly was Vera, propped up in one corner. After they'd brought Jayne onto the ship yesterday, Kaylee had deposited the rifle back here. Jayne would never have left Vera lying around like that; he would have field-stripped the gun, given it a good clean, then reassembled it and stowed it on its brackets alongside all his other weapons in the recess above his bed. Jayne regarded his firearms like they were treasured pets.

Something tugged at the periphery of Mal's thoughts, like his mind had got snagged on a thorn. Carefully he moved across the room, turning his head this way and that. He thought he could hear a faint, persistent buzzing. Where was it coming from?

The buzzing shifted in pitch. Now it sounded more like…

Children's laughter?

"Mal?" Wash, over the ship-wide intercom. "Mal, there's a wave incoming for you. Point of origin: Persephone. Caller ID: Badger. You want to take it, or shall I tell him you're washing your hair?"

Mal leaned on the intercom switch. "Patch it through to my bunk. I'll talk to him there."

He cast one last frowning look around Jayne's bunk, then exited.

In his own bunk, he activated the wave screen. A shot of Badger's head and shoulders flickered into view. Scumbag he might be, but you could say this for Badger: he was a flamboyant scumbag. His trademark bowler hat, paisley neckerchief, and flamingo lapel brooch were all present and correct.

What was missing was his habitual cocky grin.

"Badger, hey," Mal said. "I was just thinking about you. Been meanin' to call."

"Funny that," Badger said. "Might it 'ave sumfink to do wiv 'ow I 'aven't 'eard from 'Oyt Koestler in over 'arf a day? I've been expecting 'im to get in touch to tell me my cargo 'as been safely 'anded over and is now in transit. Instead, not a gorramn dicky bird. Which sets me to wondering whevver fings mightn't've gone as smoothly as one would like. Is there sumfink I should know, Reynolds?"

"Yeah, about that. I'm no longer interested in transporting your 'technical apparatus,' being as how it appears it's something has been cooked up at a Rim-planet Blue Sun R and D site. Nothing good ever came out of one of those."

"Why the bloody 'ell do you care where the cargo comes from?" Badger barked. "Provenance 'asn't been an overriding concern of yours before now."

"Maybe I'm not the man you think I am."

"You're certainly not the man you used to be. And wot's become of Koestler, then? Please don't tell me 'e's lying dead in a ditch somewhere."

"No."

"No?"

"Not in a ditch," said Mal.

Badger gritted his teeth in frustration. "For Gawd's sake, Reynolds! Seriously?"

"There was a difference of opinion. Your fella Koestler didn't take too kindly to not gettin' his way. Bullets flew." Not the whole truth but close enough. "We didn't start it," Mal added.

"Bet you finished it, though." Badger huffed a resigned sigh. "I should've known it might go south, what wiv you lot involved."

"I'm sure you didn't mean that to sound so insulting."

"I'm sure I did."

"You pay Koestler in advance?" Mal said. "If not, bright side, I've saved you some money."

"And the item you're supposed to be bringing me? Wot about that?"

"Best of my knowledge, it's sitting in its flightcase somewhere out in the barrens of Canterbury. Probably being used as a soapbox by speechifying coyotes."

"You fink this is amusing, Reynolds?"

"No, sir. Weren't no easy decision, leaving it behind, but I'm stickin' by it."

"I 'ave a very important buyer lined up. 'E finds out you've abandoned the thing wot 'e's paid me good money for, 'e's going to be less than pleased. And 'e isn't the type of man you want displeased with you."

"Well now, that would be your problem, Badger, wouldn't it? Rather'n mine."

"I'll make it your ruddy problem, Reynolds!" Badger exclaimed. "Just you see."

"Big words."

"Your wave location ping tells me you're still on Canterbury. It isn't too late. Go out there, fetch my item, bring it 'ere to Eavesdown, and there'll be no more to-do about it. 'Ow do you like that? My best and final offer."

"What's in that box anyway?" Mal said. "Maybe if I knew a bit more about it, I might reconsider."

"It's a great big pile of *mind your own business*, that's wot."

"Leaves me none the wiser. Think I'm just gonna terminate this conversation."

Seeing Mal's hand heading for the off button, Badger said quickly, "All right, all right. I'll tell you this much. It's a device for situational control."

"And what the ruttin' hell does that mean?"

"To be honest, I'm none too sure. I fink it means it has some sort of tactical civil application."

"In other words it's something the Alliance—to pluck a name out of the air completely at random—might use against folk. To, well, control them."

Badger shrugged. "Could be. I'm just repeating wot I've been told meself, which ain't much. It's a delicate piece of kit, apparently, so it's to be 'andled with care and not dropped or jarred. The flightcase has an inner layer of protective foam, but still, you could damage the mechanism."

Oops, Mal thought, remembering how the float-sled carrying the flightcase had bumped to the ground when he'd shot it.

"Only other fing I know about it," Badger went on, "is its nickname is the Ghost Machine."

"The what now?"

"Ghost Machine."

"Brrr. I guess all the non-creepy names were taken." Mal was making light of it, but the words *Ghost Machine* had nonetheless sent a small chill through him.

"They could call it Magic Rainbow Fun Time Machine for all I care," Badger said. "Wot it represents to me is a sizable amount of time, effort, and investment which I don't want flushed down the toilet by some jumped-up space jockey who 'as no right deciding wot freight 'e will and won't allow on 'is ship."

"Oh hell now, you just hurt my feelings. Space jockey?"

"Get me my cargo, Reynolds." Badger lurched towards the camera, and from the other end of the connection Mal heard the sound of a fist thumping a desktop and ornaments jumping. "No ifs, buts, or maybes. Come back empty-'anded and you'll never get a job round Eavesdown again. I'll 'ave you blacklisted."

Just then, *Serenity*'s engines began cycling. A deep, resonant thrum filled the ship from stem to stern.

As the sound rapidly increased in volume, Mal cupped a hand behind one ear. "What's that you're saying, Badger? It's getting kinda noisy this end."

Badger raised his voice. "I said, Reynolds, you'll be unemployable."

"Nuh-uh. Still can't hear."

Badger spoke louder still. "There won't be a trader in this town—on this whole gorramn planet, for that matter—that'll touch you with a bargepole. You mark my words."

The thrusters kicked in, making *Serenity* quake.

Mal mouthed words at the screen.

"I know you can 'ear me, Reynolds," Badger bellowed.

Shrugging his shoulders in fake apology, Mal reached out to cut the connection.

"You're making a big mist—"

The image of Badger disappeared.

With a thundering rumble and a tremendous lurch, *Serenity* lifted off.

16

As *Serenity* exchanged atmo for vacuum, Wash felt a familiar sense of liberty. The grip of Canterbury's gravity eased, to be replaced by the ship's own slightly lighter artificial gravity, which activated automatically. The pale blue of planetary exosphere gave way to the indigo of space. *Serenity* herself became less cumbersome to handle, a nimbler, more responsive beast in frictionless vacuum. Pinpricks of light began to fill the bridge's forward view ports, massing into a shimmering starscape.

Out here in the Black was where Wash was most at home. Not that he minded the occasional spell planetside, but give him a helm, a nav computer, and a functioning set of engines, and he was as happy as a dog with a chew toy. The surface of a world or a moon was so *limited*, whereas in space there were countless places you could go. The possibilities were literally infinite—or, to put it another way, the 'verse was your oyster.

He sat back in his seat, fingertips resting lightly on the yoke, and let *Serenity* soar through the emptiness. Mal had not yet given him a destination, but that was okay. The only thing Wash need be concerned about was Alliance vessels, and so he had the proximity detector dialed to full gain. Any ship within a thousand-klick radius would register, and if it pinged as the Feds, he would have ample time to take evasive action. Aside from that, he was content simply to fly.

To starboard, the lesser of Canterbury's two moons edged into view. On the way in, Wash had steered *Serenity* into the shadow of this planetary satellite so as to mask the ship from the sensors of a passing I.A.V. cruiser. The moon was the only piece of cover in the vicinity, and Wash thought it prudent to plot a course for it now, in case they needed to hide again.

Just as he finished inputting the necessary corrections, the door to the bridge opened and closed.

"Honey?"

Wash turned to see Zoë come sashaying towards him. "Oh, hi, babe," he said. "I was wondering where you'd got to. Been looking forward to that coffee you promised."

Then his brows knitted in a small frown of puzzlement.

Not only had Zoë come back from the galley empty-handed, without the cup of coffee she had gone to make him, she wasn't wearing the clothes she'd had on quarter of an hour ago, either— her customary combo of leather vest, khaki pants, and a bootlace wrapped around her throat. She had exchanged these for a slinky, curve-hugging silk dress, accessorized with a velvet choker. Her hair was different too. It wasn't fastened back as normal. Instead it hung free, framing her face in a cascade of dark ringlets.

Whatever her garb, Zoë Alleyne Washburne was a spectacularly beautiful woman. But Wash could not recall ever having seen her adopt such a soft and, well, feminine look.

"Uhh, hey, Zoë," he said. "What's with the dress and stuff? Not that I'm complaining," he added quickly. "I mean, you look great. You always look great. It's just… Wow. This is really, um… not you."

Zoë picked up the hem of her skirt and swished it to and fro around her legs, revealing a pair of high-heeled, side-buttoning ankle boots, which Wash assumed she must have borrowed off Inara and neglected to return.

"Got to look the part," she said. "Dress to impress."

"Impress who? Aside from me, obviously."

"The businessmen."

"What businessmen?"

"The ones we're meeting on Beaumonde."

"Beaumonde?" said Wash, blinking. "Since when are we going to Beaumonde?"

"Since we took off. Try and keep up, Wash."

"Nobody told me anything about Beaumonde. This some new job Mal's got us? We go to Beaumonde and there's a juicy client all lined up? I knew our luck would turn eventually."

"Mal?" Zoë frowned. "Mal who?"

"Mal, Zoë. Y'know. The captain? Debonair? Floppy fringe? Looks good in tight pants? So I'm told. I mean, I don't see him and go, 'Those pants really show off his butt nicely.' Thought's never occurred to me."

"I don't know any Mal, Wash. Is he some new supplier? From the way you're describing him, maybe I should meet him. He's obviously made quite an impression on *you*." She said this with a teasing grin.

"Okay now," Wash said. "This is getting silly, Zoë. We're obviously playing some fun game, but it might help if you'd clue me in on the rules first. What's my role? Business tycoon with a smoking-hot wife-slash-business-partner? I can do that. I think."

Zoë stepped closer, still smiling. "I love it when you act dumb. It's charming."

"Who's acting? I really have no idea what's going on here. And, if I'm honest, it's starting to freak me out a little."

She stroked his hair. "What say we put this magnificent ship of ours on autopilot and have ourselves a little fun before we get to Beaumonde? We haven't inaugurated this pilot's chair yet. You always say a ship hasn't properly been launched if someone hasn't made love in the pilot's chair."

"I do? That does sound like the sort of thing I'd say, I guess." Wash blinked. "Wait. Did you just call this a 'magnificent ship'? *Serenity* is many things, but I don't think anyone'd go so far as to describe her as that."

"*Serenity*? What's a *Serenity*, Wash?"

"*Serenity*," he said, humoring her. "Our beloved, beaten-up, patched-up, Lord-knows-how-she's-still-flying Firefly."

"But this isn't a Firefly," Zoë said, bemused and with a touch of haughtiness. "As if *we* would be traveling around in a crummy little tugboat like *that*."

"Well, if this isn't a Firefly, I don't know what... it..."

The sentence trailed off. Wash was looking around in astonishment.

He was still on a ship's bridge but this one was five times larger than *Serenity*'s and about ten times as sophisticated. There weren't loose cables all over the place or lengths of duct strung along the ceiling. The surfaces weren't all scuffed and battered. Everything gleamed with high-tech newness. Crystal-sharp readout screens glistened and the console buttons were recessed and touch-sensitive—state-of-the-art instrumentation. Even the yoke was a thing of beauty, molded into a sinuous ergodynamic shape and capped with walnut-inlaid handles.

If he didn't miss his guess, this was the bridge of a Carshalton Spaceways Seraphim. Only the highest-spec private cruiser money could buy. For a mere sixty million credits you got all the onboard luxuries you could wish for, from sauna to lap pool to six lavishly appointed cabins. Inara's billionaire-industrialist pal Stanislaw L'Amour owned one of these dream machines, and when Wash had met the guy on Thetis a few weeks back, he had quizzed him about the spacecraft, all but drooling as L'Amour listed its features. While there were some who criticized the Seraphim's flight performance in atmo, nobody questioned that it was just about the ritziest and most comfortable way to travel the 'verse.

And now he himself was piloting one? Wash could only assume so. Why else would he be seated at the controls?

"Why would we have a Firefly?" Zoë said. She sounded as though the idea was absurd. "When it comes to possessions, it's nothing but the best for Mr. and Mrs. Washburne."

From the way she said their names then, with the titles, it was clear that it signified something. Something more than just their married status. Mr. and Mrs. Washburne. As if it carried weight.

"So, let me get this straight," Wash said. "This… is our ship?"

"Who else's?"

"We bought a Seraphim? You and me? Paid for it out of our own pockets?"

"Why are you making it sound so extraordinary?"

"But how can we afford it? I'm the guy who gets his shirts from overstock outlets. The guy who can barely scrape enough credits together to take you out to dinner."

"Wash, honey, you have your shirts tailor-made for you by Zhuoyue on Osiris."

She tapped his chest. Wash looked down. He wasn't wearing one of his usual lurid nylon Hawaiian shirts. Instead, this one was plain white and long-sleeved, with the couturier's logo embroidered on the breast pocket, and was made out of some sort of sleek, light material that felt like a cool breath on his skin.

"And," she went on, "we can afford to eat anywhere we want."

"But a Seraphim?"

"Why not? We could buy a half-dozen of these ships. A dozen if we felt like it."

This was beyond crazy now. Never mind that he was in a Seraphim, which, apparently, he and Zoë owned. She was telling him they were some kind of insanely wealthy power couple?

"Now come on," Zoë insisted. "Put the *Comet* on autopilot. She may not fly as well as she does with you at the helm, but she flies well enough."

Comet. When he was a kid, Wash had had several scale-model spaceships, which he'd played with endlessly. Of all of them, his favorite had been a model of a Carshalton Spaceways Paradise-class Elysium, forerunner of the Seraphim. It was the pride of his collection and he had christened it *Comet.* One of his childhood ambitions had been to own, or at least fly, an Elysium when he was grown up. And now it turned out that he was the proud owner of a Paradise-class cruiser after all, and it was even named after his toy. A dream come true.

His hand groped across the control console until it found the autopilot button.

"Autopilot activated," said a sultry computerized voice from some hidden speaker. "I have the ship. Feel free to enjoy yourselves."

"Oh, we shall," Zoë said. "While we can."

"While we can?" Wash echoed.

"The kids are tucked up in bed, fast asleep. We can count on Celeste to stay that way, but not the twins. Sooner or later, probably sooner, one of them's going to wake up and wake the other one up. I give it half an hour. Let's not waste it."

"Kids," said Wash. "Twins." By now, these miraculous revelations were starting to seem commonplace.

Zoë hoisted up her skirt and straddled him. She grabbed his face with both hands and kissed him passionately.

Wash returned the kiss just as passionately. He was still confused, but somehow, when he was this physically close to his wife, feeling the heat and heft of her body against his, it didn't seem to matter quite so much anymore.

From a small device strapped to Zoë's wrist, there came a tiny wail. She pulled back, scowling.

"Gorramn it."

A second wail joined the first. The device on her wrist was a baby monitor and it was picking up the sound of two infants crying.

"Just a half-hour's alone time," Zoë said, exasperated. "Is that too much to ask?"

She heaved herself off Wash.

"Hold that thought, honey," she said, aiming a stern finger at him. "I'll settle them and come right back. Don't go anywhere."

"I won't," said Wash, nodding eagerly.

Zoë strode out of the bridge, speaking into the baby monitor. "Mommy's coming, darlings. Hang on."

Wash watched her go, both baffled and aroused. What in the name of *wǒ de mā hé tā de fēng kuáng de wài sheng* was going on?

He didn't know.

All he knew was that he liked it.

Liked it a lot.

17

Meanwhile, down in the engine room, Kaylee was conducting a full inventory of *Serenity*'s moving parts.

The ship was not a thing of beauty, but in the time since Mal had hired Kaylee to be his engineer she had grown to love this doughty midbulk transport vessel. She knew *Serenity*'s moods. She could sense almost telepathically when the ship was ailing, when a component needed to be replaced, when the engine was becoming clogged up and required a thorough overhaul. She could sense, too, when things were running smoothly and there was even a little extra oomph to be extracted from her.

It wasn't simply a case of looking and listening. It was a case of being attuned to the ship as a whole—how she flew, any slight torque or drag, the vibrations that sang through her frame, a whole concert of cues imperceptible to most folk. Sometimes Kaylee reckoned she and *Serenity* had achieved a kind of symbiosis, like a shark and a remora, or a crocodile and one of those little birds it lets clean its teeth. The ship permitted Kaylee to tend to her needs, and in return offered safety and shelter.

Right now, the engine was a touch cranky. Kaylee reckoned the power outlay differentiator was nearing the end of its useful life.

The centrifugal compressor coupling was also misbehaving, but that wasn't surprising since she'd had to seal a crack in it with a soldering iron only last week. She had a spare on board if necessary, but the existing one would be good for another hundred thousand miles or so, she thought. Mal was all about eking maximum value from an engine part, for reasons of economy. "Ain't exactly up to my eyeballs in platinum here, Kaylee," he had told her more than once. "It's up to you to make everything on this boat last as long as you can."

Just as Kaylee was finishing up her survey, she detected the tiniest of changes in *Serenity*'s propulsion output. It was so small, nobody else would have noticed; but to her it spoke volumes. Wash had just engaged autopilot. He was prone to driving *Serenity* quite hard on the first leg of a voyage, when they had just broken free of a world's gravity well. Exuberance got the better of him and he leaned a tad too heavily on the gas pedal. Under autopilot the ship's systems took a more measured approach, easing back to the optimal level of speed.

Kaylee went to the hook where she kept a rag for wiping the grease off her hands.

For some reason, the rag wasn't hanging there.

"Looking for this, pumpkin?" said her father, holding the scrap of cloth out to her.

"Thanks, Pop." Kaylee took the rag and set to cleaning herself up.

"Shouldn't be scared of a little dirt, girl. Look at me." Her father held out his hands, fingers splayed. They were filthy all over, especially under his nails and in the folds of his knuckles. They were callused and covered in scars too. Everywhere there was evidence of wrenches that had slipped and hammer blows that had been misaimed. There was waxy burn tissue from electrical shorts and lumps of skin thickened by repeated use of screwdriver and pliers. Indeed, a chunk of one thumb tip was missing from that time a support strut had given way and the inspection port lid on an Autry-McCrea 8-series hovercraft engine block had slammed down on his hand. Kaylee, aged three at the time, had heard his cry of pain clear across the backyard, from his workshop all the way to the house. It was also the first and only time she had heard her father curse.

"These," Aloysius Frye said, "are the hands of an engineer. They're the mark of our trade, and it's something to be proud of. Show me yours, Kaylee."

Kaylee did as bidden.

"Yep," he said, clasping her hands and turning them over, palms up, palms down, several times. "Gettin' there all right. Few more years, they'll be as purty as mine."

"Aloysius," said Kaylee's mother reproachfully. "Why is it you approve so of our daughter disfiguring herself in that way? Look at her. She's a beauty. That hair. That smile. And you reckon it's okay she ends up with the roughened hands of a workman?"

"Mom..." Kaylee protested.

"No," said Jemima Frye with a stern glint in her eyes. "You've got to think about your marriage prospects, my girl. It's fine your pa reveling in how grubby and mutilated he is. Him and those fellas he likes to hang out with down at LaRue's Bar, they're all about how tough and hardy they are. Comparing cuts and bruises all the time. 'Got this one from a steer that kicked me.' 'Got this one from sharpening a plowshare.' 'Never mind that. How about this one I got when Billy Jack Travis punched me out the other day for wolf-whistlin' at his missus?' You aren't one of them. You need to keep yourself as dainty and ladylike as can be."

"I know how to be dainty and ladylike, Mom. You should have seen me at this swanky shindig I went to on Persephone not so long ago. I had the loveliest pink dress on. I was the belle of the ball. Men all around me. No shortage of offers to dance."

Her father gave her a warm "that's my girl" look.

Her mother remained frosty.

"But that's just it, Kaylee," she said. "You could have any man you want. But you're not getting any younger, and what bloom you have is tarnished if you insist on wearing bib overalls all the time and doing work that grubbies you up and damages you."

Jemima Frye, feeling that her point had been made, marched back to the house, leaving Kaylee and her father alone in the workshop together.

They tried to avoid each other's glances but couldn't. The moment their eyes locked, both started sniggering.

"'Bloom'!" he snorted.

"'Grubbies you up'!" she chortled.

"Pay your mother no mind, Kaylee," her father said after the laughter had run its course. "She means well. You're her only child, and if you'd been a son, none of this would matter. She'd be glad of you being an engineer. It's only 'cause you're a girl that it bothers her. Your ma was brought up a certain way, with certain expectations for how women should be. She don't love you any less for how you turned out. Guess she wishes you were a bit more like her and a bit less like me, but if she hasn't got used to that by now, she maybe never will. Anyways, come on. You gonna help me here with fixing this busted transaxle or what?"

So saying, Aloysius Frye strapped on a head flashlight, then got down onto his back on his wheeled creeper board and trundled himself under the chassis of the late-model Hendry six-wheeler he was working on. Kaylee grabbed another creeper board and joined him beneath the jacked-up motor wagon, down on the cement floor of his workshop with its overlapping patches of spilled fuel and lubricant.

"I know spaceship engineering's more your thing these days," he said, "but earthbound vehicles can be just as complicated, not to mention as interesting."

"You're telling me," said Kaylee. "We got this Mule bike on *Serenity*. Replacement for one we… wrote off in an accident."

Wrote off? More like *strapped a fuel tank to the front of and drove straight at Adelai Niska's henchmen who shot at it and it blew up and killed them.* But what her father didn't know couldn't hurt him.

"The new one worked like a dream half the time," she went on, "and the rest of the time is the orneriest heap of *gǒu shǐ* you ever saw."

"Mule by name, mule by nature." He started unscrewing the transaxle unit's housing. "You loved being on that ship, didn't you?"

"Yeah. Yeah, I did."

"Slight hitch in your voice when you said that. Wasn't all plain sailing, huh?"

"Won't lie, Pop. To begin with, everything was shiny. Later on, after Inara and Shepherd Book went, we kinda lost our way. Mal became just so bitter. It's like he stopped caring, most of all about himself. Without Book, we didn't have a voice of reason anymore, and without Inara, we didn't have a center. It felt as if everything was slowly falling apart and there was nothing anyone could do to stop it."

"That young man you liked. Simon is it? What about him?"

Kaylee pondered. "He just couldn't seem to get over himself, you know? So stuck in the ways of his upbringing. It made him so... *starchy.*"

"Bit like your mom in that respect."

"A bit. I know he had feelings for me. If only he'd've let them out, then we could've maybe got somewhere."

"Pity," said her father. "Still, you're back here on New Virginia now. Back home in Tankerton, 'Jewel of the Coastal State.' All that other stuff's behind you. This is your life."

"It is. It's good to be back."

"And it's good to have you back, pumpkin," her father said. "Now, see that socket set to your left? I need the ratcheting wrench, and also the extending bar and the one-and-a-half-inch socket."

Kaylee handed him the implements, and he assembled them and set to work loosening a bolt.

"If that Simon'd been as smart a man as you say he was,"

Aloysius Frye continued, grunting as the bolt proved reluctant to shift, "he'd have recognized what a prize he had in you. Some fellas just need things spelled out for them, know what I mean? You can't be subtle or just sit there hoping. Equally, you can't be too brazen about it. That can be a turn-off for guys. Your mom, after we met at the formal tea dance over in Patricksburg, made it fairly clear that she had her sights set on me and nothing was going to divert her. Traditional she may be, but she's also a determined woman. Thing was, I thought I was making all the running. I was the one asking her out on dates, doing all the things a man properly does when he's courting; but it was your mother who kept finding ways of bumping into me in the street or at the grocery store 'by accident' and who persuaded her daddy to send his farm vehicles to me to mend rather than use old Earnest MacMurray's garage out on Larkhill Road like he'd been doing for years. The woman has wiles. Women do. You do, I know. Sweet and innocent you may seem, Kaylee, but beneath it you're as shrewd an operator as they come. There'll be another Simon along soon enough, and this time around you'll be better equipped to handle him."

She lay back on the creeper board beside her father under the Hendry, down there among the smells of metal and oil and his sweat, and watched him toil away at the transaxle. Her father hummed to himself contentedly, pausing every so often to ask her to pass him a tool. When a stray spurt of transmission fluid caught him in the face, he just chuckled. Aloysius Frye was difficult to annoy.

Aloysius Frye was also dead—a fact that Kaylee had somehow conveniently forgotten.

18

The clatter of small arms. The thunder of anti-aircraft artillery. Shells howling. Tracer fire stuttering through the dark. The rumble of military vehicles rolling across uneven terrain. The voices of men and women, panicked, terrified, some crying out in agony, others yelling urgent commands. Billowing orange explosions. The reek of gunsmoke and death.

And now, adding to the chaos and cacophony, a new element: an Alliance skiff zooming overhead, strafing Independent positions, clearing a path for an oncoming horde of Alliance troops.

Sheltered behind a ridge, a handful of beleaguered Browncoats took stock of the situation.

"Sergeant!"

Radio Operator Graydon lurched towards Sergeant Reynolds, lugging his comms set with him.

"Command says air support is holding till they can assess our status."

Sergeant Reynolds snarled, "Our status is that we need some gorramn air support. Now get back on line and tell them—"

At that moment, Zoë joined the group. She skidded to a halt beside her superior officer. "That skiff is shredding us, sir."

Graydon looked up from the comms set. "They won't move without a lieutenant's authorization code, sir."

Without hesitating, Reynolds scrambled over to a two-day-old corpse sprawled nearby. He tore the rank badge off the dead man's sleeve and thrust it at Graydon. "There. There's your code. You're Lieutenant Baker. Congratulations on your promotion. Now get me some air support."

As Graydon hurried off, Reynolds turned to address the small gathering of soldiers with him, Zoë among them. To one of them he said, "Pull back just far enough to wedge 'em in here." Then, to Zoë, he said, "Get your squad to high ground. Start picking 'em off."

"High ground's death with that skiff in the air," she replied.

"That's our problem and thanks for volunteering," Reynolds shot back. He swiveled towards a very scared private. "Bendis, give us some cover fire. We're going duck hunting."

A shell crashed to earth a few yards away, showering them in rubble and dust. Zoë threw her arms over her head instinctively. When she looked up, one of their number was dead. Shrapnel had torn a chunk out of his torso.

"Just focus," Sergeant Reynolds said to everyone. "The Alliance said they were gonna waltz through Serenity Valley and we've choked 'em with those words. We've done the impossible and that makes us mighty. Just a little while longer, our angels are gonna be soaring overhead, raining fire on those arrogant cods. So you hold. You *hold*."

The last word was a throaty shout, an effort to instill courage into their faltering hearts.

And although everything seemed hopeless, the chances of victory vanishingly small, Zoë still felt emboldened. She had been fighting side by side with Malcolm Reynolds for the best part of six months now. Together they had endured unbelievable hardship and come under enemy fire countless times, and she was convinced he was one of the finest soldiers she knew. Something about him made you prepared to follow him even into the jaws of hell.

"Go!" Reynolds said, and the others scattered to carry out his orders.

Zoë reloaded her machine gun while Reynolds picked up a rifle for himself from a cache of weapons.

"Really think we can bring her down, sir?" she said.

"Do you even need to ask?"

Out of the corner of her eye, she saw him pull out a small cross that hung on a chain around his neck. He kissed it, then slipped it back inside his shirtfront. It was a discreet little gesture. He had no idea she had witnessed it. But then Zoë was well aware that Reynolds had faith.

Question was, would it protect them today?

"Ready?" Reynolds said to her.

"Always. Bendis. Bendis!"

The ashen-faced private did not move. He did not even register that Zoë was calling his name. He was a platoon's worth of terror poured into a single body.

Battle-frozen. The guy was a kid, barely out of his teens. He'd come from herding cows on the family cattle ranch to this crapstorm. He was going to be no use to her.

"Rut it," she said, and sprang up from behind cover to rake an Alliance position with a salvo of bullets.

Reynolds ran in from the side to attack the sandbagged position too, finishing what Zoë had started. Alliance soldiers screamed and died.

He ran on and ducked down behind a rock. Zoë caught up with him, and together they crouched while a hail of rounds came their way, blasting the rock.

A sudden lull. Reynolds popped up to survey the scene through the sights of his rifle. Ahead, downslope, lay an anti-aircraft gun emplacement, seemingly unmanned. Reynolds scanned this way and that, eventually picking out a lone Alliance soldier hunkered in one corner.

Reynolds's first shot flushed the man out. His second brought him down.

Reynolds and Zoë sprinted down to the emplacement. Reynolds grabbed the controls of the anti-aircraft gun and swiveled it around, centering the Alliance skiff in the sighting reticle. The automated targeting system came into play, zeroing in on the single-seater fighter and signaling a lock. Reynolds pulled the trigger, and the anti-aircraft gun roared. Both barrels spat a stream of shells at the skiff.

There was a burst of brilliant light. The skiff was hit on one wing.

"Yes. Yes!" Reynolds yelled with furious satisfaction.

Heeling over to one side, the skiff plummeted towards the ground.

Reynolds's look of triumph went to one of alarm as he realized the stricken skiff was heading straight for him. He ran full tilt to get out of the way, calling Zoë's name as he went.

The skiff pounded into the earth like the fist of an angry titan. For a moment Zoë knew only the overpressure wave of its impact and the heat flash of its fuel tanks erupting into a fireball. She and Sergeant Reynolds were thrown flat, fetching up in a heap together.

Flaming debris rained down around them. Reynolds began to chuckle. Zoë, for her part, was simply relieved. Talk about a near miss. They had come within inches of being incinerated. Her hair had been singed. She could smell it.

They returned to the Independents' rallying point. Zoë could not resist aiming a barbed comment at the still-cowering Private Bendis. "Nice cover fire."

"Did you see that?" Reynolds crowed as he passed Bendis.

He went over to Graydon, the radio operator.

"Graydon. Graydon. What's the status on that—?"

Graydon lay slumped against a stack of ammo crates, unmoving. Blood streaked his face.

"Zoë." Reynolds motioned her towards the body.

As Reynolds headed back to Bendis, Zoë bent down and began

detaching the radio headset from Graydon's remains.

Reynolds knelt beside Bendis. "Hey. Listen to me," he said. "Bendis, look at me! Listen. We're holding this valley. No matter what."

"We're gonna die," Bendis moaned.

"We're not gonna die. We can't die, Bendis, and do you know why? Because we are so very pretty. We are just too pretty for God to let us die." He grabbed the youngster's chin. "Huh? Look at that chiseled jaw. Huh? Come on!"

"I'm sorry," Bendis said haplessly.

Then, over and above the din of conflict, came a sound.

A sound Zoë couldn't believe she was hearing. Faint at first, but growing in volume.

The roar of jet engines.

She looked up to the sky, towards the east, where dawn was just starting to lighten the dark.

Reynolds looked too. He began to smile.

"You won't listen to me, listen to that," he said to Bendis. "That's our angels, come to blow the Alliance right to the hot place."

Bendis's drawn expression eased. Something like hope entered his eyes.

"Zoë," said Reynolds, "tell the Eighty-Second to hold on just a little bit longer. We're gonna be okay. Air support's coming through."

The approaching aircraft were distant specks, too tiny to identify, and for a moment—just a moment—Zoë had a notion that they were Alliance. The promised Independent air support had not been delivered, because the situation was just too hot for the pilots to make the attack run safely. Instead, the enemy had got the upper hand. Which meant the Battle of Serenity Valley was effectively over. Command would now either leave the Browncoats on the ground to be massacred or else order them to lay down arms and surrender.

She got on the radio. "Command, please confirm. Are aircraft heading for our position on a westerly bearing friendlies or hostiles? I repeat, are aircraft heading for our position friendlies or hostiles? Over."

A crackle of static, then the reply: "Confirm. Inbound aircraft are Independent."

She relayed the news to Sergeant Reynolds, who hooted in glee.

"Now you bastards are gonna get it!" he called out to any Alliance troops who might be within earshot.

Sure enough, the distant specks resolved into a squadron of Independent fighter planes that came soaring in across Serenity Valley, their airframes glinting in the early light. Wing-mounted cannons stitched the Alliance soldiers below with heavy-caliber rounds, while bomb bays dropped seeds of explosive ordnance that blossomed into flame.

The fighters wheeled around and returned for a second pass, and a third. A half-dozen of them succumbed to surface-to-air fire. The rest cut a swathe through the advancing Alliance forces, obliterating infantry, armored vehicles, and gun emplacements in a glorious blaze of destruction.

The sun rose over a scene of utter carnage. Serenity Valley no longer lived up to its name, if it ever had. Columns of smoke arose from blackened craters. Mangled bodies were strewn far and wide. Husks of burned-out vehicles smoldered.

What had looked like almost certain defeat for the Independents had turned into an Alliance rout instead.

Sergeant Reynolds gazed out over the devastation, Zoë by his side. Private Bendis was with them, too, looking as though he could scarcely believe he had come through this hell unscathed.

Zoë was having a hard time believing it herself. She had been so sure the air support wouldn't arrive. But the Independent pilots had shown phenomenal courage, and their intercession had turned the tide of the battle at the very last minute.

"Know what?" Reynolds said. Beneath the smut and the mud stains, his face showed steely resolve. "This is it. I can feel it. This is the moment when it all changes. We've shown 'em. We've shown 'em what a ragtag band of rebels can do. We've given 'em one hell of a bloody nose, and those Alliance sons-of-bitches won't forget it. I'll wager their top brass are rethinking their strategies even now. There's a little worm of fear crawlin' in their bellies that wasn't there before. They're wonderin' if maybe they've bitten off more'n they can chew. If they didn't already know we're no pushovers, they sure as hell do now."

"I'd like to think you're right, sir," Zoë said.

"You bet I'm gorramn right, Zoë. When this war started, no one on our side really thought it was winnable. Today, for the first time, I reckon it may just be. You've gotta see that, don't you, Zoë? Zoë? Zoë?"

Snap.

"Zoë? Can you hear me, Zoë?"

Snap snap snap.

"Come on, Zoë. You can hear me, can't you? Wake up."

Zoë blinked sharply. It was more of a flinch than anything, in fact.

It wasn't the war-weary Sergeant Reynolds who was talking to her anymore. It was the markedly fresher-faced Simon Tam. He was right next to her, clicking his fingers under her nose.

"There she is."

"Simon?"

Zoë was in the ship's galley. In her hand was an empty coffee pot. On the counter was a mug that was full to overflowing. Coffee covered the countertop and had spilled onto the floor as well, forming a puddle around her feet.

"*Xióng māo niào!*" she exclaimed.

"Panda piss?" said Simon, cocking an eyebrow. "I know we can't afford the most expensive beans available but it doesn't taste *that* bad."

Zoë set down the pot, grabbed a dishcloth and started mopping up the mess.

"What happened here?" Simon asked, picking up another dishcloth and helping her. "I came in and found you standing stock still with this glazed look on your face, like you were a million miles away. It's as if you started pouring coffee and completely zoned out."

"I… I think I must have."

"Took me best part of a minute to get you to snap out of it."

"I really don't know what happened, Simon," she said. "I guess I just drifted off."

"That's not like you, Zoë, if I may say."

"Tell me about it. Can't say I had the best night's sleep last night."

"Me too. And Mal said something similar. It seems there's a lot of insomnia going around."

Zoë paused from her labors. "Simon…" she began.

"Yes?"

"Is it possible you can dream while still being awake?"

"Hmmm." Simon paused, tapping fingers against chin. "I'm no expert, but there is something known as hypnagogia. I learned about it in my psych module at med school. It's a state of overlap between sleeping and waking during which you can undergo visual hallucinations and a whole load of other vivid sensory experiences besides. Sometimes it's known as lucid dreaming. You're at the threshold of consciousness but not quite, and in that halfway house the unreal can seem startlingly real. You can taste things, smell things, feel things, as if they're actually there."

Zoë nodded slowly. "Okay. And I suppose this…"

"Hypnagogia."

"Hypnagogia, it can show you what might have been rather than what was."

"Any dream can do that."

"Only, before you interrupted, I could've sworn I was back at Serenity Valley with Mal. It was a blow-by-blow replay of the battle, right up until the ending. That was when it veered off in completely another direction. This time, the Browncoats won."

Simon raised his eyebrows. "Talk about wish fulfillment."

"I know. And I had the distinct impression that it was a decisive moment, a turning point. From there, the Independent army went on to win the war. Is that strange?"

"Why should it be strange? Of course you'd like the battle to have turned out differently. The whole war, for that matter. You and Mal were betrayed by your superiors at Serenity Valley. You saw countless men and women sacrifice their lives for the Independent cause. That's going to leave a mark on your psyches. You know what I think this is?"

"What?"

"Survivor's guilt. It's common with veterans. 'Why did I make it out in one piece when so many others didn't? What did I do to deserve still being alive?' Worse when you're on the losing side. 'Was it worth it? Were all those deaths in vain?' Sometimes you even find yourself wishing you'd been killed. So now, when you happened to lapse into a hypnagogic state, that's what came bubbling up from your subconscious. You revisited one of the pivotal events of your past and you addressed it by recasting it in a positive light."

"You reckon this is something I should worry about?" she said.

"No," Simon replied. "What I do reckon, though, Zoë, is that you should maybe talk about it with someone sometime. A professional, or perhaps with someone who was there, like Mal. Just get it out of you. You are just about the strongest person I have ever met, but that strength comes at a cost. You bottle up a lot of things inside, things that you should let out. If you don't get rid of them, in time they're liable to burn a big hole through you, like holding a lump of phosphorus in your hand."

He wasn't wrong, Zoë knew that. She was the kind of person who preferred to repress darker feelings rather than admit to them. But it was the habit of a lifetime, and she doubted she'd be able to change.

"Well, I'm grateful for the lecture, Doc." She resumed wiping up the spilled coffee. She was aware of putting an impassive expression on her face, like a mask. It felt familiar there. "Fascinating stuff."

Simon gave her an appraising look, then nodded. She could tell that he knew she had gone into denial. He knew, too, that although she had opened up a tiny chink in her armor, it was now firmly closed once more.

"Perhaps we could all just do with some rest," he said. "I know I could."

19

Physician, heal thyself.

It was all very well giving advice to others, Simon thought, but no good if you didn't follow your own recommendations.

He trudged down to the infirmary in order to give Jayne a once-over. Due diligence and all that.

The big man was still sound asleep.

Simon noted that the med couch diagnostic instruments were registering an elevated level of cerebral activity.

Of course, it's all relative, he thought. *With Jayne, cerebral activity starts from a very low baseline.*

Joking aside, however, the level wasn't abnormally high. It was commensurate with that of someone dreaming: a decrease in low-frequency brain waves and an increase in high-frequency brain waves.

Jayne's eyes were darting to and fro beneath their lids in the classic REM fashion. That, too, was indicative of dreaming.

In every respect, Jayne's physical condition was nominal. Green across the board. It was safe for Simon to leave him there for another hour or so.

He headed up to his bunk, planning on taking a nap. As he climbed down the ladder into the cabin, he realized that it was his birthday. How could it have slipped his mind?

Luckily, his family were here to remind him. His mother and father, of course, but various members of the extended clan as well. There was Grampa and Nana Tam, and Silas and Zelda Buckingham, also known as Grandy and Grandmama, his mother's parents. Likewise from the Buckingham side of the family there was Uncle Holden and Aunt Isabelle, with their identical-twin daughters, Simon's cousins Cordelia and Flavia.

His father's brother, the rakishly disreputable Bryce, was present. Bryce rejected the prefix "Uncle." "Just Bryce will do," he always said. "'Uncle Bryce' makes me sound old. Worse, it makes me *feel* old."

For much the same reason—reluctance to let go of his youth—Bryce had not married and settled down to raise a family. Accompanying him was his latest in a long line of girlfriends, a glamorous, underdressed, over-made-up woman half his age whose name Simon couldn't quite recall but thought was Audrey or Aurora, something like that.

Everyone was assembled beside the dining table, on which sat a plump white cake with a plethora of lit candles on top and Simon's name piped in frosting. Front and center of the group was River, and she hopped up and down and clapped with delight as Simon entered.

"Told you he'd make it," she said, at which their mother patted her on the arm and said, "You were right, dear," while their father added, "Never doubted it for a second."

River scampered over to Simon and gave him a huge hug. She drew back, holding him by the hand, and looked at him. "I've missed you," she said.

Simon gazed deep into her big brown eyes. He saw in them a profound clarity and the light of intelligence. For some reason this struck him as significant. He had the weird feeling that River's eyes did not normally look like this, that they should instead be filled with a terrible, wild confusion.

But where could that idea have come from? River Tam was one of the most talented, brilliant young women in Rochester Peak. On all of Osiris, in fact. For a time it had appeared as though she was going to make a name for herself in the world of ballet. She was an exquisite dancer, and her teacher, Madame De Tocqueville, had made it clear that a place was available for this prodigy with any corps on the Core planets and that, in time, there was every chance she might rise to the pinnacle of her profession and become a *prima ballerina assoluta.*

River, however, had elected to pursue academic success instead. She had graduated from high school three years early, gone straight to college and earned a PhD in theoretical physics at the incredibly advanced age of seventeen, after which she had been head-hunted by every top-rank university on Osiris, all vying to take her on as a research fellow. Having accepted a position at Rochester Peak's own Tiancai U., where only the truly gifted could study, her work on loop quantum cosmology was already earning plaudits from her peers. There was talk of her ideas revolutionizing the field, particularly her hypothesis concerning the influence of T-duality on mirror symmetry—Simon wasn't sure on the specific terms, but it was something along those lines at any rate—and its applications in regard to spaceflight.

River still danced, but for pleasure only. Her mind, in its own way, also danced, pirouetting to the music of mathematics and geometry in their most complex forms.

Sometimes Simon found it hard to reconcile the fact that this woman, with her genius-level intellect, was also his little sister. They were both doctors, but the title meant so much more in her case than it did in his. He, as a surgeon, understood fairly well how the human body worked. The scope of River's discipline encompassed all of Creation, from its largest moving parts right down to its very smallest.

Bryce Tam ambled over and clapped both Simon and River on the shoulder.

"Good grief, Gabe," he said to his brother. "Look at these two. Have you ever seen such an accomplished pair? Simon saving lives every day over at AMI. River doing that fancy physics stuff I can't even begin to wrap my head around. It's a wonder they sprang from your loins, frankly."

Gabriel Tam took the fraternal teasing in good spirit. Two years Bryce's senior, he was used to being the sensible one, his younger brother the scallywag who'd never grown up. "What astonishes me, Bryce," he said, "is that they share DNA with you."

"Ha ha! I suspect their brilliance is all from Regan. Along with their good looks."

"Oh you!" Simon's mother flapped a hand.

"Is someone going to blow out these candles?" Nana Tam demanded. "They had better before the house burns down."

River led Simon over to the cake, and he bent and blew heartily. River joined in until between them they had extinguished all of the tiny flames.

"Make a wish," River said.

Simon looked around him at the gathering. He was overcome by a sudden wave of joy, so much so that he felt his eyes prickle with tears. He blinked to hold them back. A Tam male did not cry.

"I don't need to wish for anything," he told his sister. "Everything I want, I have right here."

River rose up onto the very tips of her toes—*en pointe*, as a good ballerina should—and gave him a peck on the cheek.

Simon's mother handed him a knife and he began slicing up the cake.

The party lasted all afternoon. Wine and champagne were quaffed. Grandmama Buckingham got squiffy, as she often did at these occasions, and started telling dirty jokes. The twins Cordelia and Flavia kept encouraging her, and the jokes got dirtier, until eventually her daughter-in-law Isabelle escorted her off to the living room, where Grandmama fell asleep in front of the television watching her favorite soaps on the Cortex.

Towards evening, Simon found himself out on the veranda with his father, each with a glass of New Canaan brandy in his hand. It was a perfect Osirian fall day. The trees in the yard were at their autumnal finest, their foliage all shades of gold, orange, and red. The air was warm but with a slight bite that presaged the onset of winter.

"Not a subject either of us cares to broach, Simon," said his father, "but—"

"When am I going to give you grandchildren?"

"You know me so well. You're busy, I get it. Attending physician at a top-tier hospital—well, to say that it's demanding would be an understatement. But there must be time, surely, for a personal life too. Your mother and I are concerned that you take your responsibilities too seriously. You're a handsome, eligible lad. You'd really have me believe no attractive lady has caught your eye?"

"I've been out on a few dates."

"And?"

"And dates is all they were. Nothing came of them."

"Never forget, we could set you up," Gabriel Tam said. "With your mother's connections particularly, we could find you a compatible mate in no time."

"You make it sound like animals at the zoo. 'And here we have our breeding pair. We're hoping for a cub any day now.'"

"Don't be so dismissive of the idea. Your mother and I were set up by our respective parents."

"I was not aware of that." *And*, Simon thought, *I rather wish you hadn't told me.*

"Oh yes. I'm surprised you didn't know. It was… Well, 'arranged' is such a pejorative-sounding word. But it was felt on both sides that she and I would be a match, and so we were introduced to each other, and we soon found that we got along."

"Got along."

"Yes. We had plenty in common. A love of horse riding. A penchant for composers such as Bach, Brahms, and Xiaosong. And, of course, we both come from the same social milieu. These things are important, Simon. You may not think it, but they are."

Blame the brandy, along with all the wine that had preceded it, but Simon couldn't help snorting in derision.

His father shot him a look of rebuke.

"I'm sorry, sir," Simon said. "Maybe I'm wrong, but I've always thought that when I marry, I'll marry someone I love."

"Love!" Gabriel Tam said the word as though it were something quaint and faintly implausible. "Love doesn't last, Simon. What makes a marriage work is shared values, mutual interests, a similar outlook on life. Don't ever make the mistake of marrying for *love*. You could end up with simply anyone as a wife. Some sordid little gold-digger, for example. Or some low-rent creature who works with her hands."

"I work with my hands."

"Getting them dirty, I mean."

"I get mine dirty."

"You know what I mean. Wielding a scalpel is altogether different from, say, fixing machinery, and blood is not the same as engine oil. I'd hate to think you might let the side down, Simon, that's all I'm saying. We're Tams. We have certain standards; appearances to keep up."

"Like Bryce, you mean?"

"Bryce." Gabriel Tam shook his head sadly. "Bryce, alas, is a lost cause. My brother is what he is. There's no changing him and no redeeming him. Whereas of you, my boy, much is expected. You carry the Tam name. It's an honor but also, I'm afraid, a burden. Someone has to continue the line, and when you do"—a subtle but firm emphasis on the *when*—"it's vital that your offspring hail from good stock on both sides."

"Question, Dad. Would you have this same conversation with River?"

"Don't be ridiculous. Of course not."

"Then why are you having it with me?"

"Are you being deliberately obtuse, Simon, or are you really that naïve? Either way, I don't much care for your attitude. You are not River. River is not you. She is free to choose her own path."

"And I'm not?" Simon said.

"Not so much, no. If River were in danger of becoming wayward, naturally your mother and I would intervene. However, she has a glittering career in the making and she seems eager to embrace it. We have no fears for her."

"No fears for who?" said River. She had just stepped out onto the veranda.

"It's nothing, dear," said her father benignly. "Nothing that need concern you."

River smiled. "Well, if you two aren't too busy, perhaps you'd like to come back inside. Uncle Holden has sat down at the piano and we're all set for a sing-along."

"Sounds marvelous." Gabriel Tam got to his feet. "Simon? Come. Join us. At these get-togethers, as in all family affairs, it's crucial that everyone takes part, don't you agree?"

As if his point needed underscoring, Simon's father added a slow, sly wink.

"Yes, grumpy face," River said to Simon. "Come and have a singsong with the rest of us."

Simon was reluctant, until his sister grabbed his hand and started hauling. He couldn't refuse her. There was nothing he would not do for River.

He followed her and their father into the house, and in no time all of the partygoers were standing around the piano—Grandmama Buckingham included, having awoken from her snooze—and singing their hearts out, accompanied by Uncle Holden's enthusiastic if not always accurate playing. On the program of this impromptu recital were classics such as "The Ships That Sailed From Earth-That-Was," the slightly risqué "My Darling Dwells On Dyton (But My Honey's Home Is Hera)" and that old standard "Blue Sun, Bright Future." The whole shebang was rounded off with a rousing rendition of the Alliance anthem, during which Cordelia and Flavia attempted harmonies they weren't quite able to pull off.

Memories of his exchange of views with his father out on the veranda soon faded and Simon was singing as lustily as the rest of them and laughing uproariously.

In the warmth of the family home, surrounded by loved ones— that was where happiness lay.

20

Jayne and Matty were out riding the range.

The Cobb herd needed moving from its current, played-out pasture to a new one. The brothers rounded up the eighty-odd head of cattle and set them on the trail. Matty's dog Jip played his part as per usual, chasing after stragglers and giving them a nip on the hock if they wouldn't willingly fall in line. It was another glorious summer's day on Sycorax, the sun beating down but not so hot as to be unpleasant. The sky was an unbroken sheet of cornflower blue from horizon to horizon.

Jayne had thought he'd never have a day like this with Matty again. The kid had been dying, no question about it. The damplung had got its hooks into him deep, and when that disease took ahold, there was only one direction things could go and that was downhill all the way to the inevitable end.

Now, he kept aiming sidelong glances at his little brother while they rode, checking to be sure. But there wasn't the least visible indication of the disease. Matty appeared to be in perfect health.

"I see the way you're lookin' at me, Jayne," Matty said at last. "You can't hide it. You're lookin' at me like you're waiting for me to just cough, maybe, or be a tiny bit off-color. It's gone, my brother. Damplung's up and gone, and it ain't never comin' back."

"You sure? Don't get me wrong, Matty. I don't want you gettin' sick again. I'm just finding all of this hard to take in."

"Know what? Me too. But the doc said to Mama, when he realized I was on the mend, he said that every once in a while there's a case where damplung goes into—what's the word? Remission. Spontaneously, as it were. The body's immune system figures out how to beat the disease after all, on its ownsome, and you get better. It's, like, a one-in-a-million chance, but it happens."

"So all this time, the money I kept sending home to buy you medicines, you're saying I needn't have troubled?"

Matty laughed. "Hell, no. Those drugs kept me going, kept me functioning long enough for nature to kick in and start doing its bit. Without them, I'd have been six feet under ages ago. Only reason I'm here today, Jayne, is you. I can't thank you enough for that."

"You bein' alive and well is all the thanks I need, Matty."

His brother's face turned somber. "Haveta tell you, there were times when it got real dark. More'n once I had thoughts about eatin' my own gun, just to bring an end to the misery. But I knew I couldn't do that to you and Mama."

"Damn straight you couldn't," Jayne growled. "If you'd gone and committed suicide, Mama would've killed you!"

"That makes no—" It dawned on Matty that Jayne was ribbing him. "Oh yeah. I get it."

"You always were slow on the uptake."

"And you're the smart one in the family," Matty said. "God help us."

They rounded a bend in the trail, with the cattle still following dutifully, uttering the occasional inquisitive moo. Before them lay the meadow known as Gospel Acre, named after the brothers' great-grandfather Gospel Cobb, the full-time rancher and part-time lay preacher who'd first settled this patch of land. His mortal remains were buried somewhere out in this field, and it certainly was a favored spot for a person's last resting place. A glittering silvery creek meandered to the south, forming the field's perimeter on that side, while to the north there was a copse of oak and hickory and, beyond, a line of hills that ran along the horizon, pale purple in the distance. You couldn't see aught but land and sky, and whenever Jayne viewed the scene it did not fail to stir his soul. Maybe one day he would end up being interred here just like his great-grandfather, forever a part of the soil. He could think of worse fates.

The cattle filed down into the meadow and straight away set to munching on the grass. Jayne and Matty headed for the copse to sit in the shade, eat the sandwiches Mama Cobb had prepared them, and swig whiskey from a hip flask. Jip settled down beside them, his muzzle on his forepaws. He was a no-breed dog, wire-haired and rangy, with sharp-pointed ears perched atop an unduly large head. Matty reckoned there was wolf somewhere in his ancestry; Jayne was more of the opinion that it was coyote.

All at once, Jip sprang up, his ears pricked. He let out a soft whine.

"What's that, boy?" said Matty.

"Something's got his attention," Jayne observed.

Jip let out a couple of short barks, then looked pleadingly at his master.

"His tail's not down, so he ain't scared," Matty said.

"Ain't up neither," Jayne said, "so he ain't happy. Hear that?"

Hoofbeats. A good mile away. Rippling through the still air. Sounded like three, maybe four horses.

Jip barked again.

Jayne had an uneasy feeling. He reached for Vera, which was sleeved in a rifle scabbard attached to his horse's saddle.

"Could just be a posse passing by," Matty said.

"Could be. Probably is. But I ain't taking no chances. Been rumors 'bout a gang of cattle rustlers up Beacon Levels way."

"Yeah. I heard. But nobody'd try it in broad daylight, would they?"

"Depends," Jayne said. Both men were on their feet now and peering hard in the direction of the sound.

"On?"

"Far as most folk are concerned, there's just two people living at the Cobb ranch right now. You and Mama. A middle-aged woman and her son who ain't in the best of health. I've been on Sycorax less than a week, and hardly anybody knows I'm back."

"But everyone round these parts knows I'm not sick anymore," Matty said.

"The rustlers don't come from round these parts. Their intel may not be up to date. If that's them coming our way right now, they're probably thinkin' there's no one defending this here herd. No one worth considerin', at least. They're thinkin' its easy pickings, and that's made 'em bold."

Solemnly Matty drew his own guns, both of them. Like his older brother he was something of a firearms connoisseur. For his personal sidearm he favored the much-vaunted Van Heflin 9mm recoilless semiautomatic and carried a pair of them in cross-slung buscadero holster belts. Each pistol was customized with mother-of-pearl panels inlaid on the grip and an extra-capacity magazine that held eighteen rounds rather than the usual ten.

Finally the approaching riders came into sight. There were four of them in all, and as if to confirm Jayne's supposition, each had a bandana fastened around the lower portion of his face.

"Covering their noses and mouths against dust?" Matty suggested.

"Ain't dusty country," said Jayne. "That's disguise."

Jip's fur was up. He began barking furiously.

"Hush, Jip!" Matty said, but the dog would not be silenced.

The sound drew the riders' attention. Spying two men, two horses, and a dog at the edge of the copse, they wheeled their mounts in that direction. If Jayne had any last lingering doubts as to their intentions, these were dispelled as the riders spurred their horses to a gallop, at the same time drawing their guns.

"We got us a fight on our hands, Matty," Jayne said. "You up for it?"

"You have to ask?"

The cattle rustlers fired first.

The Cobb brothers were not slow about retaliating.

They weren't on horseback either, which gave them a clear advantage. It was harder to shoot accurately from a fast-moving horse than when standing on your own two feet on firm ground.

Vera accounted for the frontmost rider. The Van Heflins, fired simultaneously, unhorsed two of the others.

The fourth rustler about-turned and fled for the hills.

"Should we chase him?" Matty asked.

"Nah. We've scared the *gǒu shǐ* out of the fella. He ain't comin' back."

Two of the rustlers the brothers had shot were stone dead. The third lay on the ground, groaning and writhing in agony.

"Gotta be regrettin' your decision to try and steal these cows now, huh?" Jayne said, standing over him. The cattle, though startled by the exchange of gunfire, had remained in the meadow. The grass of Gospel Acre was just too sweet-tasting to abandon, whatever the circumstances.

"Doctor," the man whimpered. "Please. Fetch a doctor."

"Not gonna happen," said Matty. "Nearest town's ten miles away. You're bleeding out fast. By the time we bring a doctor back, you'll be long gone."

"Asshole." The rustler spat out the word along with a sizable quantity of blood.

"You're the cow thief, and you're callin' *me* an asshole?"

The man's mouth parted in a gruesome grin. "You two are so screwed, you know that? You messed with the wrong gang."

"Seems I could say the same about you," Jayne remarked.

"There's more of us. Plenty more. My people learn we've been killed, they'll come, and they'll be out for blood."

"Sure, sure," said Matty, "and I'm president of the Alliance."

"No kidding." The rustler coughed horribly, spewing crimson down the front of his shirt. "You dipsticks have just... just signed your own... death... warrrrr..."

A last gurgle of breath. The rustler's head sank back to the ground. His eyes rolled up in their sockets.

Gone.

Matty toe-nudged the corpse, just to be sure.

"Reckon what he was saying's true?" he asked Jayne. "There's more of them and they'll be gunning for us?"

Jayne shrugged. "Dunno. Coulda just been bravado."

He didn't think so, though.

It seemed that the Cobbs had just made some enemies.

The notion filled Jayne with apprehension.

But also, because he was a man who relished a fight, excitement.

21

In *Serenity*'s cargo bay, Mal sat down heavily on an empty oblong packing crate.

Tired. So gorramn tired.

He guessed there was something he ought to be doing around the ship, some captainly duty or other he should be carrying out. If nothing else, he could get on the Cortex and start chasing up business contacts. Shake the tree, see what fruit fell.

All he wanted, however, was some shuteye.

He reclined back on the packing crate.

He reclined on an ottoman in his and Inara's house.

No, it was a packing crate. A hard steel packing crate in the cargo bay.

No, it was a soft, cushioned ottoman.

Packing crate.

Ottoman.

Mal hadn't known what an ottoman even was until he'd moved in with Inara. He just wasn't an ottoman sort of guy.

He hadn't known what a lot of other things were, for that matter. Avocados. He'd heard about them, sure. Never seen one in the flesh, so to speak. Absolutely never eaten one until Inara served them for dinner one day. They looked repulsive on the outside. Skin all brown and warty like a toad's. The taste? Well, that was pretty repulsive too. He'd maybe have preferred eating a toad.

And hair pomade. Inara had bought him a tin of the stuff five Christmases ago. He'd used it just once, and thereafter it had stayed in a drawer. The smell had been acrid and he'd not been able to get away from it because it was attached to him. His own approach to male grooming was much less refined. Soap, water, a dab of cologne on special occasions: that was it.

The pomade wasn't the only gift Inara had given him that December. The main one had been a bouncing baby daughter, Samadhi. And Mal knew which of the two he preferred. The black-haired, blue-eyed beauty who'd gurgled and drooled and peed all over him the first time he changed her diaper. That one by far.

This same Samadhi now came hurtling into the room, took a running jump at her father, and landed with her knees smack dab in his crotch.

Mal jackknifed under his daughter. "Oof! Easy there! Mind your poppa's poor cods. You want another brother or sister sometime in the future?"

Samadhi regarded him with puzzlement. "No. I got Jackson already. Don't want another smelly brother. Or sister."

The aforementioned Jackson Serra-Reynolds entered the room in hot pursuit of Samadhi. "There you are!" he cried. "Found you! My turn to hide now."

"Wasn't hiding," Samadhi retorted. "I'm not playing that game anymore. Now I'm trampolining on Daddy."

Suiting the action to the word, she began jumping up and down on Mal's pelvis.

Out of sheer self-preservation, Mal snatched her up and began zooming her through the air in figures-of-eight. Samadhi squealed with delight.

"Fly, little Firefly!" Mal said.

"My turn! My turn!" Jackson said, leaping up and down on the spot with his hand in the air. "I wanna be a Firefly too!"

Mal set his daughter down and picked up his son. "Whoa. You're gettin' heavy there, hoss. How old are you now? Twenty-five?"

"Don't be silly, Daddy. I'm seven. Now Firefly me."

Mal whooshed Jackson around the room, setting him down occasionally on a piece of furniture then lifting him off again. Each stop was a planetfall: "Lilac. Santo. Greenleaf. Silverhold."

Samadhi joined in, chasing after Firefly Jackson.

"Hey, Jackson," said Mal, "we got the I.A.V. *Samadhi* hot on our tail. We gonna let those pesky Feds catch us?"

"No!" Jackson said fiercely.

The pursuit continued through the house, ending up in the kitchen where Inara was preparing a meal. Mal tumbled to the floor with Jackson, and Samadhi bundled in on top of them. After three minutes of roughhousing, when Mal started begging for mercy, Inara stepped in.

"Kids. Go wash up for lunch."

Jackson and Samadhi raced to be first to the bathroom.

Inara looked down pityingly at her husband. "I swear, Mal, I've seen you in gunfights, I've seen you in fistfights, but I have never seen you more battered and bruised than when you horseplay with those two."

"They're gonna be the death of me," said a rumpled-looking Mal. "Help me up."

He extended a hand to her, and when she reached out to grasp it, he yanked her onto the floor with him.

"Come here," he said, smothering Inara in kisses. "My Mrs. Reynolds."

"Mrs. *Serra*-Reynolds."

"Sure, sure. Have I told you how much you mean to me, woman?"

"Not as a I recall."

"Could've sworn I did just this morning. Or was that *showing* you how much you mean to me?"

"If you mean when you lay on top of me for three seconds grunting, then I guess I got the message."

"Three seconds? It was five at least!"

"I was looking at my watch, Mal. It was three."

"Gorramn Companion. Always keepin' one eye on the time."

"Former Companion."

"Let's not let the facts get in the way of a good joke."

"I'll remember that for if you ever make one."

"Ouch," said Mal. "Seriously, though, Inara. You're everything to me. I know we got the fancy house and a thousand acres all our own and those two little hellions who run us ragged, but without you, it wouldn't be nothing."

"Double negative. It's either 'It wouldn't be anything' or 'It would be nothing.' Not both."

"Woman, don't correct my grammar when I'm bein' romantic."

"Mal," Inara said, her smile turning sincere. "Are you happy?"

"I am."

"Is this all you ever wanted?"

"It is."

She wrapped her arms around him and kissed him tenderly. "Then stay," she said.

It wasn't even an issue. Mal had no intention of leaving.

22

Wash guided the *Comet* from one Core world to the next. He could have hired another pilot to do the job for him, or just engage autopilot, but he preferred to spend as much time at the controls of a ship as he could. It reminded him of the old days, when he was young and had nothing. Nothing but a rattlesome old freighter he could barely afford to keep running.

Back then, work was thin on the ground. Wash lived hand to mouth. It was sheer love of flying that kept him going, and he was content, just about.

Then Zoë Alleyne entered his life, and everything changed.

They met at a party on Persephone, held by Atherton Wing, a mutual friend. Wash, by that time, was making considerable strides forward with his transportation company Pteranodon Incorporated. His client list now included the likes of Wing and other nobles and plutocrats. Still, he was relatively small beer. Parties like this were a good chance to network, and Wash was doing his best. Chummy banter, backslapping, the niceties of upper-class etiquette—these things didn't come naturally to him, but he was learning.

He and Zoë bumped into each other. Literally. Wash was backing away from the buffet table with a canapé in either hand. Zoë was reversing from the opposite direction. They collided, and the canapés fell to the floor.

One look at her, and Wash forgot all about food. He forgot he had even been carrying the canapés.

"I'm so clumsy," he said.

"Seems you are," she said.

"But not normally."

"No?"

"Normally I'm like a ballet dancer. Poised. Light on my feet."

He did a very bad impersonation of a ballet dancer.

Zoë laughed. "I didn't realize people with two left feet could be ballet dancers."

"Oh, there's more of us around than you'd think. Hoban Washburne, by the way."

"Zoë Alleyne."

"Friends call me Wash."

"Would you like me to call you that?"

"Would you like to be my friend?"

"Know what?" said Zoë, her eyes reflecting the dazzle of the chandelier overhead. "I reckon I just might."

They spent the rest of the evening together.

And the rest of the night.

And pretty soon it was clear to Wash they were going to spend the rest of their lives together.

Zoë became not just his wife but his business partner. Thanks to her sharp brain and no-nonsense deal brokering, Pteranodon Inc. grew in leaps and bounds, far quicker than it might have if Wash were running it on his own. Within the space of a decade it had become a mighty, 'verse-spanning empire, with a fleet of nearly a thousand ships of various sizes shuttling back and forth between planets.

During that time Zoë also brought him children, their eldest Celeste and the twins Ulysses and Uriah. Those three were the center of Wash's world. They went everywhere with him and Zoë. The twins were still too young for education, but Celeste got her schooling remotely using the Cortex curriculum plan. She was whip-smart, like her mother, and oh-so pretty. One day she would be breaking boys' hearts left and right. That was if Wash ever allowed any to take her out. He knew how boys were, having been one himself. He liked to say that Celeste could start dating when she was old enough, and by old enough he meant forty. It wasn't entirely a joke.

His life, looked at objectively, was an incredible success story. Pteranodon was the envy of its rivals. Everybody wanted to hire the company's services. And if Zoë was the driving force behind Pteranodon's rise to the top, if it was her that clients listened to, her they were impressed with and intimidated by, more so than him, what did it matter? Whatever worked.

Even when Wash overheard people refer to the two of them as Mrs. Washburne and her husband, that was okay with him too. Somebody had to be the face of Pteranodon. Why not Zoë?

At Beaumonde, Bellerophon, Ariel, and beyond, the *Comet* put in. There were meetings in conference rooms, in rooftop gardens, in penthouse suites, in floating palaces, on beachfront decks; and usually there were boozy dinners afterwards to celebrate the signing of some contract or other. Business could always be conducted via wave, but in person was better. That was when Zoë could really work her magic.

Sometimes Wash would just sit back and watch her go. She was a whirlwind. A tsunami. Nothing could stand in her way. Clients caved before the force of her personality, readily doing whatever she asked, cutting margins, agreeing to bulk discounts, you name it.

Between deals there was always the chance to grab a little downtime. Wash and Zoë owned a number of houses across the Core but their favorite was the mansion on Persephone. There they could roam the spacious grounds, swim in their private lake, entertain guests, and play racquetball with the neighbors. The children loved that place, Celeste most of all. She talked about it all the time aboard the *Comet*. "Are we going back to the Persephone house soon?" she would ask. "Can we, Poppa? Please?"

One night, Wash and Zoë were lying in bed together, her head on his chest, in their huge room at the Persephone mansion. By some miracle, the twins had gone to bed without much fuss and were actually staying asleep. It helped that Wash had spent much of the afternoon playing with them, wearing them out—and himself—by pretending to be a hungry Tyrannosaurus Rex whose favorite snack was small boys, especially ones whose names began with the letter U.

"Are you happy, Wash?" Zoë asked, running a finger over the contours of his chest.

"Of course I am," was his reply. "What's there not to be happy about? I've got everything. Everything a man could need."

"Is this all you ever wanted?"

"All," said Wash sleepily, "and more."

23

Zoë Alleyne got horrendously drunk the day independence was declared.

The celebrations went on long into the night. Her recollections were hazy but she had a distinct memory of bedding some beefy, broad-shouldered hunk from the 19th Sunbeamers, a space commando who made up for what he lacked in the brains department with what he had in the trouser department, and who knew his way around a woman's body, to boot. There was also a bar brawl between a half-dozen Browncoats and a similar number of Alliance sympathizers who just couldn't accept that not only had they been on the losing side, they had been on the wrong side. A rut and a fight, fueled by beer and bourbon chasers—pretty much the perfect night out as far as Zoë was concerned.

All this took place on Londinium, where just twenty-four hours earlier the Alliance Parliament had declared formally that the war was over and begun drawing up terms of surrender. Proceedings in the Upper Chamber of the House were being broadcast 'verse-wide on the Cortex, with one politician after another stepping up to the speaker's microphone and declaring how sorry he or she was for the pain, suffering, and loss the conflict had caused.

With these announcements came the inevitable denouncements, as scapegoats were sought. Alliance generals were pulled from their beds in the dead of night and imprisoned pending trial. Leaders on every major Core world were rounded up and placed under house arrest. Even a handful of Blue Sun executives found themselves being led away from corporate headquarters in handcuffs. Heads rolled, figuratively for the most part, although there were summary lynchings of authority figures on a couple of the less civilized planets.

The morning after, an extremely hungover Zoë emerged into the brilliance of Bai Hu, the White Sun. The light was like a dagger between the eyeballs. She staggered to the nearest diner and helped herself to the largest breakfast imaginable, washed down with about a quart of black coffee. The proprietor, identifying her as a Browncoat, waived her bill. "For one of the valiant folks who won us our freedom?" he said. "No charge." Her guess was the man had been pro-unification during the war—like most on Londinium—but now saw the wisdom in ingratiating himself with the victors.

On her way out, she bumped into Sergeant Reynolds. Judging by his bloodshot eyes and deathly pallor, he wasn't in much better shape than she was. To Zoë's no great surprise, he had a girl hanging off of either arm.

"Sir," she said.

"None of that now, Zoë," he replied. "Ain't you heard? War's over. You can call me Mal."

"And who are these lovely ladies, Mal?" It felt weird calling him that. "Aren't you going to introduce me?"

"Sure. This is, um… I want to say Marie?"

"Marnie," said the one on his left. She had the Independent emblem—blue star on two yellow stripes against a green triangular background—painted on her cheek.

"That's it. Marnie. And this is Carina."

"Katrina."

"Close enough. We're heading off to find us some hair of the dog. Care to join us?"

Zoë didn't think conversation with Marnie and Katrina was going to be what you'd call stimulating. "Thanks, but no. I'm probably just going to hit the sack."

"You do that. Zoë?"

Reynolds leaned close to her and said, with a wink, "You happy?"

"If my head would stop pounding, yes."

"Is this all you ever wanted?"

Zoë nodded, regretting nothing, even the pain spiking through her cranium.

It was true. This *was* all she had ever wanted.

24

At the end of a sixteen-hour rotation at AMI, a weary Simon made his way not back to his penthouse apartment in Merriweather Heights but instead towards Rochester Peak's spaceport and a certain repair yard. He entered the premises via the front gate and found the owner in the workshop, bent over a rocket pod with an acetylene torch. He stood and watched as some expert spot-welding was performed. Sparks flew like fireworks, and the smell of scorched metal was pungent.

Finally the person straightened up, turned to him and raised the visor of the welder's mask on their head to reveal a heart-shaped face and a pair of bright, lively hazel eyes.

"Can I help you?" the woman said.

"Are you Kaywinnet Lee Frye?"

"That's the name on the shingle outside, sir. But you can call me Kaylee. Whom do I have the pleasure of addressing?"

"Dr. Simon Tam."

"Ooh. A doctor. Shiny! And what can I do for you today, Doctor?"

"I have, um… A problem."

"An engineering problem?"

"You could say that. It's, er, a wiring fault which needs correcting."

"Well, you've certainly come to the right place. I fix faults." Kaylee Frye removed the welder's mask. She was wearing her thick chestnut hair scraped tightly back in a ponytail. She unfastened it and let it fall. "Let's go to my office, huh? And you can tell me all about it."

Her office was a partitioned-off corner of the workshop, furnished with a metal-framed desk, a battered chair on wheels, a wall calendar, and not much else. Kaylee parked her behind on the edge of the desk and looked Simon up and down.

"Well?" she said. "You gonna explain what this wiring fault is? Can't fix what I don't know about."

Simon moved closer to her, until their noses were almost touching. "I lied, Kaylee," he said. "I don't have any problem. Especially now that I'm here."

Kaylee angled her face up to his. "Why, Dr. Tam," she said breathlessly. "I do declare! Are you trying to seduce me?"

"Trying and succeeding, I hope."

Later, as they gathered up their strewn clothing off the floor, Simon said, "I hate to say this, but I think my father knows about us, Kaylee."

She frowned. "How? We've been discreet. We never meet anywhere but here."

"He has his ways. I wouldn't be surprised if he's paying someone at the hospital to keep an eye on me. Some first-year intern desperate for a little extra cash. That would be like him."

"Your own father spying on you?"

"You have no idea what kind of a man he is," Simon said. "And how important lineage is to him."

"Are you sure he knows?"

"No. It's just, the other day, he dropped hints. He talked about 'girls who work with their hands' and about 'engine oil.' It might have been coincidence. It might also have been him sounding me out, trying to gauge my reaction."

"How *did* you react?"

"I don't think I gave anything away."

"Then we're okay," Kaylee said. "I know this is difficult for you, Simon."

"It's not," he said, but the protest sounded unconvincing even to his own ears.

"I get it. I'm not the kind of girl your daddy wants you to be with. But you have to ask yourself, are you happy?"

"With you? Yes. Yes, I am."

"And is this all you ever wanted?"

"You and me?" Simon didn't have to think twice. "Yes. Yes, it is."

25

Kaylee and her mother spent the afternoon shopping at the Belle Reve mall in downtown Tankerton, near the seafront boardwalk. Kaylee hadn't been keen to go but Jemima Frye had insisted.

"A little mother–daughter bonding time, Kaylee. That isn't too much to ask, is it? Your father gets you to himself practically all day, every day. All I'm after is a few hours. You can spare that, surely."

"When you put it like that, Mom," Kaylee had replied, "yes, I can."

In actual fact, Kaylee didn't mind shopping. She tried on several dresses, compared different shades of eyeshadow, and helped her mother pick out a silk blouse and a tight-waisted formal jacket with puff shoulders. Jemima sat on the board of the local women's guild and also performed unpaid secretarial and administrative duties on behalf of Shepherd Driscoll at church. She was a tireless community volunteer and liked to look smart while carrying out her good works.

When they returned home from their spree, Kaylee was footsore and exhausted. She could work on an engine without pause, hammering, lifting, crawling under, for hours on end. Traipsing around shops, however, tuckered her right out.

She almost didn't notice that the sign above the street entrance to her father's workshop had changed.

Where the sign had once said ALOYSIUS FRYE, MECHANICAL REPAIRS, now it had been replaced with one that said ALOYSIUS FRYE AND DAUGHTER, MECHANICAL REPAIRS.

Kaylee was so stunned, she could hardly speak.

"Pop?"

Her father came out from the workshop grinning. "Like it, pumpkin? Why else do you think your mother dragged you away the whole darned afternoon?"

Jemima Frye smiled conspiratorially.

Kaylee hugged them both. "What's brought this on, Pop?" she said, adding, "Not that I'm not thrilled."

"Your mom, for one. She's been nagging at me to take things a bit easier. Haven't you, Jemima?"

"What you call nagging, Aloysius, I call expressing wifely concern," Kaylee's mother said. "You aren't getting any younger."

"Then there was that health scare I had, earlier in the year." Aloysius Frye patted his chest. "Old ticker's fit as a fiddle now, of course. Been fixed up good and proper. But it was a shock to the system all the same, falling sick like that. Got me thinking I shouldn't be flogging myself half to death keeping the money coming in. Got me thinking I need to ease up and concentrate on enjoying the life I have left to me. Got me thinking I could do with someone to share the load. And who better, pumpkin, than you? You coming back from the Black, the timing was just right. It was like an omen from God. You're one heck of a mechanic, maybe even better than me. I'd be a fool not to want you by my side."

"Oh, Pop."

"We're business partners now, girl. Everything split fifty-fifty. If you're agreeable, that is."

"You bet I am."

"This make you happy?"
"You know it does."
"Is this all you ever wanted?"
"You even need to ask?" said Kaylee.

26

Radiant Cobb took the news about the cattle rustlers about as well as can be expected.

"Those no-good, low-down, snake-sucking *yān guò de hún dàn!*" she bellowed. "Tryin' to take my cows! Who in the name of *wǒ de mā* do they think they are? *Hé chù sheng zá jiāo de zāng huò!*"

"I'm not sure they actually want to fornicate with livestock, Mama," Matty said. "Just steal it."

"You keep your smart-mouth remarks to yourself, my boy," Radiant said. "Jayne, you're sure there are more of them?"

"So the fella told us," Jayne replied. "He was at death's door, so I don't reckon he had any reason to be lyin'."

"And you let one of them get away, so now he's gonna tell his accomplices about what happened and they're gonna be out for some payback. You shoulda chased after him and brung him down."

"He was too far gone," Jayne said. "We'd never have overtaken him."

"And we didn't know there was any more of them, anyway," Matty chimed in. "Not straight off. We assumed it was just the four, and we didn't learn otherwise until too late."

Their mother raged at them some more, and Jayne and Matty stood back and took it. It was like weathering a storm. You knew it'd blow itself out sooner or later. All you could do in the interim was endure.

When eventually she calmed, Jayne asked her what their plan of action was.

"Get ready," Radiant said. "That's all we can do. Them bastards'll be back, you can count on it. But they won't find us unprepared. You two go bring the cattle into the barn. That's first on the list of priorities. Meanwhile I'll fetch out every last gun we have in the house and give 'em a good clean. We'll need to put up barricades too."

"How about going into town and asking for help?" Matty said.

"From who exactly?" Radiant snapped. "The Cobbs ain't much loved round here. We weren't that popular to begin with, and it only got worse after your father, God rest his soul, went on that bender and torched Chad-Michael Wu's grain silo to the ground, then shot up the Happy-Go-Lucky Casino."

"Wu owed him money," Jayne said, "and Dad owed the casino."

"What he did might, arguably, have been justified," said Mama Cobb, "but it don't change the fact that he caused injury and property damage. Wilmington County folk have been even less kindly disposed towards us since he did it, and there's no shortage of 'em that'd gladly see us run out on a rail. In fact, this rustler gang might well be the answer to everyone's prayers if they think it could mean an end to the Cobb family. No, we got no one to rely on but ourselves, boys. And ourselves, I reckon, is more than enough."

As Jayne and Matty were setting off towards Gospel Acre to retrieve the herd, Radiant Cobb drew her elder son aside.

"Jayne?"

"Yeah, Mama?"

"I can't say I'm not pleased you've come back to us. I only wish this rustler situation hadn't arisen to muddy up the well-water."

"It's okay, Mama," Jayne said. "Ain't no other place a man ought to be than his homestead when it's threatened."

"Spoken like a true Cobb. Your daddy'd be proud. Are you happy, Jayne?"

"In a funny way, yeah, I am."

"Is this all you ever wanted?"

"All things considered, gorramn it, yes."

27

Badger, if he was being honest with himself, was not having the best of days.

The conversation with Malcolm Reynolds had put him in a right foul mood. The nerve of the bloke! Rejecting a perfectly good cargo. Who died and made him King of all Londinium?

Adding insult to injury was the way Reynolds had hung up on him. All that malarkey about not being able to hear what Badger was saying. The connection had been clear. Reynolds had just been dicking about.

Rut that wanker.

Badger's real problem, however, was not the transporter of the item so much as the intended recipient. At some point he was going to have to break the news to the guy who'd paid for the Ghost Machine that he wouldn't be getting his Ghost Machine after all, at least not any time soon.

And the longer he put off making that call, the better.

There weren't many people in the 'verse whom Badger was afraid of, but the man in question was one of them. Afraid of? That was putting it mildly. Dreaded, more like.

All morning Badger fretted and fumed, stomping around his lair in Eavesdown and peeling apple after apple in an effort to quell his anxiety. The apple therapy usually worked, but not this time.

He wondered if there was a way he could still get ahold of that flightcase with its valuable contents. However, he didn't know anyone on Canterbury apart from the late, unlamented Hoyt Koestler. He could order some of his own men to fly out there and search for the item. That'd cost money, but the expenditure would be worth it. How long would it take, though? Three or four days, and that was assuming they'd even be able to find the box.

Within three or four days, his buyer would be wanting to know what had become of his purchase. He'd expect Badger to have it in his possession and be ready to forward it on. The buyer would not be best pleased to learn that the Ghost Machine was still on Canterbury and possibly lost.

Alone in his office, Badger steeled himself to send the man a wave, then recanted at the last moment.

He did this several times. Finally, after perhaps his tenth aborted attempt, the matter was taken out of his hands. The person in question got in touch.

Badger knew he had no choice but to take the call. With trembling finger he pressed Accept.

"Ahh, Meester Badger," said Adelai Niska.

The old man's smiling face filled the screen. Bald-pated, bespectacled, he looked like your favorite grandfather, the one who bounced you on his knee and gave you toffees even after you'd already eaten too many.

"There you are," Niska continued. "All day I am waiting to hear from you. How nice, I am thinking, will it be to have communication from my friend the Badger. But nothing comes, and I ask myself, have I offended? Have I, how you say it, made him pissed?"

Though his mouth had gone dry, Badger managed to say, "Mr. Niska, I was just about to—"

"Ah, ah, ah." Niska wagged a finger. "Excuses. They are the things that are like... The leaky bucket, yes? They are no good use."

"I wasn't making exc—"

"And the lies," Niska said, interrupting again, "they are worse. The bucket with no handle. Do you understand this image?"

Badger wasn't sure he did, but nodded regardless.

"Now then," Niska said, "I have words I must be having with you."

Badger gulped. "Shoot," he said, then wished he hadn't used that particular word. Where dealings with Adelai Niska was concerned, the verb in its literal sense was often a likely outcome.

Not for the first time, Badger rued the day he had agreed to be Niska's go-between with regard to the Ghost Machine. If only the sums involved hadn't been so juicily tempting.

"You see, Meester Badger, it transpires that..."

Niska broke off as a woman's pain-wracked scream issued from somewhere nearby him.

"W-wot was that?" Badger said, regretting asking the question as soon as it left his lips.

"Nothing you need pay any heed to," Niska said. "A friend's wife. She has been unfaithful to him. Lesson must be taught. A woman cannot be loose with her favors, especially not to important husband. Sets a poor precedent."

Another scream came, this one even more tormented than the last, a mindless howl of agony.

"Please!" Niska barked at someone behind him, out of the camera's sightline. "I am trying to make wave here. Keep her quiet until I am done." He looked back at Badger. "My men have the enthusiasm but they are not—I want to say delicacy? The finesse, yes, is better describing it. After you and I finish, I will give demonstration to them. They try out new toy, you see. The Scorpion is its name. Like my Spider, but next-generation. A most interesting tail it has, this instrument of persuasion, but they have not good understanding of its proper using yet."

Badger was very ready for this conversation to be over. At the same time, he was not looking forward to its conclusion. He had a hunch that it was no mere happenstance Niska had waved while there was torture going on in the background. The unfaithful wife of Niska's friend wasn't the only one who was being taught a lesson.

"I must discuss with you a subject now," said Niska. "Our little deal. Or not so little."

"Yes," said Badger. "Yes, of course. I assumed that's wot this is about. Mr. Niska, fing is, you see, there's been a spot of bovver."

"A spot of bother. I know this phrase."

"Yes. And—"

"But I have," Niska went on, "my own spot of bother, which makes me not so much concerned about any spot of bother of yours."

"You do?"

"The Ghost Machine. I do not want it anymore."

Badger gaped. Had he misheard? Was this a trick? "You... don't want it?"

"No. I am going off the idea."

"Wot?"

"In the two days since we are last speaking, Meester Badger, new information has come to light. From someone, I may say it, high-placed in Alliance. Ghost Machine, you remember, is part of consignment of twenty-four. Others have been delivered to Alliance, but it seems Blue Sun have not been entirely truthful about their product. It is a shame, a great shame. Dishonesty in business practices. Is like warped mirror. It reflects bad on us all."

"Wot 'aven't Blue Sun been truthful about?"

"Ghost Machine is supposed pacification device."

"So you told me."

"And so my contact at Alliance told *me*," said Niska. "It has purpose of making crowd of unruly people—a mob—tranquil. How does it do this?"

"No idea, Mr. Niska. You tell me."

"I shall. Infrasound. Machine, when activated, sends out subsonic frequencies which work on part of human brain. Very specific soundwaves which target very specific portion of brain known as septal nuclei. Septal nuclei are also known as brain's 'pleasure center.' They make happiness."

"Okay…"

"When septal nuclei are stimulated by Ghost Machine's infrasound, person quickly slips into tranquil dream-state. Like on psychotropic drug but much faster-acting. Almost instant. So, if mob is rioting, Ghost Machine may be deployed to stop them in their tracks. Nobody hurt. Everyone safe. Is better, for sake of appearance, than to use water cannon or make unconscious with gas, never mind to hit with batons or shoot with the guns. Then Alliance officers can say, 'Look, problem is dealt with quietly. No mess, no fuss. Aren't we good people?'"

"Rioters, all blissed out, can be rounded up and carted off in paddywagons. No aggro. Bosh. Job done."

"But Blue Sun, it is regrettable to tell, their test results have fudged," said Niska. "Fudged is another way of saying made false, no? Test results tell some of story but not whole story. Because Ghost Machine has secondary effect. Soon after it is first used on people, it begins to influence another part of brain. Part next door to septal nuclei. Part called the—I hope to pronounce this right. Amygdala."

To Badger, it sounded like some kind of exotic foreign food. "And that is…?"

"Amygdala," said Niska, "is organ which deals with fear and aggression responses. It causes us to be scared and to be hostile. For person exposed to Ghost Machine for more than a few minutes, magically peaceful dreams turn rotten. There is the panic, the confusion, the phobias. Uncontrollable horrors of the mind. Some, they even die from it. The blood pressure rises sharply. A stroke. A cardiac arrest. Others become violent, a danger to themselves and to those around."

"Oh," said Badger. "So the Ghost Machine ends up 'aving the opposite result it's meant to."

"Exactly. Exactly. Exactly. You see the spot of bother now, Meester Badger, do you not? Ghost Machine makes angry people calm but then straight away angry again—angrier than before—or terrified or both at once. Is counterproductive. Blue Sun cover up this unfortunate fact, because they wish Alliance to buy device, but Alliance have found out. Alliance no longer want Ghost Machines after all. And I, I do not want Ghost Machine either."

"Wot were you going to use one for anyway?" Badger inquired. "If I may ask."

"You may."

"Was it because you could 'ave applied the technology as a kind of drug? You said the Ghost Machine worked like a drug. You could 'ave got people 'ooked on it. Sold them 'its of it."

"No. Too complicated," said Niska. "My reason was more simple. A man in my line of work sometimes finds himself in difficult position. To take example, not so long ago my skyplex in orbit around Ezra came under assault. I will not trouble with details. Long and short, there was gunfire and I lost employees."

Badger had heard something about this. It was rumored that the attackers concerned were none other than Mal Reynolds's crew, come to rescue the man and his pilot from Niska's clutches.

Bloody Reynolds. Everything seems to revolve around that geezer. Mal? Maladjusted, more like.

"Now," said Niska, "imagine if I have Ghost Machine. There is attack. I fire up machine. Everyone suddenly docile. Incident resolved without bloodshed and destruction. Intruders easy to make captive. In theory. But now I know Ghost Machine is ineffective. Could make whole situation worse. So, I not want anymore."

"All right," said Badger. "I understand." He strove to remain outwardly calm. Inside, he was feeling the first faint inklings of hope. Could it be that he was off the hook? Was it possible? "Then you're canceling our arrangement?"

"I am."

"Let me get this absolutely straight. You aren't after 'aving your Ghost Machine at all?"

A philosophical shrug from Niska. "It disappoints, but no. I have no interest in it now."

"Where might that leave us financially?" Badger asked. "You've paid up front. I presume you'll be wanting your money back."

"No, Meester Badger. No." That winning smile again. To the casual observer, Niska would seem like the nicest person in the 'verse. "Who has reneged on this deal? Not you. It is I. I am the one who has changed mind. You have discharged your end of the obligation. For the sake of my reputation, I cannot force you to give back what was handed over in good faith. You may keep every credit you have received, and we part on good terms."

Badger felt close to fainting. If this wasn't the most extraordinary turn of events, he didn't know what was.

"And your Ghost Machine?" he said. "What should I do with it?"

"Is on its way, yes?"

"Yes," Badger lied.

"Your spot of bother was only minor one?"

"Very minor."

"Well, when you receive machine, do as you please. Sell to some unsuspecting third party. Throw on junk heap. What do I care?"

"Mr. Niska, really, this is too generous of you."

"Pfah! Generous? You have been inconvenienced, as much as I. Now we are all square, as the saying is. Goodbye, Meester Badger. Have a pleasant rest of the day."

The wave screen went blank.

Badger let out one of the biggest, most heartfelt sighs of his life.

Had that really just happened? Had Adelai Niska really just told him he could keep a sizable chunk of money even though he hadn't delivered the goods and indeed might not have been able to?

More to the point: where Badger had anticipated threats and fury from one of the most terrifying crime bosses alive, there had been nothing but cordial politeness. Apology, even.

In that moment, Badger had never felt gladder to be alive.

He began to chuckle.

Soon he was guffawing helplessly.

"Take that, Malcolm Reynolds," he declared to the empty room, tears of mirth pouring down his face. "You screwed me over, only it turns out the joke's on you. I've got off scot-free. I've got my fee in my pocket *and* your cut of it, and best of all Adelai Niska isn't going to roast my innards over a slow fire. In fact, 'e finks I'm some kind of 'onorable gent. Adelai ruddy Niska!"

So saying, Badger sprang to his feet, grabbed his bowler hat, and headed out into the stews of Eavesdown to celebrate his stroke of remarkable good fortune.

28

Days of idyll.

On Sihnon, Inara's homeworld and now Mal's planet of residence, the weather was always clement. Here, as on the other of the Core's two capital planets, Londinium, the terraforming process had worked to perfection. The temperate zone extended across a broad band of latitude in both hemispheres, and even at the equator the climate was merely subtropical. A midsummer noontide was balmy but never sweltered.

For the Serra-Reynolds family, life was leisurely. Jackson and Samadhi were visited by a tutor every morning for school lessons, while their parents might fly by skimmer to the nearest town, Tiantang, to meet friends for coffee, or else go pony trekking in the hills, or just laze by the side of their infinity pool, taking the occasional dip.

Afternoon was a time for all four of them to take part in a shared activity. It might be meditation practice, led by Inara, or target practice, led by Mal. They might go out hiking. They might head for the big city to visit a museum or an art gallery or catch a film. Jackson was into movies about the Unification War, which Mal tolerated even though they rarely showed the Independents in a good light. His least favorite was a recent one called *Serenity*, where the

Battle of Serenity Valley was presented as an out-and-out victory for the Alliance. The Browncoats were not seen to surrender. They were simply annihilated by a squad of Alliance soldiers led by a very charismatic actor with blue eyes, tidy hair, and a fixedly earnest demeanor. Several times Browncoats were referred to in the dialogue as "vermin" and "scum," the screenplay dehumanizing them to the point where not a single Independent character was given a name.

On a visceral level Mal found this offensive. He had been one of those anonymous "vermin." He'd fought alongside brave men and women in the mud and blood of conflict, and to see them reduced to wild-eyed, fanatical nobodies was an outrage.

Inara had initiated him in the ways of Buddhism, however, and as the family left the movie theater Mal centered himself with breathing, in order to assimilate and disperse the indignation he felt. Holding on to old animosities was unhealthy. Hatred hurt no one but the hater. The war was long past. Mal was in a different place now, a different life. He even called an Alliance planet home these days, something the old Mal wouldn't have dreamed of doing. Too angry then. Too grudgeful. Letting go, forgiving, detaching, rising above— these were the paths to enlightenment.

Still, he couldn't resist pointing out to Jackson that *Serenity* presented a very one-sided view of the hostilities. "I know you see something like that onscreen, son," he said as they flew homeward, "and it's cool and exciting, all the explosions and bullets and such. Weren't that way in reality. The war wasn't good guys, bad guys. It was people. Terrified, courageous, hopeful people, fightin' 'cause they believed in something—Alliance and Independents alike. Fightin' and in many cases dying. You'd best remember that."

Financially speaking, the Serra-Reynoldses didn't have a care. They owned their house and land outright, and could live well on the interest from the capital Inara had accrued during her time as a Companion. There were times when Mal felt he ought to be holding down some kind of job, providing for his wife and children. But Inara would always argue that if he didn't need to work, why work? He had spent so much of his life hustling, chasing hither and yon across the 'verse, scraping by. Now that he had the opportunity just to kick back and enjoy himself, he should make the most of it.

Every once in a while a nagging thought would catch him. Usually it came during the small hours. Mal would wake up with a sense that this life wasn't *his* life. It was some kind of impostor life. He didn't belong in this house. He didn't deserve Inara as his wife and Jackson and Samadhi as his kids. It was all some fantastic *error*.

Dispelling this insidious notion was like locating an angry possum in a darkened cellar and evicting it by hand. It took vigilance and effort, but Mal invariably managed. He might go into Jackson's bedroom for a while, and then Samadhi's, and watch each of them sleeping, so sweetly, so soundly. He might step onto the balcony and gaze out at the view—the moonlit valley with its whispering trees, the far mountains, the superbly star-studded sky. He might even wake Inara and tell her he loved her. These simple expedients helped still his whirling doubts. They reminded him, with their beauty, how blessed he was, and he should never question his existence.

The day when everything changed began like any other day. Before breakfast, Inara led the family in chanting salutations to the Buddha, his teachings, and his disciples, finishing off the ritual by striking a singing bowl and intoning "*Namaste.*" A little later, Master DaSilva arrived to give Jackson and Samadhi lessons in math, history, and Mandarin. He was a prissy, fastidious little man whose impeccable good manners Mal sometimes found a little grating. But the kids loved him and were blossoming under his tutelage, so Mal was prepared to overlook his foibles.

Just as DaSilva was taking his leave, a tumultuous roar shook the house.

"Oh my!" the tutor cried. "What in heaven…?"

Mal rushed out onto the balcony, just in time to see a midsize spacecraft hurtle overhead. It was on a shallow-angled descent and was veering wildly in the air, as though out of control. Its course was taking it roughly along the line of the valley, but if the pilot didn't pull up soon, the seesawing spacecraft was going to crash-land.

As disturbing a sight as this was, more disturbing still was the condition of the ship. It wasn't any single kind of vessel in particular but rather an amalgamation of several. Somewhere in there Mal identified the basic frame of a freighter, but the majority was bolted-on sections from any number of other craft. In addition, there were spikes and fins protruding from it in all directions. These added nothing in aerodynamic terms but gave the ship a profoundly menacing appearance, like some sort of reptile with ridges of scales across its back. Further adornment came in the form of random stripes and flashes spray-painted on the hull plates in fluorescent hues.

Most alarming of all was the cloud of fumes spouting from its engine exhaust, leaving a great black billowing trail in the ship's wake.

Mal's stomach clenched into a tight knot.

"Inara!" he yelled. "Grab Jackson and Samadhi. We are getting out of here."

"What is it, Mal?" Inara replied from the house.

"No time. Just do as I say."

Master DaSilva emerged onto the balcony beside him in time to see the underside of the spacecraft scrape the treetops perhaps a mile down the valley. Next moment, the ship went into a spin, around and around like a cartwheel on its side. It plowed through the forest amid a welter of splintering trunks and shattered branches, before eventually coming to rest on its belly. A pancake landing that would have jarred the bones of all aboard, but the spacecraft was essentially intact, as far as Mal could tell. It sat at the end of the furrow of devastation it had cut, canted at a slight angle, amid a dissipating miasma of smoke.

"Well I never," said DaSilva. "There's a sight you don't see every day. Those poor people inside. I hope they're all right."

"I hope to hell they ain't," Mal said, a discernible tremor in his voice. "But I doubt we're gonna be that lucky."

"Why do you say that?"

"Clearly you don't recognize what you're looking at, Master DaSilva."

"I'm looking at a crashed spacecraft whose occupants may well be injured. We must go to their aid."

"No. We must do precisely the opposite. We must run, as fast and as far as we can, and we must do it now."

"Mr. Reynolds, far be it for me to disagree with you, but—"

"But nothin'!" Mal snapped, right in DaSilva's face. "I don't know how and I don't know why this can have happened, here on a Core planet, but that there ship is gonna mean the death of all of us if we do not leave this instant."

"But why?" DaSilva protested. "Whom does it belong to?"

"Reavers."

29

In its first few months of trading, Aloysius Frye and Daughter, Mechanical Repairs did solid if not spectacular business. The workshop's location on the outskirts of Tankerton placed it near both the city's seaport and spaceport, meaning that Aloysius and Kaylee were conveniently close by for emergency callouts when the engines of ships of either kind needed mending. Aloysius had already established a name for himself as an industrious and meticulous mechanic, and while there were some customers who were skeptical as to whether Kaylee had inherited his talents, those doubts were soon put to rest when they saw her handiwork. It wasn't long before people were asking her father why he hadn't brought her into the business sooner. He replied that Kaylee had had to go out and see the 'verse first, find herself out there in the Black, before she could return home and settle down. A spell crewing aboard a Firefly had done wonders for her. She had gone out a girl and come back an adult woman.

Kaylee herself looked back on her *Serenity* days fondly but had no regrets about leaving the ship. Nothing had been the same since Inara and Book went. Then there were the threats to life and limb— the shootouts, the pursuits, the run-ins with the authorities—which had seemed to plague *Serenity*'s crew constantly. She didn't miss any of that.

She did miss Simon. Good-looking, infuriatingly indecisive Simon. But him and her, it just hadn't worked out. The stars hadn't aligned for them. Maybe in some other life...

One afternoon, when her father was out tending to a private yacht with a faulty magnetohydrodynamic drive, a sharp-dressed man called by the workshop. He was inquiring about reconditioning a vintage spaceplane, an Ellison Z-Type no less.

"A slingshotter," said Kaylee with admiration. "Are we talking the old-old Ellison with the chemical fuel thrusters or the less old one with the liquid air-cycle engine?"

"The less old," said the man. "I know it had its critics, back in the day, what with the extra time it'd spend in lower atmo so as to collect enough oxygen for the engines to burn."

"Not to mention the increase in aerodynamic drag. Then there's the size of the fuel tank. Gotta fit in all that liquid hydrogen somewhere. All told, the thrust-to-weight ratio on the newer-model Ellison was a *zhēng qì de gǒu shǐ duī*. Plus, the helical-coil heat exchanger, even though it was supposed to be a self-cleaning one, had a tendency to foul like crazy. Thing went through filters like somebody with a head-cold goes through tissues."

The man shook his head self-deprecatingly. "Okay, okay, I get it. I've bought myself a money sink. But damn if, when it's up and running again, it won't get me halfway around the planet like *that*." He snapped his fingers.

Kaylee laughed. "Can't put a price on speed, I guess. Nor on classic style."

"Amen to that." The sharp-dressed man held out a hand. "Caleb Dahl."

"Kaylee Frye. I'd shake, but..." She showed him her grease-stained right hand.

"I'm not scared of a touch of dirt, Miz Frye."

"In that case, put her there, Mr. Dahl. So, what kind of state of repair is your Z-Type in?"

"One previous not-so-careful owner. It's been sitting in a hangar best part of a decade."

"A fixer-upper, then."

"You got it."

"Well, I'm the woman for the job," Kaylee said brightly. "I love me a challenge."

"I'm right glad you said so."

"Can't promise it's gonna come cheap, however."

"I understand," said Dahl, "and I appreciate your candor. Put it this way. Money's no object."

"Music to my ears."

"Marvelous. Here's my card."

The text on the card read CALEB DAHL—IMPORTS & EXPORTS, followed by his home address and sourcebox number.

"That's a swanky card," Kaylee said, admiring the creamy smoothness of the paper stock and the crisply embossed lettering. "Harmsworth Avenue? I don't think I know that street."

"It's in the Clearcrest Bay district."

Kaylee let out a low whistle. "That's a swanky part of town."

"Then I guess, on present evidence—swanky card, swanky address—I must be a swanky kind of guy."

"And what do you import and export, might I ask?"

"Oh, this and that. Whatever pays. But look at the time. Must dash. It's been a considerable pleasure meeting with you, Miz Frye." Bending smartly from the waist, Dahl took her hand and kissed the back of it, grease smudges notwithstanding.

To say Kaylee was charmed would be an understatement.

When her father got back, she couldn't wait to tell him about the dashing Mr. Dahl and his Ellison Z-Type.

Aloysius Frye's face darkened. "Give me that card of his, Kaylee."

She handed it to him, and he promptly tore it up into tiny shreds.

"Word of warning," he went on, gravely, "and I'll say this only once. You have nothing to do with Caleb Dahl. You do not go near the man. You send him a wave to tell him you won't be doing business with him. From then on, never contact him again. Ever."

"But why, Pop?"

"Because I say so."

"But he's rich. He'd be a great client to have. Maybe he'd recommend us to all his rich friends. This could be the making of us."

"I've told you how it's gonna be, Kaylee, and that's final."

"Pop…"

"Uh-uh."

Her father wouldn't brook another word of it. Caleb Dahl was a no-go subject. Aloysius Frye said he didn't even want the name mentioned again in his hearing.

Puzzled, Kaylee nonetheless dutifully waved Dahl. She didn't need his card for his sourcebox number, since it was listed publicly on the Cortex.

"I won't be able to take on your Z-Type after all," she said. "I guess I… I thought I was up to the task but I'm not. I shouldn't have misled you. I'm sorry."

"Nowhere near as sorry as I am, Miz Frye. Are you sure you won't reconsider?"

Kaylee gnawed her lower lip. "Sure as I can ever be."

"Well, that is a mighty shame," said Dahl. A shadow briefly crossed his face. It could have been disappointment. It could equally have been anger, as if he did not like having his wishes thwarted. "Should there be a change in circumstances, please don't hesitate to get in touch. Goodbye."

As she cut the connection, Kaylee pondered.

Aloysius Frye and Daughter, Mechanical Repairs was an equal

partnership, was it not? Everything split fifty-fifty, that was what her father had said.

Which meant she had as much say in how the company was run as he did.

Which, in turn, meant that if she wanted to pursue importer/ exporter Caleb Dahl as a customer, what was to prevent her?

Later that day, after her parents had gone to bed, Kaylee disobeyed her father's edict and waved Dahl a second time.

"I'm delighted you've been able to see your way to providing me with your services after all, Miz Frye," Dahl said. "You will not regret it."

And he smiled at her and gave her a look, which, if his smile hadn't been so dazzling, might have reminded her of the look a cat gets when it has a small bird in its jaws.

30

For maybe the eighth or ninth time, Wash perused the article in the *Azure Illuminator*:

HOBAN AND ZOË WASHBURNE - A PROFILE
BY WILHELMINA ASCOT

Hoban and Zoë Washburne are two of the business titans of the post-war 'verse. Their company Pteranodon Incorporated is the premier freight transportation line in the Core and beyond. If you need something sent, large or small, chances are it's Pteranodon Inc. that will be doing the shipping.

I'm greeted by the male half of this partnership, known to his friends as "Wash," in the hallway of their sumptuous mansion in Persephone's upscale Westborough enclave, not far from Cadrie Pond. Westborough, for those not fortunate enough to have visited, is a cluster of multiple-acre estates patrolled by private security and surrounded by high fences.

The first thing I'm struck by is how much better-looking Wash is in real life than in any onscreen image I've seen of him. Although his eyes are set perhaps a tad close together, they are piercingly blue and radiate a rare warmth and charm. His sandy-blond hair is neatly trimmed. He looks to be in excellent physical shape. He is in his early forties but one would imagine he was a good decade younger.

Over a glass of the finest Beaumonde Beaujolais, we discuss mutual Persephonean acquaintances such as Atherton Wing and Sir Warwick Harrow. Wash says he counts both men as "close personal friends." Then Zoë Washburne enters. She is a stunning-looking woman, oozing dynamism, and manages successfully to maintain the tricky balance between a working life and being a mother. I see this in the way she ushers out the twin toddlers who have followed her into the room. She is firm but gentle with them, saying, "Ulysses, Uriah, Mommy has to talk with the nice lady now. Go play with your big sister." The two darling things beg to stay, and when again told no, they stick their tongues out in unison, whereupon Mrs. Washburne sticks her tongue out in return, then sends them packing with a gentle swat on the behind.

Once the twins withdraw, our pleasant little *tête à tête* can at last commence…

It was a classic *Illuminator* society pages puff piece, fifteen hundred fawning words penned by a journalist with aspirations to aristocracy.

Sitting at his desk and rereading the article now, however, Wash felt only resentment. In the month since it was published, things had taken a sharp downturn.

At first it seemed merely a run of bad luck.

A consignment of propoxin went astray somewhere in the Kalidasa System. Presumably the medicine was pilfered during a ship-to-ship transfer and was even now being sold on the black market.

There was a labor dispute at a psilomelane mine on Regina, which resulted in a week-long stoppage. A Pteranodon freighter was supposed to be conveying several hundred tons of the manganese ore to a refinery on Santo, but instead just sat on the landing pad all that time. An idle ship was a ship losing money.

Several Pteranodon crews came down with a mystery malady that was traced eventually to a batch of bad protein bars. The break in the supply chain cost the company in the region of half a million credits.

Aggravating though all this was, Wash and Zoë took it in reasonably good humor. These things happened in business. You had setbacks. You dealt with them.

Then came the news that a Pteranodon subsidiary had posted false results for the last fiscal cycle. Astrocline, one of the lesser freight haulers the company had swallowed up during its rapid expansion, had registered profits 150 percent in excess of its actual profits. The problem was traced to an accounting error, and the relevant personnel were sacked, but investor confidence was shaken and share prices in Pteranodon took a significant hit.

Around the same time, a hostile takeover was launched against another Pteranodon subsidiary, Konglong Shipping, which had a lock on the Red Sun System routes. A group of shareholders engaged in a proxy fight and very nearly succeeded in wresting control of Konglong from the board of directors, until Wash and Zoë themselves weighed in. They deployed an army of lawyers to declare the takeover bid illegal and threatened to take the rebel shareholders to court. The rebels, rightly fearful that the Washburnes's pockets were deeper than their own and their appetite for victory stronger, backed down.

A third major blow came in the form of a class action suit from the same crewmembers who had fallen ill due to the bad protein bars, which had been found to contain a measurable quantity of rat feces. Their complaint pertained to unsafe and unsanitary working conditions, and they were petitioning for compensation. The Washburnes's defense team countered by demanding proof that Pteranodon had knowingly supplied foodstuffs that were unfit for purpose. The crews' lawyers could not, and the judge, who happened to be a friend of Wash's friend Sir Warwick Harrow, threw the case out.

While Pteranodon Inc. emerged from these misfortunes more or less unscathed, Wash was left with a deep sense of unease. Before, the company's voyage through the seas of commerce had been plain sailing. These choppy waters it had lately encountered disquieted him. It was almost as though someone was gunning for him and Zoë. Someone was trying to undermine everything the Washburnes had so painstakingly built up.

Or was that just paranoia?

Looking back at the *Illuminator* article filled him with a weird nostalgia. Only a handful of weeks had passed, and yet the Hoban Washburne described by Wilhelmina Ascot seemed like a very different person. The image she gave of a sleek, suave freight magnate was not one he recognized right now.

A knock at the door of his home office roused Wash from his somewhat bitter reverie. Zoë entered.

Spotting the *Illuminator* piece open in front of him, she said, "Looking at that *again*, my love?"

"Sure. Why not?"

"No need to be defensive."

"It was a big deal for us. A Wilhelmina Ascot profile is a badge of honor. Anybody who's anybody has had one. It means you've made it. And then there's this picture."

He indicated one of the photos that accompanied the article. It showed him, Zoë, and the children on the mansion's front steps. He and Zoë each had an arm around the other's waist and were smiling broadly for the camera. Celeste, meanwhile, was resting a hand on each twin's shoulder. The gesture looked affectionate but in fact she was holding Ulysses and Uriah steady. Otherwise the pair of them simply wouldn't keep still long enough for the photographer to take the shot.

"Look at us," he said.

"What's wrong with it? It's a lovely picture."

"But we look so gorramn... *smug*. Grinning like that. Not a care in the 'verse. Little did we know that in just a few days' time everything would turn to *niú fèn*."

"*We're* not *niú fèn*, though, are we, Wash?" Zoë said, moving closer. "You and me? We're still good."

She laid a hand on the back of his neck.

Brusquely, almost petulantly, Wash shrugged it off.

"I get it," said Zoë, a certain frostiness entering her voice. "You're pissed. I'm pissed too. But don't take it out on me. Relax. It's going to be fine."

"Relax?" he retorted. "How can I? It's been one crisis after another, and I'm just waiting for the next to hit. And when it does, people are going to start to wonder about us, if they aren't already. They're going to wonder just how firm our grip is. Pteranodon's looking weak right now, and weakness is like blood in the water. It brings out the sharks."

"And if they start circling, we'll see them off. You and me, hun. Together. Let 'em try to take us on. See how that works out for them."

None of this was making Wash feel any better. Normally when he was down in the dumps, it only took a few encouraging words from Zoë to rally him. This time, everything she said just seemed to compound his misery. During Pteranodon's meteoric rise to preeminence, they hadn't failed. Not once. Any obstacles had been brushed aside. Everything had just fallen into their laps.

But how much of that had been his doing, and how much Zoë's? What had he actually contributed to the company over the years?

The more Wash thought about it, the more it seemed he was the junior partner, both at work and at home. The Wilhelmina Ascot article had painted a very traditional portrait of the Washburnes, depicting Wash as the man of the household and Zoë as a mother who happened to have a job as well; but then the *Azure Illuminator* catered to a conservative readership. The truth was otherwise. When it came to business, Zoë did most of the running. Staging a buyout, opening up a new route, purchasing new ships—it was Zoë who made these decisions. Wash just went along with them, and up until now he hadn't had a problem with that.

But maybe he should have. Maybe he needed to be more involved with the company. Maybe that was what Pteranodon Inc. was crying out for. What if all these recent troubles stemmed from him relying too much on Zoë and not trusting his own judgment?

Over the next few days, Wash's misgivings continued to simmer. There were no more upsets, business-wise, but neither was there any notable upswing in Pteranodon's fortunes. Wash moped around the mansion, tetchy with the staff and even with his family. One time, he snapped at Celeste for a relatively minor piece of misbehavior. After stubbing her toe against a table leg, she uttered the words "rutting hell," when one of Zoë's cast-iron household rules was no profanity from, or in front of, children. Wash totally overreacted, scolding Celeste with such vehemence that she burst into tears and called him "a big stinky buttface," adding that he was also "a bad daddy." That earned her a half-hour time-out in her room, although if Wash was honest, the punishment was as much for hurting his feelings with the "bad daddy" comment as for the backchat.

It all came to a head at a dinner party, as these things often do. Among the invitees was Durran Haymer, who came over to Persephone from his floating estate on Bellerophon especially for the occasion. Haymer had sent plenty of work Pteranodon's way and was considered a valued client. The main purpose of the evening was sucking up to him.

Haymer sat on Zoë's right, and throughout dinner she fawned on him, laughing extravagantly at his every quip and touching his arm at least once every five minutes. Subsequently she took him on a tour of the house, showing him the various Earth-That-Was artifacts she and Wash had amassed over the years. "Of course, our collection's not a patch on yours, Durran," Wash heard her say as the two of them left the dining room. "But we try."

When they rejoined the rest of the party, Zoë and Haymer had their arms linked and were leaning together, chuckling about something. They had been gone nearly twenty minutes. That, to Wash, seemed a long time. The Washburnes didn't have *that* many antiques.

Watching Zoë with Haymer during the meal and afterwards, Wash felt an obscure pang that he gradually was able to identify: jealousy. He hadn't known her to behave this way with another man before, not even in the name of making a deal. He'd seen men try to flirt with her during business meetings, but all it took was one steely glare from her to shut them down. Zoë Washburne was having none of *that*.

But the way she was all cozy with Durran Haymer now…

It went beyond just "sucking up," in Wash's view, and it set him to wondering whether looks and touches and shared laughter was as far as it went.

Haymer was a handsome guy. Sophisticated. Well connected. More obviously a match for Zoë than Hoban Washburne ever was. If there wasn't something already going on between those two, it seemed to be starting right now, before Wash's very eyes.

Some while later, Wash found himself out on the back terrace with Haymer, under a full moon. The two of them were smoking cheroots and discussing a transaction. During a lull in the conversation, almost as an aside, Haymer said, "That wife of yours is some woman, Washburne. Gotta say, you're punching well above your weight there, pal. No offense." He accompanied the remark with a jovial biff on the arm, like a more vigorous version of a knowing wink.

At that moment, Wash could quite happily have punched him back.

In the face.

Hard.

As it was, he just nodded, and resolved never to have Haymer over to his house again. Never to leave Zoë alone with him again, either.

By the time everyone left to go home, Wash had got himself steaming drunk. As he and Zoë were undressing for bed, there was a row. Wash was sure he started it but wasn't quite sure what it was about. Something trivial. There was yelling, there was name-calling, and he ended up spending the night in the guest room.

In the morning, he brought breakfast up to her and tried to apologize. This, too, deteriorated into a row. Zoë told him he had said some harsh things to her last night. Things that were hard to forgive. Wash's retaliation was to accuse her of carrying on with Durran Haymer behind his back. Even if he didn't believe it was true, he still hoped to see a flicker of guilt on her face, an unspoken admission that she had cheated on him. Maybe not with Haymer but with someone else.

Because Haymer was right. What was a woman like Zoë Alleyne doing with Hoban Washburne? What did she ever see in him? She was way out of his league. There had to be something to account for her attraction to him, some ulterior motive on her part. It was the only explanation that made sense. It couldn't just be love, could it?

The argument escalated. The children, hearing the ruckus, came to investigate. The twins began to cry. Celeste looked on aghast. They had never seen their parents like this. It terrified them.

That didn't stop Wash and Zoë. They ended up bent towards each other, screaming in each other's face.

Wash wasn't even aware of attempting to hit Zoë until all of a sudden she reared back, her eyes glinting with sheer venom.

"Raise a hand to me, Hoban Washburne?" she snarled. "Don't you gorramn dare."

Wash looked at his hand. It was poised level with his head, ready to deliver a slap. He wanted to lower it but somehow could not. If he did, he would be capitulating to her, and he was too angry for that. Equally, no way could he go through with the slap. If he struck Zoë, there'd be no coming back from it. Everything he believed in, everything he held dear, would be destroyed.

Meekly, shoulders slumped, he turned and exited the room.

All day long he hid in his office, seething. Zoë did not come to see how he was. He didn't expect her to but hoped she might. The kids left him alone too. He heard Celeste shushing the twins as they walked past the door, like he was a hibernating grizzly you mustn't disturb.

He wracked his brains thinking how to mend the rip he had torn in the fabric of their marriage. At the same time, a voice in his head was telling him that Zoë should be reaching out to him, not the other way around. If his accusations were false and she hadn't been unfaithful, she ought to come and say so. Put it beyond doubt. The fact that she didn't was tantamount to a confession.

Eventually, as evening was falling, there was a light tap at the door.

"Yeah?"

Zoë walked in.

Wash tried to read her body language. She had her hands behind her back. That could mean anything from contrite to antagonistic. As for her expression, it was impassive. Zoë could put on a hell of a poker face when she wanted.

"Wash," she said. Her voice was neutral too.

"What?"

"Now's the time."

"The time for…?"

"Boot up your sourcebox."

"Huh? Why?"

"There's some people want a word."

"Who?"

"Stop asking questions and do as I say."

Wash was feeling belligerent. "Not unless you give me a good reason to."

"I don't think you understand, Wash."

Zoë showed her hands. In one of them was a pistol. She leveled it at him.

"This isn't a request," she said, thumbing back the hammer. "It's an order."

31

Aiming her Mare's Leg point-blank at Colonel Hiram Tregarvon, Zoë said, "You have a choice. Come quietly, or I blow your brains out on the spot. Either's fine with me. Bring you in alive or dead, I still get paid the same. But you should know that alive's a bigger pain in my ass. I'll have to keep an eye on you all the way back to Londinium. Dead's a whole lot simpler."

It had taken three weeks for Zoë to get to this point. Three weeks of following trails. Prying intel out of various informants, sometimes with money, other times with threats, occasionally with violence. Traveling from one pissant Rim planet to another even more pissant Rim planet. Until at last she'd tracked Colonel Tregarvon down to Haven and a shack surrounded by an expanse of prairie, the nearest outpost of civilization a good hundred miles away. This was a man who definitely did not want to be found. Which was one reason why the bounty on his head was so skyscrapingly high.

Another reason was the massacre at Cooper's Hollow, one of the worst Alliance wartime atrocities, which Tregarvon had masterminded. Three hundred civilians murdered, an entire town razed to the ground, and along with them the platoon of Independents they'd been harboring.

For protection on Haven, Tregarvon had brought a pair of still-loyal ex-Alliance soldiers with him. They had been patrolling outside the shack when Zoë crept up on them. Both now lay dead, one with a broken neck, the other with a crushed windpipe. She had felt little compunction about dispatching them. They had sided with a monster and had got no more than their due.

For a coldblooded murderer, Tregarvon himself, in the flesh, was a less than impressive sight. He was puny-framed, with a pathetic comb-over and a mustache so threadbare it barely qualified for the name. When Zoë kicked in the door to the shack, he had let out a little squeak of shock and scrambled to grab a gun. She had decked him with a single punch, and now he was on his knees with her rifle to his head, and he was gibbering in terror. The crotch of his pants was soaked. His eyes rolled in their sockets.

"Come on, you *liú kǒu shuǐ de biǎo zi hé hóu zi de bèn ér zi*," Zoë intoned. "What's it going to be? If you're going to let me take you back to Londinium to face a war crimes tribunal, say yes. That's all you have to do. Just nod, even, if you've lost the power of speech."

Tregarvon seemed terrified beyond the capacity to make the decision.

Which was no skin off Zoë's nose.

"Okay. Can't say I didn't give you a chance."

She fired.

As she wiped spatters of blood and brain off the barrel of the Mare's Leg, Zoë reflected that she had shown Tregarvon more mercy than he had shown the residents of Cooper's Hollow. When they had refused to capitulate to his ultimatum—give up the Browncoats who were hiding in their midst—he had ordered an artillery division to bombard the town until not a single building was left standing. He hadn't even attempted to flush out the Independent soldiers by means of house-to-house raids. That might have cost Alliance infantry lives. His solution, for all its savagery, had prevented casualties among his own men, and that in turn had reflected well on him in the eyes of the troops he commanded and of his superior officers.

Zoë returned to the war crimes bureau on Londinium with sufficient photographic and physical evidence to prove that Colonel Hiram Tregarvon was dead. Hannah Hsiao, the official in charge of the bureau, processed her claim with the usual thoroughness. When Zoë asked if there were any new warrants, Hsiao shook her head.

"None but the usual. Take your pick."

Zoë looked at the posters that adorned the wall of Hsiao's office, a rogues' gallery of the Alliance's worst committers of wartime atrocities. Each featured a headshot of the person concerned, along with physical characteristics and identifying marks, names of known associates and a list of possible whereabouts.

"What about him?" she said, pointing to one that showed only a blank, generic silhouette, with no additional information whatsoever.

"The Butcher of Beylix?"

"Yeah. Any fresh intel come in about him?"

"Not a thing. Man wasn't only the most feared interrogator in the whole Alliance, he was a gorramn ghost. Still is. No photographic evidence. Not a trace of him in any Alliance database or on the Cortex. Nobody knows his real name. Weren't for the stories that came out about him during the war, you might think he never even existed."

"Yeah," Zoë said. "Most of the Browncoats I served with thought the Butcher of Beylix was just some kind of legend. A boogeyman. Or Alliance propaganda, maybe. Me, I reckon what he did to people, the tortures he devised—stuff like that ain't made up. It had to have come from somewhere."

"Frankly, I'm not sure why we even keep him on the wall," said Hsiao. "I guess there's a chance he might slip up one day. Someone who knew him might spot him and rat on him, or else one of you bounty hunters gets phenomenally lucky. Even then we'd have a job proving it was *the* actual Butcher of Beylix. All's we've got to nail him with is a set of bloodstained battle fatigues the Butcher supposedly wore."

"What's the betting the blood on them isn't his own?"

"High probability it belongs to one or more of his victims. Main thing is, his DNA will be all over the fabric. We get a match, and we can prove the fatigues were his, then we get our man." Hsiao waved a hand casually. "You want to try tracking him down, Zoë, be my guest. He could be just about anywhere in the 'verse. That's why the bounty on his head's so damn steep. But you could spend your whole life looking and never find him. I were you, I'd stick to the ones we have names and faces for. Leave the phantoms be."

After Hsiao had confirmed Zoë's claim on Colonel Tregarvon and authorized the payment transfer, Zoë headed straight to the nearest bar and embarked on the process of getting rip-roaringly drunk.

Midway through the evening, Mal Reynolds appeared. Zoë greeted him and bought him a drink, and for a while they sat companionably together, talking about anything except the war.

Reynolds had not been having a good peace. On various occasions since the armistice, his and Zoë's paths had crossed, and each time he had looked that little bit more haggard, that little bit less cocksure. It was as though he didn't know what to do with himself now that the Independent cause was won. The Rim planets were free from the Alliance's authoritarian influence at last, while the political infrastructure of the Core planets was in the throes of being dismantled and replaced by something more democratically accountable and, it was hoped, fairer. The system wasn't perfect yet. Within the new Independent government—an interim arrangement known as the Accord—there was factional infighting and frequent policymaking paralysis. The Accord was a coalition of former Browncoat brass from the length and breadth of the 'verse who had been focused and effective when combating oppression but less so when it came to the day-to-day management of hundreds of planets.

To Zoë, Reynolds seemed to epitomize the problems the Accord was experiencing. His objective achieved, he had lost his way.

"Tried running a transport business for a while," he told her, referring to his latest attempt to scrape an income as a civilian.

"How'd that work out?"

"Not so great. Bought a Firefly, about tenth-hand, only the gorramn thing turns out to be the money-suck to end all money-sucks. Maybe if I'd had a decent engineer I could've kept her flying, only instead I had this useless *tā mā de hún dàn*, name of Bester, who was more interested in chasin' tail than in, y'know, fixing stuff. Asshole didn't even know what a reg couple is."

"Maybe you should've checked his credentials before you hired him."

"When you put it like that, it sounds so sensible. Anyways, that heap-of-garbage Firefly's now sittin' in an Eavesdown Docks scrapyard waiting to be broken down for parts, and I'm more credits in the hole than I care to think. Apart from that, life's peachy. How 'bout you? The bounty-hunting biz treating you well?"

"It's a living," Zoë said with a shrug. "What skills I have, it's a way of putting 'em to good use."

"Word is you just brought in Colonel Tregarvon."

"Brought in *pieces* of him. Left most of him on Haven."

"Shame. Couldn't have happened to a nicer guy."

Zoë glimpsed a flash of the old Sergeant Reynolds swagger as he said this. The thought of Tregarvon and other similar Alliance creeps was bringing back good memories for him—memories of a time when he had known what was what and who was who. She wondered whether he would have been happier if the Independents had lost. Maybe Mal Reynolds always needed someone to fight against. He defined himself by what he resisted, and therefore without anything to oppose, he was nothing.

"You could always join me, you know," she said. "There's money to be earned, and you'd make a damn fine bounty hunter, I reckon. We could be a team."

She might have been drunk, but the offer was sincere. She thought she would quite enjoy working alongside Reynolds again.

"Dunno," he said. "Is it really 'me'?"

"Think about it. There are dozens of war criminals still out there, perhaps even hundreds. Holed up in out-of-the-way places, praying justice doesn't catch up. Some of 'em may even think they're safe and won't ever have to pay for what they did. Don't you want to see them in jail?"

"I had a choice, I'd rather see 'em six feet under."

"That's always an option. They don't comply, a bounty hunter is authorized to employ lethal force. For me, it's not what I prefer, but in some cases—Tregarvon to name but one—it's not exactly regrettable."

"Well, okay," Reynolds said. "Maybe." He motioned at their empty glasses. "Say, you considerin'…?"

"You buyin'?"

Ruefully Reynolds shook his head. "I was kinda hoping you would do the honors."

Zoë didn't mind paying for another drink, or another after that. Reynolds had saved her ass more than once during the war. Least she could do in return was treat him to a little liquor. Especially since he had fallen on hard times and seemed in dire need of getting drunk.

At closing time, Zoë, Reynolds, and the last few remaining patrons staggered out of the bar.

"There's this place I know," Reynolds said to her. "Ain't far."

"Yeah? What do they do there?"

"They serve alcohol, late into the night. And there are women in their scanties. But mostly it's about the alcohol. Interested?"

"Not in women in their scanties," Zoë said, "but in alcohol? Sure. Why not? Lead the way."

Reynolds ventured down some winding back alleys, Zoë

stumbling after him. She had been more inebriated than this in the past, but she had also been a lot soberer. Her buzz was just about the right level for that hour. And she was with her trusty old pal Reynolds, heading off for some dubious-sounding dive where there was a fair chance they might end up embroiled in a fistfight.

Good times.

Even when they strayed into an ill-lit area of town where the buildings clustered a little too close together for comfort and the alleys grew ever narrower and windier, Zoë wasn't worried. She knew how physically capable she was. Reynolds was the same. Anything untoward came their way, the two of them could handle it.

Still, when the moment happened, it happened fast—faster, almost, than she was able to cope with.

She felt a familiar tingle. Call it a sixth sense. Call it situational awareness drummed into her at Browncoat bootcamp and honed in battle. There was the whisper of a footfall behind her. Furtive, shadowy movement ahead.

"Mal..." she murmured.

They struck from all sides at once. Two sprang from the shelter of doorways. A third rushed in from behind. A fourth and fifth descended from above, dropping from their place of concealment on a fire escape. A sixth sidled out in front of the two ex-Browncoats from the junction with an adjoining alley.

Zoë may have been drunk but her reflexes were only somewhat impaired. Sinking into a crouch, she swept her leg around in an arc, knocking the nearest attacker's feet out from under him. As he fell to the ground, she hurled herself at him, landing with her knee on his throat. The man started wheezing helplessly and didn't stop.

Wheeling on the spot, Zoë glimpsed another attacker lunging for her. He was wielding a blunt weapon, a baton of some kind. No, a crowbar. He brought it down at her, but Zoë, keeping low, parried, moved inside his descending arm, and delivered an uppercut to his solar plexus. The breath whooshed out of him, and as he sank to his knees, she grabbed his weapon arm and twisted the wrist over sharply until ligament snapped. The man yelped, and Zoë snatched the crowbar out of his grasp and clobbered him senseless with it.

She straightened up, looking around for Reynolds. He wasn't to be seen, only the four remaining assailants, who formed a semicircle around her. All of them were armed with striking implements that ranged from a billy club to a tire iron.

"If this is a mugging," Zoë said to them, hefting the crowbar, "you sorry bastards picked the wrong gorramn victims, that's all I can tell you."

"Sadly," said Reynolds, from right behind her, "they didn't."

A sun exploded inside Zoë's brain.

Then came pain. Pain searing through her skull.

The crowbar fell from her grasp. She collapsed, clutching the back of her head with both hands. The world seemed to have turned to jelly, everything soft and unsteady. The already dim alleyway began to darken further.

Grimly she fought to stay conscious.

"Zoë," Reynolds said, "for what it's worth, I'm mighty regretful about this."

With a supreme effort, she turned to look at him.

He had a small leather sap in his hand.

He raised it aloft and whacked her with it again, and this time the blow fulfilled its intended purpose. Zoë's lights went out.

32

The Cobb house was barricaded, the windows boarded up, pieces of heavy furniture ready beside the doors to be shoved into place when necessary. The larder had been stocked, enough food and fresh water to keep body and soul together for a month. Jayne, Matty, and their mother were all set for a siege.

For a while, it did not come.

They kept watch in shifts, from the widow's walk that capped the roof. Perched up in that vantage point, like an eagle in its roost, you had a clear view for miles around. No creature larger than a gopher could approach without you seeing.

When he wasn't on lookout duty, Jayne got on his mother's sourcebox and scanned the Cortex for information about the gang of rustlers. From snippets here and there, he gathered that they had been plaguing this region of Sycorax for nigh on half a year now. They were known as the Beavertail Gang, and their numbers were estimated at anything between a dozen and forty, depending on which news outlet you consulted.

Their leader was a woman called Ottoline Beavertail. Only one picture of her existed, a grainy shot of a gaunt, formidable-looking middle-aged lady with close-cropped gray hair and a patch over one eye. She owned a spread over in Bitter Hampton, which was just about the driest, least fertile piece of land imaginable, a hellscape of salt pan, slot canyon, and granite bluff. Raising cattle there was a struggle at the best of times, and lately a drought had taken ahold, alleviated only by torrential downpours of rain that caused flash-flooding, property damage, and generally more problems than it solved. By all accounts, Ottoline Beavertail had seen a quarter of her herd succumb to fatal dehydration. Added to that, the remaining livestock had contracted redspot, a respiratory disease with a nine-in-ten mortality rate. She had obviously come to the conclusion that the only logical way to replace her lost cows was to steal other people's.

Her gang consisted of various local guns-for-hire, a couple of farmers who'd suffered significant livestock depletion like her, and a passel of malcontents just glad of the opportunity to raise some hell. It was a mixed bag, which she held together through a combination of sheer force of will and being meaner than any of them.

There wasn't a hope in hell of law enforcement getting involved in the affair. The nearest sheriff's office was in Grover City, half a continent away. As for the Feds, Sycorax was one of those unproductive Border worlds that the Alliance considered beneath its notice. The Feds couldn't have given two hoots what went on there. It was up to civilians to deal with the Beavertail Gang, and so far, in and around Wilmington, and elsewhere, there had been precious little appetite for tangling with them. Some had tried and had come to grief.

None of them, mind you, was the Cobb family.

At least Jayne had a slightly clearer idea now what he, Matty, and their mother were up against. Desperados, under the command of a woman with a grudge against the world and no hesitation about mowing down anyone who got in her way.

The wait dragged on, and Matty suggested that maybe the Beavertail Gang weren't coming after all. "That guy, he could just have been braggin'. Tryin' to intimidate us. And the one that got away, he could've gone back to the others and told 'em not to bother with us. We showed him we're too badass to mix it up with."

"Maybe," said Jayne.

"You don't think so."

"All's I know is, Ottoline Beavertail don't seem like the kind of person you mess with and there ain't repercussions. I'd like to think she and her gang are gonna leave us alone, but I wouldn't bet on it."

Radiant Cobb nodded in agreement. "You listen to your big brother, Matty. Unlike you, he's been out there in the 'verse. Worked all manner of jobs in all manner of places. Hooked up with that bunch of ne'er-do-wells on a transport ship for a spell, under that captain—what was his name? Reynolds. He's seen things, and he's gotten a pretty shrewd idea how it all works."

Three more days passed. It was Radiant who was on sentry duty when the Beavertail Gang finally showed.

She hollered down through the hatchway that gave access to the widow's walk. "We got riders closing in from the east. And not just a few, either. They're comin' mob-handed."

"You get yourself back down into the house, Mama," Jayne called up.

"On my way," said Radiant, shutting the hatch and shinning down the ladder to the second-floor landing.

The Cobbs shoved furniture up against the backs of doors. Jip ran agitatedly around their legs, yipping and growling.

Through a crack between two boards nailed over a window, Jayne saw the Beavertail Gang as they thundered into the farmyard. His mother wasn't wrong: mob-handed. There were a good forty of them, maybe as many as fifty. Ottoline Beavertail had clearly spent the time since Jayne and Matty killed three of her gang members recruiting new additions. The woman wasn't taking any chances.

The cattle rustlers drew to a halt in front of the house. Ottoline Beavertail herself was at the forefront, astride a noble-looking palomino with a coat like spun gold. She held a repeater rifle one-handed with the butt wedged against her hip, barrel pointing to the sky.

"I'm addressin' the people in the house," she said in a loud voice. "I know you're in there. I'm told you're called Cobb and there's three of you. Give me a shout, let me know you can hear me."

Matty, crouching on the floor, looked at Jayne and their mother. "What do we do?" he hissed. He was holding Jip by the scruff of the neck, to reassure the dog and keep him from barking.

"I just want to talk," Ottoline Beavertail continued. "Hold a negotiation, like. You have to be able to see how many of us there are. The math ain't hard. You're outnumbered fifteen to one, and we're copiously armed too. This ain't a situation you can fight your way out of. Come on out, and we'll see if we can't settle things some other way."

Jayne ran through the scenarios in his head. The Cobbs went out, and the Beavertail Gang would simply blow them to kingdom come. They didn't go out, and the gang would surround the house and start blasting away. With their superior numbers and firepower, it wouldn't be long before they ground the defenders down.

Neither outcome promised the Cobb family much chance of survival.

"This is an honest offer," Ottoline Beavertail said. "No tricks. Show your faces, me and my fellas will stay our trigger fingers, and you and me'll just powwow. I'll give you a couple minutes to decide. We don't see any sign of you by the time those two minutes are up, we start shootin'."

"Only one thing for it," Jayne said to his mother and brother. "Matty? Help me shift this." He nodded to the chest of drawers that was wedged against the front door.

"We're gonna parley with her?" Matty asked as he and Jayne slid the chest of drawers to one side.

"*We* ain't. *I* am, my own self. No point all three of us gettin' ourselves killed if there's the possibility we don't have to. But here's the thing, Matty. I want you up in the widow's walk when I'm out there. Take the thirty-cal Heyes and Curry, stay low so no one sees you, and cover me. It looks for one moment like I'm in trouble, you plant a round in that there Beavertail woman's skull. I reckon, without her telling 'em what to do, it'll be headless chicken time for the rest of the gang. They might even turn tail and run for the hills."

"I don't like this plan," Matty said.

"Me either," said Radiant Cobb. "Seems like a damnfool idea."

"Ain't as if we have many other viable options, Mama," Jayne said. "I didn't expect there'd be quite so many of those folks outside as there are. This way, at least we can see if there's some room for maneuver. Things don't go well, I'll scoot back into the house fast as I can and we'll hold out against 'em."

His mother's hard face broke into a soft smile. She laid a hand on Jayne's cheek. "You really are the spit of your daddy, you know that? Same eyes. Same brass-balled attitude. Hopefully without the womanizing or the loose way with money."

I have my moments on both those fronts, Jayne thought.

"Matty?" he said. "Upstairs with you. Mama? I'll be right back."

Holding Vera at port arms, Jayne opened the front door and stepped out. He left the door slightly ajar, in case he had to beat a hasty retreat.

"There we are," said Ottoline Beavertail. "Just the one of you?"

"For now," said Jayne. He cast an eye around the assembled gang members. They were a shabby, ragtag bunch. Sycorax's dregs. The horses they were mounted on weren't much better—slat-ribbed and droop-headed nags, the lot of them. Only Ottoline Beavertail's palomino was groomed and in any way well looked after.

"You must be the oldest Cobb boy," the gang's leader said. "Jayne? That right?"

A few of her henchmen sniggered.

"Kind of a funny name for a fella," Ottoline Beavertail said.

"Don't know how to take that," Jayne retorted, "comin' from a woman with the surname Beavertail."

A few of the gang sniggered again, if a little more surreptitiously this time.

"Still, it was fairly cruel of your ma and pa to give you a girl's name."

"Well, since we're talking cruel names—'Ottoline'?"

"It means 'prospers in battle.' My mom and dad mightn't have been kind but you *could* argue they were prophetic." Ottoline Beavertail gestured at Vera. "That a Callahan you got there?"

"Yep."

"Customized trigger. Double cartridge thorough gauge. Harwood laser-calibrated scope."

"You know your guns."

"So do you, it seems. It's a fine specimen. A person could do a lot of damage with a gun like that."

"This is nice and all, chattin' about weaponry," Jayne said, "but it ain't the reason I'm out here."

"Me either." The woman sat back in her saddle, her good eye glittering. "It'd appear we have a score to settle, Jayne Cobb. I have it on good authority you and your brother killed three of my guys."

"Won't deny it."

"Glad you won't, 'cause otherwise that'd've made you a liar."

"Weren't without provocation, neither. Those men came to steal our cattle."

"And you had every right to defend your livestock and your livelihood," said Ottoline Beavertail. "I shan't dispute that. I guess what it comes down to is this. I want those cows of yours and I aim to have them. It ain't a matter of whether or not I get them, it's a matter of how willingly you're gonna give them up."

"Easy way or hard way, huh?"

"That's about the size of it. You've got 'em corralled in that barn over there, am I right? Rhetorical question, 'cause I can hear them lowing and stamping."

The herd were indeed restless. They didn't enjoy being cooped up indoors, and they could doubtless sense the tension among the nearby humans too. Cows picked up on such things.

"Here's the nub of it," Ottoline Beavertail said. "You let me and my guys mosey over and open up the barn doors and herd them cattle out, and there will be the end of the story. No shots fired. No more deaths. Seeing as how three of my people are expired because of you, that seems like the fairest I can be. I ain't after no pound of flesh. All I'm after is several hundredweight of cow."

"You can see that that ain't reasonable, Miz Beavertail," Jayne said. "You take all of our cattle, we're left with nothin'. This here's a working ranch. We rely on those cows for income."

"You have arable crops as well. Saw 'em on the way in. Fields of alfalfa, maize, sugar beet. This place ain't just about cows. But nobody can say Ottoline Beavertail ain't a fair woman. We'll take only half the herd. Best and final offer."

Jayne paused, giving the idea serious consideration. It'd be tough, losing half the herd, but it'd be tolerable. The family could scrape by, and he had a bit of cash saved up from his days as a mercenary, enough to buy perhaps twenty new head of cattle.

No, gorramn it. This wasn't about keeping or giving up cows. It was the principle of the thing. Cattle rustling was just plain wrong, and the lowlifes who did it shouldn't be allowed to get away with it. Besides, who was to say that the Beavertail Gang, having made off with half the herd, mightn't come back for the rest at a later date? And who was to say they wouldn't just open fire regardless, even if Jayne let them take the cows? His gut was telling him this one-eyed woman was about as trustworthy as a trodden-on rattlesnake.

"So?" said Ottoline Beavertail. "What's the verdict, Mr. Cobb? We got us an agreement or what?"

"We don't."

"You sure about that?"

"I am."

"Well," she said with a sincere-sounding sigh, "I'm right sorry to hear it. Fellas?"

As one, her gang members trained their guns on Jayne.

Jayne responded by snapping Vera to his shoulder and taking aim at their leader.

Ottoline Beavertail merely grinned. "Reckon you can drill a hole in me before any of these two-score of shooters drills a hole in you?"

"Reckon I can give it a damn good try," Jayne said, squinting down Vera's barrel.

Come on, Matty, he thought. *What're you waiting for? If this ain't a case of "I'm in trouble," I don't know what is.*

At that moment there came a ferocious snarling from within the house, accompanied by the sound of claws scrabbling on varnished hardwood as Jip shot out through the partway-open door. His ears were flattened and his fangs were bared. He had sensed that Jayne was vulnerable and needed support. To Jip, he himself and the Cobbs were all one pack, and when a pack member was in danger, the rest should rally round to help.

Fearlessly, Jip made a beeline for the assembled Beavertail Gang.

One of them was so startled by the dog's sudden appearance that he fired off a shot.

The bullet caught Jip in the flank. The impact sent him rolling over, while his throat gave vent to a sharp yelp of distress.

From up on the roof, a cry of anguish was swiftly followed by a volley of gunfire. Matty had started shooting at last, but indiscriminately. Incensed by the fact that someone had hurt his dog, he loosed round after round into the gang's midst. His target wasn't Ottoline Beavertail, as had been the plan, but just anybody.

Consternation reigned. Horses reared, whinnying. Some of the gang returned fire in Matty's direction. Others started plugging away at Jayne, who was already making for the house, Vera booming in his hands.

He threw himself through the doorway, still firing. Radiant Cobb slammed the door behind him.

She and Jayne shunted the chest of drawers back into place. Then Jayne hurried to the nearest window and peered out.

Up in the widow's walk, Matty continued to rain down bullets at the gang. Some of them were retaliating but the majority were busy dispersing, seeking cover. Jayne counted five bodies sprawled on the ground, two of them writhing in pain, the other three inert. None of them, sad to say, was Ottoline Beavertail.

Jip was also on the ground, twitching. To judge by the ragged bloody wound in his ribcage and the way his jaws hung slack, he would never be getting up again.

"Well, ain't this a damn pickle," said Radiant Cobb.

Jayne's only reply was a grunt of determination.

33

The invitation came out of the blue.

It took the form of a recorded wave message from his father.

"Simon. Would you come up to the hunting lodge this weekend? It'll be me, Bryce, Holden, and you. A boys' outing."

Simon knew his father well enough to realize that Gabriel Tam wasn't anticipating the answer no. It wasn't an invitation; it was a summons.

Simon had had plans for the weekend. The plans had revolved around Kaylee Frye. He called her to apologize.

"Something's come up," he said. "A family thing. I have to go."

"It's okay," Kaylee said, just about masking her disappointment. "I understand. Family's important. It is to everyone but especially to someone like you. We'll see each other next week?"

"Absolutely we will. And Kaylee?"

"Yeah?"

He wanted to say, *I love you*. What he ended up saying was: "See you next week, then."

He hoped she would somehow know what he really meant.

The hunting lodge sat in a large tract of hilly forest some thirty miles north of Rochester Peak. The land was owned by a consortium of which Gabriel Tam was a member. It was there for the members' personal recreational use, and trespassers were unwelcome. Automated hover-drones with stun-gun attachments and facial recognition systems patrolled the perimeter and made sure that trespassers learned exactly how unwelcome they were.

As Simon drove along the dirt track that led to the hunting lodge, he wished he had the courage to stand up to his father. Why couldn't he simply refuse his demands? Why did he always jump to attention like a soldier when Gabriel Tam commanded?

The reason, he supposed, was that he owed his parents for everything: his life, his private education, even his attending position at AMI, which his father had pulled strings to get him. That debt came with obligations. Simon had never been under any illusion about this. His parents—his mother less so than his father—had always made it clear that his cozy existence depended on their continued goodwill. The threat was unstated but implicit: they had made him; they could break him.

Simon had grown up wanting nothing other than to please his parents. Nowadays, more and more, he was wondering when he would ever be allowed to please *himself*.

His relationship with Kaylee was, under these circumstances, a small act of rebellion. They had met when he was working an ER rotation at AMI and she had come in bleeding from a bad gash in her hand. A laser cutter accident, she said. "Gorramn thing just slipped."

She was lucky. The laser cutter had missed any of the major tendons. Simon put in sutures and bandaged the wound. Throughout the procedure, his gaze kept straying to his patient's face. He couldn't keep his eyes off this woman. He was utterly captivated. It was amazing he managed to do even a halfway proficient job with the suturing.

As he prepared her discharge notes, he deliberately dragged the process out. He didn't want her to go.

"Keep the wound clean," he said. "Change the dressing regularly.

THE GHOST MACHINE

Take the full course of antibiotics I've prescribed. Try not to use the hand for the next couple of weeks, until it's fully healed. If you need anything, anything at all, here's my private wave address. You can contact me any time of day or night."

"Okay, Doc, okay," Kaylee said. "I get it. So when are you gonna ask me out?"

"Uh, I beg your pardon?"

"You ain't saying it, but you're trying to. Just ask me. Handy hint: I won't turn you down."

"Out on a date? Is that what you mean?"

"That's just what I mean."

"I can't, Miz Frye. You're my patient. It would be unethical."

"Sign that there discharge document. Then I ain't your patient no more and everything's shiny."

"Shiny?"

"Sure," Kaylee said, her eyes sparkling. "Shiny. You've heard the expression before?"

"I don't believe so."

"Well, you have now."

Simon put his signature in the onscreen box with a flourish. "There. One Kaywinnet Lee Frye, officially discharged."

"Friday night," Kaylee said. "You choose the place."

Simon chose a low-key, out-of-the-way bar, somewhere where nobody he knew would ever go.

It was the start of something wonderful. A secret his family would never know about and therefore could never interfere with. His very own special thing.

He pulled up in front of the hunting lodge, which was essentially a glorified A-frame log cabin that sprawled over three stories. Vehicles belonging to his father, Bryce, and Uncle Holden were already parked outside. Bryce Tam's car was, typically, a racy little maglev number, all chrome trim and undulating bodywork.

Simon walked up to the lodge, fallen leaves crackling underfoot. He climbed the front steps and entered the building to find the three senior men seated around the spacious main room. Each had a glass of whiskey in his hand. A fire roared in the grate.

The atmosphere was… *off.*

Simon couldn't put his finger on what it was exactly, but something was up. None of the three men was smiling. He had been expecting the mood to be congenial, hearty. From his experience, that was how these male-bonding sessions went. There'd be drinking, a bit of shooting in the woods, the odd off-color joke or two, and plenty of talk about the family's past. The Tams were able to trace a clear line of ancestry to occupants of the very first of the generation starships that left Earth-That-Was and traveled to the 'verse. Their Original Settler status was a source of great pride to them, setting them apart from others. Moreover, throughout recorded history Tams had been at the center of key events, here on Osiris but elsewhere too. The surname carried weight, as Simon's father never tired of reminding him.

Today, however, Simon got the sense that things were going to be different. This was no ordinary occasion.

His feeling of creeping unease deepened as Gabriel Tam said, "Son. Sit yourself down."

He sat, and Uncle Holden pressed a whiskey tumbler into his hand.

"Simon," his father said. "Something has come to our attention. Something regrettable."

"Oh?" Simon said, as casually as he could. "And what would that be?"

"I'm hoping you'll do the decent thing and just fess up, without having to be pushed to it."

"I can't fess up if I don't know what I'm meant to be fessing up to."

Gabriel Tam let out an exasperated sigh. "Really, Simon, you can be so obtuse at times."

"Allow me to handle this, Gabe," said Bryce, patting his brother on the shoulder. "Simon." He was putting on a jovial air, but Simon could see through it. Beneath, Bryce Tam was in deadly earnest, coldblooded as a lizard. "I'm a man of the world. I know what it's like. A girl catches your eye. She's pretty. She's flirtatious. You just can't resist, and why should you? You're a man, with a man's needs. There's no harm in a quick little fling. Doesn't matter what type of girl she is. If she's fanciable, by golly you should have her. It just shouldn't be allowed to develop into anything serious."

"I really have no idea what you're talking about," Simon said. But he did. This was about Kaylee. Somehow they had found out. His secret wasn't a secret after all.

Bryce edged closer to his nephew. His smile was as great in breadth as it was devoid of warmth. "Now, now. You must understand that we only have your best interests at heart. Your father, Holden, myself—all we want is for you to be happy. Sometimes, though, being happy means making others happy. Do you understand?"

Simon understood all too well. But since they knew, he wasn't willing to buckle under and admit to the relationship. Why give them that satisfaction? Let *them* do the work.

"We're giving you an opportunity here, Simon," said Uncle Holden. "All you have to do is own up, accept you've made a mistake, and do whatever it takes to repair it. In this instance, that means ditching the slattern and allowing your father and mother to set you up with someone far more befitting your rank and status. For what it's worth, I'd be willing to consider either Cordelia or Flavia as a potential future Mrs. Simon Tam."

"I'm sorry, what?" Simon said, genuinely aghast.

"I appreciate they're your cousins, but a cousin is entitled to wed a cousin. And I know for a fact that both of the girls have admired you since they were very small."

"With all due respect to Cordelia and Flavia, Uncle Holden, they're a decade younger than me. They're also, well... I refer you back to my previous remark about them being my cousins."

"It isn't a problem, Simon. I even checked with my local Shepherd, just to make sure the church sanctions cousinly marriage. It does. And it'd be keeping things in the family, wouldn't it?"

Simon almost felt like laughing. "So you're happy to pimp out your daughters to me? But which of them should I choose? I know. Why don't I just have both?"

Uncle Holden's face darkened. "Pimp out? How dare you speak to me like that, boy! The impertinence!"

"No, but wait," Simon went on, raising a forefinger. Anger was making him bold. "Hear me out. They're identical twins. I could alternate between them and probably wouldn't even notice the difference. Mondays, Wednesdays, Fridays—Cordelia. Tuesdays, Thursdays, Saturdays—Flavia. They can both have Sundays off, of course. That'd make life easier for them. Sharing the workload."

"Such crude flippancy is uncalled for. These are my daughters you're talking about."

"I think it's very much called for, Uncle Holden. This whole situation is absurd. I'm not staying a moment longer." Simon rose to his feet, setting down his untouched glass of whiskey with a thud. He glared around at all three men imperiously. "You can't control me. You can't legislate what I can and cannot do. I will love who I want to love and marry who I want to marry."

It felt unbelievably good to be saying these things. Simon knew he would pay for them in the long run. The consequences would doubtless be dire. It might well mean the ruin of him.

But in that moment, standing up to these three—to his father in particular—and seeing the shocked, indignant looks on their faces; it was glorious. This had been a long time coming. A festering boil was at last being lanced.

"Simon," said Gabriel Tam sternly. "Sit your backside down. Now."

"No, sir. I'm leaving."

His father stood. "Then I regret what's going to happen next. Just remember, you forced our hand. This is all your own fault."

"What are you talking about?"

Gabriel Tam nodded to his brother. Bryce disappeared into one of the adjacent rooms, the lodge's pantry. He emerged dragging someone by the arm.

Simon's jaw dropped.

It was Kaylee. Her arms were tied behind her back and there was a gag around her mouth.

She looked at him with frightened, imploring eyes.

Bryce dragged her over to a wooden ladder-back chair and plonked her down in it.

"Let her go," Simon said in a voice that sounded like sparks being struck off a flint. "This instant. Let her go, or I swear to God..."

"You swear to God *what*, Simon?" said Gabriel Tam. "You'll kill us? Don't be such a gorramn idiot."

"Kaylee," Simon said. "Look at me. I'm getting you out of here. I'm so sorry about this. Trust me, they're not going to get away with it."

"Kaylee," said his father, "pay your boyfriend no heed. He's just posturing. Simon faces a choice now, and I'm afraid to say that whatever his decision may be, you aren't going to like the result. That's just how it is."

"Rest assured, Simon," said Uncle Holden, "we've been looking after her. When we abducted her from her workplace, we used minimum coercion—although I must say I bear a few bruises I didn't have before. She was quite the spitfire. Since then, she's been fed and watered, her needs tended to. We may be her captors but we're not barbarians."

"I can see what you see in her," said Bryce, eyeing Kaylee speculatively. "If I were in your shoes, I'd have gone for it. Can't blame you at all. My own type's a touch more glamorous, I would say. More into fashion and dolling herself up. But put this one in a nice frock, slap a bit of mascara and lipstick on, she'd be perfectly presentable."

Simon's hands balled into fists. Right then, he would gladly have punched Bryce Tam. In fact, he would gladly have throttled him.

Gabriel Tam went to a sideboard and slid open a drawer. He produced a hunting knife in a leather sheath, which he carried over to his son.

"To make everything better," he said, "you don't have to do much. Just use this on her. We'll take care of the rest."

Kaylee's eyes bulged in terror. She struggled against her bonds. Her yells of panic and rage were muffled by the gag.

Bryce Tam placed a hand firmly on each of Kaylee's shoulders to hold her in place. "This is the only way," he said to Simon. "She's a liability. She'll be nothing but trouble if you let her live."

"She's a stain on the family name," said Uncle Holden, "and you have to make it go away."

"You're a surgeon, my boy," Simon's father said. "You know full well how to make incisions. You must know, too, the quickest, least painful means of ending a person's life. Where to cut. How deep."

He handed Simon the sheathed knife.

"If you don't do it, one of us will," Gabriel Tam said. "But wouldn't it be preferable—indeed fitting—if the one who loves her is the one who slays her?"

34

In the deep sleep of sedation, River was beyond the reach of the siren. Its sinuous, skirling song could not affect her as it was affecting her fellow crewmembers.

Still she dreamed.

And she roamed.

From one crewmember to another she moved, seeing as if through their eyes, experiencing what they were experiencing, feeling all they felt.

She was Mal. Mal, married to Inara and the father of two heartbreakingly beautiful children. A Mal who had found some kind of contentment, until what appeared to be a Reaver ship inexplicably came down close by his home. Now he was experiencing a visceral terror—shared by River—at the thought of Reavers getting their hands on his loved ones.

She was Jayne. Jayne on his homeworld Sycorax, gearing up for a confrontation with a gang of cattle rustlers, alongside his brother and his mother. She felt his eagerness—Jayne relished a good scrap—and beneath that his fear. Jayne always hid fear from the eyes of others, revealing it only rarely, in unguarded moments. He could not bear to show that there might be vulnerability behind that gruff exterior. His fear, in this context, was not so much for his own safety as for that of Radiant and Matty Cobb. They were the two things in his life he could least afford to lose.

She was Kaylee. Kaylee, who had just become her father's business partner. Kaylee had spoken with River about her family a few times, saying how much she had loved her father but how there had always been a slight, chilly distance between her and her mother. In real life, Aloysius Frye had died of heart disease. In the dream he was bright, vibrant, alive, just as Kaylee liked to remember him. But there was a man, Caleb Dahl, whom Aloysius Frye did not want his daughter associating with. And Kaylee was associating with him all the same.

She was Zoë. Zoë in a version of the 'verse where the Browncoats won the Unification War. Zoë, restless, rootless, attempting to make the best of the peace by hunting down Alliance war criminals for money but also drinking too much in order to drown out the voices in her head, the voices of the dead. Mal featured in the dream too, but this Mal was not Mal. This Mal was a haunted man, and also, as it transpired, an unreliable man.

She was Wash. A Wash with wealth, position, all the material possessions a person could want. A Wash with Zoë, the love of his life, by his side, and three children he adored. A Wash who should have been satisfied with his lot but was ruining it through self-doubt and jealousy. And a Wash who, it appeared, was about to learn a cold, hard truth.

She was Simon. Her beloved Simon, who had finally allowed himself to open his heart to Kaylee, even if it was just in a dream. River herself was depicted in the dream, a River who had not been sent by her parents to the Academy to suffer and be cruelly transmogrified into the River she now was, but rather a River who was smart and vivacious and above all *free*. Simon's relationships with the other members of his family, though, and especially with their parents, unsettled her. How fraught they were, how filled with anxiety and mistrust. A set of weighing scales forever tipping one way or the other, never achieving equilibrium. And now Simon was discovering the true, horrific cost of his upbringing.

In the deep sleep of sedation, River dreamed all these dreams, the dreams of others, and she was perturbed.

Because what had begun as harmless fantasies were, as she had known they would, slowly and inexorably degenerating into nightmares.

35

The Serra-Reynolds family might have made a clean getaway if it hadn't been for Master DaSilva.

Jackson and Samadhi's tutor simply would not give credence to Mal's assertion that the crashed spaceship was a Reaver vessel.

"It's just not possible," he said, staring down the valley to where the patched-together, graffiti-bedecked craft had come to rest. "Reavers? They're not even real. They're just some spacefarers' myth. A tall tale to tell around the campfire."

"Oh, they're gorramn real, all right," Mal said.

"But even if they are, this is Sihnon. We're about as far from their supposed territory as can be imagined. They haunt the outer reaches of the 'verse, way beyond the Rim. It can't be Reavers. Perhaps it's someone playing at being a Reaver, some practical joker."

"Could be, but I ain't taking that chance." Mal grabbed DaSilva by the arm. "Now, come on. We need to get our asses into our skimmer."

"No." DaSilva planted his feet. "Kindly unhand me, Mr. Reynolds. I will not give in to this—this irrational panic which seems to have overcome you."

"Ain't nothin' irrational about running from Reavers. Irrational is staying put and risking getting caught by 'em. Know what happens to people who get caught by Reavers?"

"I have heard a few lurid stories."

"They ain't stories!" Mal insisted. "They're the gospel truth. You want one of 'em to peel your skin off and wear it like a suit, right before your eyes? You want to be force-fed your own entrails? You want to be raped with your own shinbone?"

DaSilva gasped. "What a revolting proposition. Surely nobody is capable of doing such a thing to their fellow man."

"Reavers are capable of that and a whole lot else." Mal yanked at DaSilva again.

The tutor still would not be swayed. "I object to this manhandling, sir. It is quite improper. I have told you that I feel it is our duty to go to the aid of those people down there. I stand by that call. To flee the scene like some coward, all because of a few baseless reports about cannibalistic savages living out in the—"

Mal coldcocked him with a roundhouse to the temple. DaSilva crumpled, and Mal caught him, scooped him up, and slung him over his shoulder. Just as he was about to turn to enter the house, he cast a glance towards the Reaver ship. He saw a hatch opening near the rear and a rag-clad leg emerge.

He didn't need to see any more. Carrying DaSilva, he raced in from the balcony, through the house, and out onto the landing pad at the front. Inara was already there beside the skimmer, standing in the shadow of its starboard delta wing with Jackson and Samadhi. DaSilva's one-person short-range hopper sat a little way off. The children looked frightened, and Mal thought, *Good. They need to be frightened. Frightened will help keep them alive.*

Inara said, "What's this all about, Mal? Did I hear you say Reavers?"

"Crazy as it sounds, they're out there. That was a Reaver ship just came over."

"But it's not poss—"

"I know it's not possible and I don't gorramn care!" Mal said.

"Jackson, Samadhi, get on board the skimmer."

"Is Master DaSilva okay, Daddy?" Jackson asked.

"Is he asleep?" said Samadhi.

"He'll be fine," Mal said. "In you get. Quick-smart."

The children climbed into the skimmer's backseat. Mal bundled DaSilva's limp form in beside them. Inara was already slipping into the pilot's seat.

"Start her up," Mal said to her. "I won't be but a moment."

"Where are you going?"

"To get something from the house."

As Inara cycled up the skimmer's engine, Mal sprinted back indoors and made straight for the gun safe. He input the code number and put his eye to the retinal scanner. The door unlocked and swung open.

Mal kept a .22-caliber rifle for the kids to learn on, an over-and-under shotgun with double-aught shells for hunting small game, and a pump-action 12-gauge for larger game. Some might think it ran contrary to the family's Buddhist beliefs even to have these firearms in the house, let alone use them. Mal, however, held the view that a household that wasn't gun-savvy was a household that wasn't savvy, period.

He did not select the rifle or either of the shotguns, however. Too big, too unwieldy. He opted instead for the long-barreled pistol that had been by his side throughout the Unification War.

He hadn't held his Liberty Hammer in a long time but it felt as comfortable in his hand as ever, like having back a part of him that had been missing.

He snatched up a box of ammo, slammed the gun safe door shut and sprinted back outside.

The skimmer's two counter-rotating fans were a shimmering blur inside their cylindrical shroud. The aircraft seemed to dance on the landing pad, eager for liftoff. Mal ran for the passenger side door, which Inara had thrown open for him. He hurled himself into the seat, feeling a rush of relief as Inara thrust the joystick forward and the skimmer sprang to the sky in a steep-angled takeoff. Master DaSilva's vacillation had cost them time, but the delay, it appeared, was not crucial.

How wrong could you be?

The skimmer was perhaps fifteen feet off the ground when something slammed into its rear end. The entire aircraft juddered wildly in the air. Jackson and Samadhi screamed. Mal looked back to see flames billowing from the charred wreck that had been the skimmer's propulsion unit.

Emergency lights blazed on the dashboard. A warning message intoned: "ENGINE FAILURE. BRACE, BRACE, BRACE. ENGINE FAILURE. BRACE, BRACE, BRACE."

"Kids," Mal shouted. "Head on your knees. Arms over your head."

Jackson and Samadhi complied.

Inara clung onto the joystick, even though it was now useless. Her main focus was the rudder pedals, which she stamped on, trying desperately to use the wing flaps to control the skimmer's rapid descent.

She succeeded, up to a point. The skimmer came down flat on its belly rather than slewing to the side and rolling over. The impact was mighty nonetheless, a windshield-shattering, fuselage-crushing tumult that seemed to go on forever.

Mal was thrown violently forward, his head colliding with the dashboard. He saw stars. He heard choirs of angels.

As his vision cleared, he blinked around the interior of the skimmer. Jackson and Samadhi were still in the brace position in the back. Both were sobbing but appeared unhurt. Master DaSilva remained out cold. Inara looked as dazed and banged-up as Mal felt. There was blood trickling from one of her nostrils.

The skimmer had come down at the very edge of the house's upper lawn. Its nosecone was buried in the undergrowth of the surrounding forest. Mal smelled smoke and didn't know if it was just from the explosion that had destroyed the fans or if the aircraft was on fire. Either way, they had to evacuate. Immediately.

He shoved open the passenger door and stumbled out, shaking off shards of windshield glass from his clothing. The Reavers had hit the skimmer with a rocket-propelled grenade, he reckoned, which meant they could be anything up to five hundred yards away. That was five hundred yards closer to a Reaver than Mal ever wanted to get. They must have moved incredibly fast up the valley, but then they were known to ingest homemade stimulants that jacked up their strength, speed, stamina, and somatic reflexes to superhuman levels.

He hauled open the rear door and reached in to grab DaSilva. Inara, meanwhile, was struggling with her own door, which had been distended by the impact and was jammed in its frame. Mal dumped DaSilva on the grass and hurried around to help her. Between them they managed to wrench it open. Mal then got Jackson and Samadhi out.

"Into the woods," he said, pointing in that direction. "It's our only chance."

He ran back around to fetch DaSilva. Just briefly, he considered leaving the tutor there. It was thanks to him that the Reavers had been able to bring down the skimmer. If DaSilva hadn't dithered, the aircraft would have taken off several seconds earlier and there was every chance it would have flown out of range of the Reavers' RPG launcher. Carrying him now would only slow Mal down. The man didn't deserve to live.

But then no one deserved being left to die at Reavers' hands. That was a fate Mal wouldn't have wished on his worst enemy.

Figures were moving at the other end of the lawn—raggedy scarecrow-like silhouettes flitting between the trees.

Mal hoisted Master DaSilva back onto his shoulder and turned.

Inara, Jackson, and Samadhi were waiting for him.

"Don't just stand there!" he yelled at them. "Go! Go! Go!"

36

Kaylee could not fathom what her father's problem was with Caleb Dahl. In all her dealings with the man, he was nothing but courteous and respectful.

His house out on Harmsworth Avenue was a rambling, turreted mansion, set in a gated compound on a clifftop with a sweeping view across the whole of Clearcrest Bay. At the rear, a flight of steps led down the cliffside to a private cove with a sandy beach and a jetty where Dahl's junk-rigged trimaran and sleek motor launch were moored.

Caleb Dahl obviously had money, and plenty of it. Was that what Aloysius Frye objected to? His wealth? But Kaylee's father had never been the covetous or jealous sort. In fact, many was the time he had spoken admiringly of those who were better off than himself. "Anybody who's earned themselves a fortune or even inherited one, good luck to 'em," he would say. "Let 'em enjoy it. Ain't for me to judge them harshly just because they can afford what I can't."

On the couple of occasions Kaylee visited Dahl at his home, he displayed impeccable hospitality. Servants brought her mint juleps and dim sum, and then Dahl ferried her personally, in his own limousine, to the private spaceport where his Ellison Z-Type was berthed. She worked on the slingshotter at intervals, whenever was convenient for

Dahl. Each time, she lied to her father about where she was off to. She invented a couple of bogus clients—a Mr. Calabash and a Mrs. Darlington—even going so far as to make entries for them in the company's books. Dahl always paid her bills promptly, and he would usually give her a little bit more than she invoiced him for. She kept this from her father, too, so as not to arouse suspicion. She squirreled the extra money away in a private bank account, a rainy-day fund in case the Fryes should find themselves in financial difficulties.

She found Caleb Dahl attractive, there was no pussyfooting around that. He was well turned out, his dress sense showy but not flamboyant, if a little heavy on the paisley and the gold braid. He had a loose, cockeyed smile and a way about him that spoke of complete self-assurance, along with that flowery eloquence of his that in others might seem affected but in him seemed natural. He might have been perhaps a tad too old for her, but since when did that really matter? She could see no evidence around the house of a Mrs. Dahl or of any significant other, meaning he was fair game.

"There'll be another Simon along soon enough," her father had said. Could be Caleb Dahl was that "another Simon." If so, this time she'd make sure he didn't slip through her fingers as Simon Tam had.

What she couldn't tell was whether the attraction was mutual. Did Dahl like her—as in *like* like? Or was he in the habit of showing everyone the same solicitous gentility he showed her? The kind of gentility that could be mistaken for attraction.

Many was the night Kaylee lay awake in bed thinking about Caleb Dahl, imagining what it would be like to have him 'twixt her nethers. It crossed her mind that his inclinations might not lie in a womanward direction, but even if that were the case, she was still permitted to fantasize about him, wasn't she?

His Z-Type turned into an epic project. Every repair Kaylee made seemed to instigate a fresh problem, a cascade of malfunction. The previous owner had not looked after the spaceplane as they ought, and a decade of being mothballed hadn't helped.

Another difficulty was sourcing spare parts. Ellison Manufacturing had gone out of business a quarter of a century back, and some of its parts had been exclusive to the company, custom-built. You couldn't swap them out with generic parts, or easily adapt parts from other aircraft to fit.

Nonetheless, Kaylee was in her element. A handsome vintage spaceplane like this came along once in a blue moon. Getting it up and running again was a paying job, yes, but it was also a labor of love.

It was a small triumph for her when she finally managed to track down a helical-coil heat exchanger in good working order. The engine part had to be freighted all the way over from Athens, in the Georgia System, but when it arrived Kaylee was delighted to discover that it needed very little in the way of overhauling. It scrubbed up nicely, and she couldn't wait to tell Dahl about it. It was the final piece of the jigsaw puzzle. Once it was installed, there was every chance the Z-Type would finally fly once more.

She waved Dahl but got no answer. This didn't deter her. She decided to take the heat exchanger out to his house to show him in person. It'd be a nice surprise, she thought. And also a good excuse to see him again. They hadn't had any contact in over a month. When they'd last met, Dahl had said something about some business that was taking him offworld and he wasn't sure when he would be back.

She rode out to Harmsworth Avenue on a new acquisition, a 170 bhp Silver Scout sports-tourer motorcycle, with the heat exchanger sitting snugly in a rucksack on her back. She arrived at the mansion, only to be informed by Dahl's butler that Dahl hadn't yet returned from his work trip. The butler, Evans, advised her not to drop by unannounced again. "Mr. Dahl," he said with a disdainful sniff, "will get in touch with you when he sees fit, young lady. That is the way of these things."

"Gotcha," said Kaylee. "Message received." She noted that

Evans was nowhere near this snooty when his boss was around. Technically he and she were both employees of Dahl, and therefore equals, but Evans seemed to think his frock coat and starched collar somehow made him her better.

Kaylee was in a quandary, but not for long. The Z-Type was so close to being airworthy again. Maybe she could just fit the heat exchanger without Dahl knowing, run a few basic diagnostics on the spaceplane, see if it was as ready as she thought it was going to be. Then, when he came back, she could announce to him that the job was done. *One Ellison slingshotter, good as new, courtesy of the magic hands of Kaylee Frye. Ta-dah!* It would be an even nicer surprise for him than the heat exchanger alone.

She headed on out to the spaceport.

It was a fateful decision.

A life-changing one, in point of fact.

The spaceport was shared by Dahl with a half-dozen persons of similar means. Private docking meant that, unlike at a major commercial and passenger spaceport, ships were subject to fewer customs checks and a light-touch regulation. Excise duties, for instance, were paid on a voluntary basis, and the general feeling was that as long as sufficiently sizable amounts of money ended up in the revenue service's coffers, users of a private spaceport were free to come and go more or less as they pleased.

Over the past few weeks Kaylee had struck up a rapport with Gerard, the spaceport's security guard. When she pulled up at the gate on the Silver Scout, he simply raised the barrier and beckoned her through.

"Mr. Dahl not with you today, huh, Kaylee?" Gerard said. "Well, guess there's no harm lettin' you in on your ownsome. He trusts you with his slingshotter, no reason I shouldn't trust you either. Be a miracle if you ever get that crate off the ground, mind."

"Miracles do happen, Gerard," said Kaylee.

She passed the afternoon removing the old, worn-out heat

exchanger and bolting in the new one. Hooking up the intake and outlet tubes was a far trickier affair than she had thought. Really, the Ellison designers hadn't made life easy for anyone working on their ships. It seemed they'd taken a perverse pleasure in forcing mechanics to squeeze into the tightest of crannies and pretty much have to hang upside down by their toes sometimes in order to access hard-to-reach junctions and connector ports. The Z-Type was a triumph of aesthetics over practicality.

Sunset had fallen by the time Kaylee got the job done. She sat herself down in the spaceplane's cockpit and booted up the control panel. One by one, lights and screens came on. Everything read nominal. Green across the board.

Kaylee awarded herself a small pat on the back.

She tapped a few keys and waited for the engine to respond.

"Come on, come on, come on," she murmured, like a parent cajoling an infant into eating kale.

There was a low grumble from the Z-Type's rear end.

"Oh yeah! Attagirl!"

The grumble eased out into a smooth purr. The sound of a liquid air-cycle engine contentedly warming up.

"Kaylee Frye, you are nothing short of an engineering genius."

The purr stuttered.

"No. No, no, no."

Then the sound petered out altogether, terminating in a kind of tragic death rattle.

Kaylee banged her fist on the control console. "*Nǐ tā mā de! Tiān xià suǒ yǒu de rén dōu gāi sǐ!*"

Wearily she clambered out of the cockpit. Just as she was about to reopen the Z-Type's engine cowl and see what she could do to make the heat exchanger function as it ought—bashing it into submission with a hammer sprang to mind—the reverberation of a spaceship at mid-altitude caught her attention. She identified the noise straight away, by ear alone, as that generated by the dual thruster pods of a Series 03 Firefly-class midbulk transport vessel.

She looked up and, sure enough, a Firefly was coming in to land at the spaceport. Her thoughts immediately went back to *Serenity* and the time she had spent as that ship's resident engineer, and she felt a brief ache of nostalgia.

The Firefly descended from the night sky with grace and majesty, tail end aglow with coruscating amber light. Unlike *Serenity*, this was a ship that had been well maintained throughout its working life. Kaylee could hear how slickly its trace compression block engine was running. No pieces of wire and elastic band holding *that* puppy together, that was for sure.

As the Firefly touched down, Gerard the security guard came running over. Actually, being as he was rather a portly man, "running" didn't describe his locomotion so much as "energetic waddling."

"Kaylee, I weren't expectin' this particular arrival today. It weren't scheduled till tomorrow at the earliest. I gotta ask you to vacate the premises immediately. Don't even ask questions. Just get on your bike and go."

His sudden anxiety discomfited her. Normally Gerard was as laidback and affable as they came.

"What's the big fuss?" Kaylee said.

"I mean it. No questions. Hustle! It's dark, so there's maybe a chance Mr. Dahl ain't seen you yet, and if he hasn't, it's best you keep it that way."

"Caleb's on that ship?"

"Yeah, he is." Gerard's face was serious and his eyes were alight with concern.

"But he's my friend."

"No, Kaylee. No, he ain't. Not if he catches you here. He won't be mine, neither, for lettin' you in. Now please, I beg of you. Git!"

She was confused, but she couldn't miss the frantic urgency in

Gerard's voice. She decided to heed his instruction. Whatever was going on here, she would discuss it with Dahl at a later date. Maybe this was all just some misunderstanding.

The Firefly was firmly settled on the ground now, like a cat with its paws tucked in, and its cargo ramp was lowering at the rear. As Kaylee set off across the asphalt towards where her motorcycle stood leaning on its kickstand, she caught sight of figures inside the cargo bay. Men, women, children, a couple dozen of them. They were huddled together on the floor, looking lost and bewildered.

And they were wearing manacles.

She halted mid-step.

Manacles?

She looked closer and saw a pair of gun-toting men with slab-like faces keeping watch over them.

Not just shackled like slaves but under armed guard as well!

Gerard, who had been following her, gave her a forceful shove between the shoulder blades. "Don't hang around. Don't even look. Ain't for the likes of you, knowing what goes on at this place."

But Kaylee dug her heels in. "What *is* this?" she exclaimed.

"This," said Caleb Dahl, walking down the incline of the cargo ramp, "is how someone like me makes his living." He strode over to Kaylee and Gerard. "I'm not even going to ask why you're here, Kaylee. Ten to one you've been working on my Z-Type. Nor am I going to ask how you gained access. Gerard, it would seem, has overstepped the mark."

"I'm sorry, Mr. Dahl," Gerard began. "This is all my fault."

"Tsk-tsk," said Dahl, wagging a finger at the security guard. "Naughty boy. I shall deal with you in a second. As for you, Kaylee, believe me when I say this is a most lamentable turn of events. You and I were getting along so well, and I truly value your diligence and your expertise. I doubt most sincerely that I am going to find another mechanic of your caliber."

Kaylee did her best to ignore the valedictory note in his voice. "Those folks in the Firefly. Where are they from? Why have you brought them here? Because it don't look to me as though they came all voluntary-like."

"You're aware that I am in imports and exports. I just never told you what it is that I import and export."

"Human beings," Kaylee said coldly.

"Among other things."

"What for?"

"For reasons that should not concern you." Dahl turned back to Gerard. "Now then, what are we going to do about you, my friend?"

"Mr. Dahl," said Gerard, "I done wrong, I know. I shouldn't've let her in. I made a bad call. If only you hadn't come back so soon. You weren't supposed to."

"We made good time from Whitefall."

"All's I can say is, do what you like with me. But Kaylee, you let her go, and she's not gonna breathe a word of this to no one. I'm certain of it."

"Gerard, that really is most noble of you," said Dahl. "You're a good man."

"Not *so* good," said Gerard, "given what I've had to turn a blind eye to over the years."

"What you were *paid well* to turn a blind eye to."

"All the more reason for saying I ain't so good." Tears had sprung in Gerard's eyes. "At the very least, don't let Kaylee see. When you… you know."

"When I shoot you dead?" Dahl pulled a pistol from a shoulder rig inside his jacket. "Like this?"

Blam!

Kaylee let out a shrill cry of alarm and horror.

Gerard sagged to the ground. There was a neat bullet hole in the front of his head, a ragged-edged cavity big as a baseball in the back.

"And you, Kaylee," Dahl said, turning the gun's smoking barrel on her. "What, I wonder, are we going to do with *you*?"

37

Zoë came round with a splitting headache, the taste of copper in her mouth, and a burning sense of indignation.

Mal Reynolds. *Mal Reynolds* had bushwhacked her.

Gū yáng zhōng de gū yáng!

In hindsight, she should've known something like this might happen. Reynolds had been struggling financially. He'd told her he was short of money. That whole happening-to-bump-into-her-at-the-bar thing, it hadn't been coincidence. He'd been hired to have a few drinks with her and then lead her down that maze of alleyways, into the waiting clutches of those ambushers. Somebody had wanted Zoë Alleyne taken captive, and Malcolm Reynolds, one of the few people Zoë had ever really trusted, had helped engineer that result.

At least he'd had the decency to sound genuinely rueful as he'd whacked her with that leather sap of his. Like he'd known exactly how much of a betrayal it was.

Through the haze of pain, Zoë took stock of her surroundings. Damp brick walls glistening in the scorching-bright light of a battery-powered carbon/magnesium lantern. No windows. A small, confined space with a single wooden door. Some kind of cellar?

And she herself was bound hand and foot, propped up in one

corner of this room. Said appendages were going numb, and she moved them around as much as her bonds would allow, in order to get the circulation going again.

Her Mare's Leg was gone, naturally. So was the serrated-bladed automatic knife she kept down her left boot for emergencies. She had been body-searched while she'd been unconscious, and whoever had done it had done it well.

There was still the coil of thread concealed in her right boot heel, however, a length of unbreakable monofilament polymer that could serve both as cutting implement and garrote. They'd missed that. Or so Zoë thought, until she managed to swing the heel open on its swivel hinge to find just an empty cavity within.

Dammit.

Time passed. Half an hour. An hour. No one came.

Zoë butt-shuffled herself over to the door, put an ear to it, listened. No sound from outside.

She tried calling out. "Hey. Hey! Anybody? Woman here not liking how cold and damp she's getting. Needing to pee too. If someone can hear me, I'd surely appreciate a restroom break."

This was no lie. She had drunk copiously at the bar, and her bladder was straining.

She kicked the door a few times with both feet. It was sturdy and did not budge.

There was no response to her cries or the sound of her kicks.

Ah well. She would just have to hold it. *Cross your legs and think of cactuses*, as her mother used to say on long journeys.

The fact that she wasn't gagged implied to Zoë that she was in some unfrequented part of town or else way out in the back of beyond. Whoever was holding her prisoner wasn't worried about her shouting to attract attention. She was somewhere where no one would hear.

She wasn't dead. That was the main thing. Her captor or captors wanted her alive. For now.

And while Zoë was alive, she was dangerous. It was far from game over.

Another hour crept by, and Zoë occupied her mind by speculating who her captor or captors might be. Someone with ties to the Alliance, was her guess. Not that there was still an Alliance worth mentioning. These days, with the 'verse sheltering under the umbrella of the Accord, the rifts of the past were—theoretically—mended. Papered over, at any rate.

However, an old guard existed, a rump of former Alliance soldiers and Alliance sympathizers who were unhappy about the outcome of the war and wished it had gone otherwise. Someone like the late Colonel Hiram Tregarvon could count on these disgruntled souls to, say, smuggle them to far-off worlds and act as their bodyguards. There was even talk of agitators who met in secret and were plotting the restoration of the Alliance. The embers of the war were not quite cold, and it might not take much to fan them back into life and thus undo all the work of reconciliation and healing the Accord had so far accomplished.

The safe bet, to Zoë's way of thinking, was that she had fallen foul of one of these seditionary groups. She—ex-Browncoat bounty hunter with dozens of Alliance war criminal scalps to her credit—was just the sort of person they would be keen to make an example of.

Which made Reynolds's betrayal all the more hypocritical for him and all the more embittering for her.

If she got out of this, there'd be a reckoning with Mal Reynolds. No, not if. When.

For the umpteenth time, Zoë tested the ropes that bound her. The knots were tied good and fast. Straining at them served only to tighten them. She searched for a sharp edge somewhere in the cellar, a patch of roughened brickwork or mortar, a metal spar sticking out, something she could try rubbing the ropes against to wear through them. No dice.

Finally, footsteps from beyond the door. Echoing along a corridor. Approaching.

Zoë braced herself. Trussed up though she was, she wouldn't make it easy for these bastards to do whatever it was they intended to do to her. She would fight, tooth and nail, to the last.

A key turned in the door.

In walked a trim, well-built man in his late fifties with iron-gray hair that was cropped close to his scalp and a neat, matching-colored mustache. He was good-looking in a sage sort of way and held himself with a cool, aloof detachment, as if he found everything he beheld quietly intriguing. He crossed the room in a few short steps, then stopped beside Zoë with his legs apart and his hands behind his back.

Looking down at her, he said, "Zoë Alleyne. Scourge of Alliance war criminals the whole 'verse over." His voice was warm, mellow. A voice you would not automatically associate with someone who meant you ill.

"That's me," Zoë said. "And you're, presumably, the asshole I'm going to kill, moment I get free."

The man chuckled. "As fierce as your reputation suggests. But your threats, while they do you credit, will serve you naught. You had best accustom yourself to that fact. Making your peace with God, if you believe in Him, would be a more profitable use of the little time remaining to you. That and developing an unusually high tolerance to pain."

"You can at least tell me who you are," Zoë said, unfazed. "'Less you're too smug to."

"It can't do any harm, I suppose," said the man, after a moment's thought. "Book. Derrial Book. You might not be familiar with the name, but you'll doubtless have heard of me by another sobriquet: the Butcher of Beylix. I'm the man, Miz Zoë Alleyne, who is going to make you rue the day you ever signed up to fight for the Independent cause."

38

"We don't have all day, son," said Gabriel Tam, still proffering the hunting knife to Simon. "Take it. Use it. Make the act as swift as you can. Be merciful to the girl."

Simon stood paralyzed with horror and disbelief.

"Knew it," said Bryce Tam. "I told you, didn't I, Gabe? I said he'd freeze up. Boy just doesn't have the cods to do what needs to be done."

"Give him a few moments to process," Uncle Holden counseled. "It's a lot to take in."

Kaylee kept her gaze fixed on Simon. Eyes he had stared into longingly, wistfully, so many times.

Maybe this is all just a test, Simon thought. *They're seeing how far I'm prepared to go. They won't actually make me go through with it all the way. They just want to know that I'm willing to put family before self.*

"No," said his father. "I can tell what you're thinking, Simon. I raised you. You're an open book to me. You're thinking all you have to do is take the knife, and we'll call a halt to the whole thing, let the girl go free, end of the matter. You're thinking this is all symbolic, nothing more. But you're sorely mistaken. Nobody is leaving here until that girl is dead. Now, it can be you who delivers the fatal strike, or it can be one of us. Makes no difference in the long run. It would simply be better for everyone concerned if it were you."

"Then we'd know that you're fully a Tam," said Bryce.

Simon at last found his voice again. "This… this is evil. You have no right to do this. Kaylee and I haven't done anything wrong. We're two people who have fallen in love. You can't punish us for that."

Two people who have fallen in love. Only now, in this terrible predicament, had Simon managed to express his feelings about Kaylee out loud. The irony would have been hilarious if it hadn't been so awful.

"You mustn't regard this as a punishment, son," said Gabriel Tam. "All it is, is a sacrifice."

"Think sensibly," said Uncle Holden. "You'd marry this girl? This grease monkey? And how do you think she would behave at social occasions? At the Archimedes Club Annual Ball, for example. Or the varsity polo meet. You think it'd be okay for her to stand there and talk *machinery* with the great and the good of Rochester Peak? She'd be an embarrassment. To all of us. The wife of a Tam does not come from the gutter. The wife of a Tam comes from a world of etiquette and refinement."

"You're not even a Tam, Holden," Simon said. "You're a Buckingham."

"A Buckingham is every bit the equal of a Tam."

"Still doesn't qualify you to pronounce on Tam family matters." It was a cheap shot, but right then Simon didn't have much else in his arsenal.

"Stop prevaricating," said his father. He grabbed Simon's hand and planted the still-sheathed knife in it. "You're only prolonging the girl's agony."

"Don't keep calling her 'the girl.' She has a name. Kaylee."

"Fine. Then do the right thing by Kaylee and put Kaylee out of her misery. Go ahead."

Simon weighed up his options. They weren't many.

He slid the knife out of its sheath. It had a ten-inch titanium-coated steel blade with sawback teeth along the top, near the hilt, and a textured rubber handle with finger grooves. Designed for skinning, gutting, and chopping up game, it was as perfect for its purpose as any of the scalpels Simon wielded in the operating theater.

He padded over towards Kaylee. The knife's blade glinted wickedly in the firelight.

"That's it, son," said Gabriel Tam with an encouraging gesture. "Don't worry about making a mess. The three of us are going to clean everything up. We'll bury the body in the woods, nice and deep so the wolves and the coyotes won't unearth it. There won't be any consequences from this. It'll be a secret the four of us will take to our graves."

Bryce stepped back from Kaylee, giving Simon free rein—and also, perhaps, so as to be out of range of any blood spray.

Kaylee's expression had gone from hope to despair. All at once she had given up on the prospect of Simon somehow rescuing her. She slumped in the ladder-back chair, defeated. It seemed she thought there was nothing she could do now except resign herself to the inevitable.

Simon firmed his grasp on the knife handle.

He squatted down in front of Kaylee.

"I do love you, Kaylee," he said. "I should have told you sooner."

She gave him a look as if to say, *Really makes no gorramn difference now, does it?*

"And that's why," he continued, "I'm going to do this."

He seized her by the elbow and hauled her to her feet.

Then he swung around, holding out the knife.

"Dad. Bryce. Holden. Don't any of you *wáng bā dàn* move a muscle."

Gabriel Tam scowled. "What did you just call us?"

"You heard." Simon brandished the knife. "I'm going now, and Kaylee is coming with me. Any of you gets in my way, I will stab you."

"He's bluffing," said Bryce.

Pivoting around, Simon jabbed the knife in his uncle's direction. "Care to test that?"

Bryce studied his nephew's face. Simon hoped he saw only pure, adamant resolve there.

Apparently he did, because Bryce took a small step backwards and raised his hands in a pacifying manner.

Simon turned around again, to face his father and Uncle Holden, and also the front door.

"Come on," he said to Kaylee, and together they began walking towards the door.

"Simon…" said Uncle Holden.

"Son," said Gabriel Tam. "You're only making matters worse. You're compounding one error of judgment with a greater error of judgment. You walk out that door, and you've sealed your fate."

"What do you mean? You mean I'll be ostracized? I can never darken the threshold of a Tam house again? I'll be an outcast the rest of my life? I think I can live with that."

"No," said his father. "I mean we can't permit you to leave this place. Not after all this. I imagine we might be able to rely on *you* not to tell anyone what's happened here, but the girl?"

"Kaylee."

"Kaylee. Her. There's no guarantee she won't report us to the authorities."

"Not that it would do her much good," Bryce chipped in. "They'd never believe her. The word of a lowly mechanic against the word of the three of *us*? We'd simply say she's a liar, a fantasist. There wouldn't even be an investigation, let alone a prosecution."

"Good point, Bryce," said Uncle Holden. "But word might get out nonetheless. There might still be a whiff of scandal. She could even go to the media. We can't afford a blot on our good name."

"Which is why, Simon," said Simon's father, "we are going to do everything we can to prevent you getting away. Both of you."

"I'll take that risk." Simon continued on towards the door, taking Kaylee with him.

"Son, please reconsider. This is your last chance. Step outside, and you'll be condemning yourself to death as well as her."

At that moment, Uncle Holden lunged at Simon from the side.

Simon lashed out with the knife. He caught Holden on the forearm, slashing through his sleeve and drawing blood. His uncle stumbled backwards, clutching his injured arm and yowling like a scalded cat.

With an elbow, Simon butted the door open. He thrust Kaylee out ahead of him, meanwhile keeping himself turned towards his three relatives, with the knife poised between him and them to hold them at bay.

"Goodbye," he said with finality, then backed out of the door after Kaylee.

They hurried across the porch. Simon knew his family members would be giving chase. They were momentarily stunned by what he had done, but they weren't going to let him and Kaylee get away.

Down the porch steps. Towards his car. Simon fished in his pocket for the keys.

A shot rang out. A ragged-edged hole appeared in the car's windshield.

Simon and Kaylee both hurled themselves to the ground. Another shot kicked up earth right by their feet. They scuttled around the side of the car on hands and knees.

Simon peeked over the car's hood to see Bryce on the porch, legs spread in a shooting stance. He had a hunting rifle in his hands, one eye to the scope.

Now his father emerged from the lodge, also carrying a hunting rifle.

Bryce drew a bead on Simon's head. Simon ducked down, and not a moment too soon. Bryce fired, and the round whanged off the car's bodywork, ricocheting into the trees.

Gabriel Tam hastened to the edge of the porch, straddled the balustrade and lowered himself over the side to the ground.

Bryce loosed off another shot to keep Simon and Kaylee pinned in place behind the car, while his brother began moving round in a wide arc. Gabriel was aiming to take up a position somewhere to the side where he would have a clear line of fire at the two targets.

Simon used the knife to saw through the rope around Kaylee's wrists. When her hands were free, she tugged the gag down from around her mouth.

"Simon…" she breathed.

"No talking. My dad's trying to flank us. We have to move."

"Can't we get in the car and drive?"

"Bryce is a good shot. He'll pick us off the moment we put our heads up above the dashboard. If we head that way"—Simon pointed—"and stay low, then we can keep the car between us and him until we reach the trees. But we have to go now, before my dad gets to where he needs to be."

Kaylee nodded acquiescence. Next moment, she and Simon were crouch-running towards the forest.

"Bryce!" Gabriel Tam called out. "They're on the move!"

"I see them," Bryce replied, and a barrage of bullets came whizzing the two fugitives' way. Tree bark splintered. Dead leaves erupted on the ground. One round passed so close by Simon's head, he not only heard its waspish buzz but felt the pressure wave of its flight on the skin of his cheek.

Back at the lodge, Uncle Holden had emerged outdoors too. His voice boomed out echoingly. "Damn you, Simon. We're coming for you! You aren't going to get away."

Even as he and Kaylee gained the cover of the trees, Simon had an inkling that Holden was correct.

Against three very determined men armed with high-velocity hunting rifles, the pair of them scarcely stood a chance.

39

After several long seconds during which Zoë looked all set to blow Wash's brains out, she relaxed her trigger finger.

"No," she said. "Tempting though it is, those aren't my orders."

"And, um, what *are* your orders?" Wash said.

"Question you should be asking is 'Who's giving them?'"

"Very next thing I was going to say."

"You're about to find out," Zoë told him. "I have to say," she added, "I'm looking forward to this."

"Looking forward to what?"

"To seeing your face when you take this call. Go on. Boot up your sourcebox like I said."

Wash eyed the Mare's Leg, then his wife, and did as requested.

"Enter your password," Zoë said.

Wash did that too.

"Now what?"

"There'll be an incoming wave. We shouldn't have long to wait."

Several minutes passed. The gun remained trained on Wash, unwaveringly.

What the hell is all this about? he wondered. The one bright spot in an otherwise fairly crappy situation was the fact that he was still alive.

How long that would remain the case, he had no idea. Was Zoë going to blackmail him? Was this some kind of robbery? He just couldn't work it out. What he did know was that she wasn't the woman he had thought she was. She was something else altogether. Something more.

An image popped up on the screen. It was a feed from what appeared to be a boardroom. Around a long oaken table sat seven men and women. The lighting was subdued, bordering on murky, so that Wash could make out little more than a face in profile here, a hand resting on the tabletop there. What he could see, however, gave an impression of wealth and influence, a center of immense corporate gravity.

"Mr. Washburne," said the man at the head of the table. "How goes it?"

"Just dandy. My own wife's holding me at gunpoint. Loving that. Who are you people?"

"We'll come to that in due course. First of all, please accept our congratulations on the course of your career so far. You have conducted business in an exemplary fashion. You started out with next to nothing, and now you have more than you can possibly have dreamed. Quite the mogul."

There was a smattering of applause from the assembled company. To Wash, it sounded bizarrely sincere.

"But then lately you have experienced the odd hitch, have you not?" said the spokesman. "A few flies in the proverbial ointment. How has that been for you?"

"An absolute joy. How do you *think* it's been?"

"It's always distressing when one's upward trajectory is hindered, even if only slightly. It gives one a sense of… Well, mortality, I suppose. Problems are for lesser beings. It is disconcerting to be reminded that one is not as exceptional and unassailable as one has come to think. That one is not a titan after all, or for that matter a god."

"Look," said Wash, "this is obviously some sort of commercial proposition. And I can't fault your sense of the dramatic. There you are, all mysterious and unidentifiable, and my wife of several years turns out to be a gun-wielding sleeper agent or some such. You have my attention. What do you want?"

"Cutting to the chase, eh?" said the spokesman. "We like that. Well then, Mr. Washburne—may I call you Wash?"

"Nope."

"All right. Mr. Washburne it is. I'll lay things out for you straight. *We* were the cause of your recent business upsets. The labor dispute, the accounting error, the attempted hostile takeover, the lawsuit—we were responsible for them all. With a little help from the dauntless and dedicated Mrs. Washburne, of course. Her inside knowledge of Pteranodon Inc.'s day-to-day affairs has proved invaluable. All this time, while you thought she was your wife and business partner, she was covertly gathering data."

Wash flicked a glance at Zoë. She just shrugged and nodded.

"Thanks to Zoë, our spy in your camp," the man onscreen continued, "we now know as much about you, professionally and personally, as you do yourself. Your habits. Your predilections. The crux of the matter is, we are perfectly capable of destroying you. You should consider the litany of difficulties Pteranodon has encountered over the past few weeks as an exercise of our power. We arranged it all with the merest lifting of a finger—a demonstration, an object lesson. Now imagine what we would be capable of if truly provoked. Not only could we bring your entire empire crashing down around your ears, we could see to it that you spend the rest of your days in abject penury and shame, a pariah."

Wash felt a chill, deep inside. It didn't occur to him for one moment that this was an idle boast. These people, whoever they were, were not messing around.

"'What is it you want from me?'" said the spokesman. "That is your next question. And the answer is perfectly straightforward. One third of Pteranodon. A thirty-three per cent stake in the company and thirty-three per cent of all its profits in perpetuity."

"That's all?" said Wash. "Why not take sixty? Eighty? And my kids while you're about it."

"Be as facetious as you like, Mr. Washburne, if it makes you feel better. This is a one-time-only offer. It will not be repeated. You have precisely sixty seconds in which to make up your mind, although I suspect you have already decided."

"And if I tell you go screw yourselves, you bunch of *xī niú* leeches? What then?"

"You are permitted that single piece of blustering bravado. That and no more. The clock is running. What's it to be?"

Wash looked at Zoë again.

"Don't expect me to give you any advice," she said. "All I'll tell you is that it makes no nevermind to me whether you give them a yes or a no. You're the one whose future is on the line. You say no, and I'll file for divorce, take a hefty alimony settlement and the kids, then watch from the sidelines as Pteranodon goes down in flames and you with it. You say yes, and you're stuck with me for a while to come, so's I can keep a close eye on you and make sure you behave and don't try anything stupid. Everything stays pretty much the same, except you'll be a mite poorer and, of course, you won't have your precious Zoë sleeping with you anymore. That particular burden, I'm glad to say, is one I'm no longer going to have to bear. Meantime, we continue to be mom and dad to Celeste, Ulysses, and Uriah. They aren't to know any different."

Wash suppressed a groan. Bad enough he was being bullied into signing over a significant chunk of his prosperity. He was also going to have to cohabit from now on with a woman who clearly didn't love him, and had never loved him? And pretend to their children that all was well? For how long? For good?

"You went to all that trouble," he said to Zoë. "Married me, had babies with me. All just to maintain your cover?"

"It wasn't *all* bad. I love those kids with every fiber of my being. You gave me them, and I'm grateful to you for that, if nothing else. But don't flatter yourself there was anything meaningful between us."

"Ever?"

"There might have been to begin with. Maybe. But all said and done, dear husband, you were only a means to an end."

Wash turned back to the boardroom on the wave screen.

In that moment, he had never hated anyone quite as much as he hated those seven faceless people. Them and the woman he had loved completely and had believed loved him back just as much.

"Okay," he said.

"Speak up," said the spokesman. "Didn't quite catch that."

"I said okay."

"Very good. You've done the right thing, Mr. Washburne. The paperwork will be on its way over. Zoë will ensure you put your signature in all the correct places. A formality, of course, but it helps to have things down in writing. If it's any consolation, Pteranodon Inc. is not the first company with whom we have come to such an arrangement, nor will it be the last. We count practically every known multimillionaire and billionaire in the 'verse as an affiliate. Your friends Atherton Wing and Sir Warwick Harrow among them. Ask them next time you meet. They will, given the appropriate, discreet prompting, tell a tale similar to your own. You could almost call this a rite of passage, much as a Wilhelmina Ascot profile is a rite of passage. It's a sure sign that you've achieved elite status and are among the true *crème de la crème*."

"Lucky me," Wash drawled.

"Lucky you indeed," the spokesman said. "This conversation is now done. I doubt we shall ever talk again, but suffice to say, it has been a pleasure doing business with you."

"Before you go, at least tell me who you are."

"I should have thought it was obvious. Who has such reach? Who has such surpassing mastery over all aspects of commerce in the 'verse? Who else but..."

"Blue Sun," Wash said, as the penny dropped. "You're Blue Sun."

"Indeed," said the spokesman. "And so are you, to some extent, from this moment on."

That night, Wash lay in the plush guest-room bed. Zoë occupied the plusher king-size he would never share with her again.

He couldn't sleep. He thought about Blue Sun. Blue Sun, whose tentacles were now insinuated into his business dealings. Blue Sun, monitoring his every action via Zoë. Blue Sun, to whom Pteranodon Inc. would be involuntarily paying a third of its income from now until doomsday.

Not because they needed his money. Blue Sun was rolling in riches.

Because they could. That was why. Because they were able to push everyone around, and there was nothing anyone could do about it.

In a way, it was almost okay. Blue Sun couldn't help itself. It was a predator. You couldn't blame it for its behavior any more than you'd blame a cougar for gnawing your leg. Pteranodon had done much the same in its time. It had eaten other companies. Swallowed them up. Now it had been swallowed itself by a bigger beast. A law of nature.

What was harder to accept was Zoë's part in all of this. How long had she been covertly working for Blue Sun? Since before Wash met her? Or was it after? Had their first encounter at Atherton Wing's been purely accidental, or had it been a setup?

Perhaps it didn't matter. Her betrayal of him was so absolute, it made no difference whether she had planned it from the start or had been recently seduced into it by Blue Sun. Either way, the result was the same. His wife was not his wife. Not anymore. Maybe she never had been. And if their marriage hadn't been a sham all along, it was certainly going to be from now on. Their business partnership too.

He should have known. He should have known there'd be a price to pay for all that happiness. He should have known it was too good to be true and too perfect to last.

Wash lay in bed, in torment, longing for the oblivion of sleep, which refused to come.

40

For the first hour or so of the siege, the Cobb family held their own.

The Beavertail Gang fanned out around the property, found defensive positions, bedded down, and started taking potshots at the house.

This was a tactical error on Ottoline Beavertail's part. If Jayne had been her, he'd have had his people rush the house from all sides at once, blasting away with their guns. A single massed assault would have severely limited the capacity of those inside to retaliate. Sure, it might have cost the gang a few lives, but the outcome was most assuredly a victory. They would have stormed the building, overrun the Cobbs, and won the day in a relatively short span of time, with casualties kept to a minimum.

Instead, their plan seemed to be trying to wear the Cobbs down. Now and then one of them would shoot, and the bullet would maybe take out a windowpane or punch a hole in the clapboard wall, maybe damage an item of décor inside—but they were effectively firing blind, and the odds that they would hit anyone were relatively low.

Furthermore, such sporadic attacks played into the hands of the people under siege. Whenever a gang member poked his or her head up in order to take aim, it gave Jayne, Matty, and Radiant Cobb a nice fat target. None of them was slow to capitalize on this. Jayne and his mother fired from between the window boards, Jayne in the front room, his mother out back. Meantime, up in the widow's walk, Matty had a commanding 360-degree view over the entire farmyard, and as long as he lay flat, he presented an almost impossible target from below. Often he and one of his relatives downstairs would bag a gang member simultaneously.

It took Ottoline Beavertail a mighty long while to cotton on to the fact that this war of attrition was not serving her well. Jayne heard her yelling at her gang. He couldn't make out the words, but it seemed clear that she was adopting a different strategy.

"Mama," he called out. "Looks like we're gonna be receivin' visitors soon."

"I'll be sure to roll out the welcome mat for 'em."

"You hear that, Matty?" Jayne said, shouting upstairs to the roof hatch. "We're liable to be a whole lot busier shortly."

"Got ammo," Matty replied. "Got the high ground. If those sumbitches ain't already sorry they killed Jip, they soon gonna be."

Peering out, Jayne spied activity to the south of the house. A pair of gang members were scuttling towards the lean-to that housed the solar converter cell array. The angle was too narrow for Jayne to get a clear shot. He watched as one of the two men gave the other a leg up onto the lean-to's corrugated iron roof. The first then hauled his counterpart up after him.

"Matty. South side. There's two of 'em going to try reachin' you via the lean-to."

"No problem, Jayne. Thanks for the heads-up."

"Jayne?" said Radiant Cobb. "I got movement out back, by the vegetable patch fence. Four, maybe five of the varmints."

Jayne looked out at the farmyard. Furtive runnings and scurryings out there suggested a frontal assault was imminent as well.

He slapped a fresh magazine into Vera. This was it. Moment of truth. Whatever happened, Jayne knew his mother and brother would give a good account of themselves, same as he would. The Cobb clan would not go quietly.

He heard gunfire from the roof. Two quick reports, then two more. A man screamed. There was the sound of a body thudding onto the lean-to's roof, then rolling off that onto the ground.

A couple more shots from up above, another scream. Matty let out a triumphant "Yessss!"

Radiant Cobb began firing from the kitchen window. "How d'you like that, you lousy cow-thievin' rats? Yeah! That's it! Run like the yellowbellies you are. This is the Cobbs you're up against. You ain't never met trouble like this in all your born days."

Out front, one of the gang crawled out from cover, carelessly straying into Jayne's crosshairs. The fella went down minus half his jaw.

Then gunfire from the farmyard started strafing the front of the house. Jayne ducked behind an upturned settee. The room erupted into bullet-riddled chaos. A table lamp toppled. A framed needlepoint sampler—"GOD BLESS THIS HOME AND ALL WHO LIVE IN IT"—fell from the wall. Crockery on the shelves of the dresser shattered.

It wasn't until the barrage ended that Jayne was able to hear Matty's panicked cries.

"Jayne! Jayne! Help!"

"On my way!"

Jayne set down Vera. A bulky weapon, and he needed to move fast, unencumbered. He scrambled on all fours towards the stairs, through the debris littering the floor. He charged up to the second-story landing and scaled the ladder to the hatch.

He got to the top in time to see a trio of gang members hauling a disarmed Matty down the pitch of the roof. They were on the north side. They must have climbed up onto the adjacent milking shed, then jumped across onto the balcony outside the master bedroom and got to the roof from there. While Matty had been preoccupied by the attackers from the south, these others had sneaked up on him from behind.

"Gorramn it!" Jayne drew a pistol and snapped off a few shots, killing one of Matty's abductors. The remaining two, however, managed to drag Matty down onto the balcony, out of Jayne's sight.

Jayne didn't hesitate. He leaped over the low iron railing that surrounded the widow's walk and slid down the roof after Matty, his hip bumping and scraping over the shingles. He slithered out past the eaves, landing heavily on the balcony below.

The two gang members were manhandling Matty over the balustrade. Matty looked dazed, and Jayne reckoned one of them must have clouted him on the head as they'd nabbed him. They all but pitched him off the balcony, to where a handful of their fellow gang members were waiting below to catch him.

Jayne dispatched one of the two on the balcony with a point-blank shot. The other returned fire. Jayne shrank to the side in the nick of time, the bullet taking out a chunk of balustrade beside his thigh. His next shot threw the gang member off his feet and sent him flying out into space, arms flailing. The man was dead before he reached the ground.

Scuttling to the edge of the balcony, Jayne saw Matty being hustled around the side of the milking shed. Without even thinking, he vaulted the balustrade. He rolled as his feet hit the dirt, coming up in a combat-ready crouch. He began to run after Matty and Matty's abductors, only to realize that he had sprained his ankle. That was what you got for leaping precipitously off a balcony ten feet up.

He limped onwards, rounding the angle of the milking shed. The gang members and Matty were nowhere to be seen. Growling in anger, Jayne lumbered after them. There was only one way for them to go and that was along the far side of the milking shed, back towards the farmyard. Once past the corner, he'd have clear line of sight. He'd pick the bastards off like bottles on a fence.

The moment he stepped out past the shed, he knew he'd been suckered.

Ottoline Beavertail herself, along with a half-dozen of her gang, were lying in wait for him. Every one of them had a gun trained on Jayne.

"Drop it," Ottoline Beavertail said, "or we drop you."

"Whoa. Easy there. Okay." Jayne held up his pistol by the barrel, then bent and placed it down.

"Good boy. Jared? Nate? Take the rest of his weapons off of him, then tie his hands."

The two gang members did as their boss ordered. Jayne did not resist.

"You got me," he said as they yanked his hands behind his back and bound his wrists. "You caught the big fish. You can let the small fry go." He nodded to indicate Matty, whom another couple of gang members were busy tying up just behind Ottoline Beavertail.

She looked over her shoulder, then back at Jayne. "Don't reckon it's a matter you have any say in, Jayne Cobb. Ain't as if you're in any position to dictate terms. All's you can do is accept you've been outsmarted and deal with the consequences."

Gunfire erupted from the rear of the house.

"That's your momma, I suppose," Ottoline Beavertail said. "The last holdout. Well, she's welcome to stay indoors, snug as a bug. My guess is, though, she'll lay down her arms and come on out, once she sees what we have in store for you people, out in the farmyard."

"Which is?"

"You'll see in a moment."

A resigned, chagrined Jayne let the gang members finish knotting rope around his wrists. The ones who were securing Matty, however, were being far more thorough in their efforts. They had him down on his stomach and were fastening both his wrists and his ankles.

Not only that, they then ran a rope around the two sets of bindings, attaching them together. Matty was now helplessly hogtied.

Four of the gang picked Matty up and carried him to the farmyard, his head hanging limply towards the ground. Ottoline Beavertail gestured, and Jayne was dragged by the elbows after his brother. A couple of times his bum ankle twisted under him. He hissed with the pain but kept walking.

They all gathered in front of the house, and after a bit of organizing, Matty was slung onto a pole that was suspended horizontally between a handcart and a fence rail, his belly towards the ground.

Jayne began to have a fairly good idea what the Beavertail Gang had planned for his brother. He felt sick to his stomach.

"Please," he said to Ottoline Beavertail. "You don't have to do this. The cows, they're all yours. Take 'em."

"Oh, we're gonna take 'em all right. But first we're gonna teach y'all a lesson. You shoulda given up your herd without a fight, but since you didn't, you're gonna have to pay the penalty."

"Not Matty." Jayne was pleading, as close to tears as Jayne Cobb ever might come. "Do it to me by all means, but not him."

"And where would be the fun in that?" said the eye-patched gang leader.

There was a fresh rattle of gunfire from the rear of the house.

"Mrs. Cobb!" Ottoline Beavertail hollered, her hands cupped either side of her mouth. "Hope you can hear me. I got both your sons out here. Holdin' 'em captive. You can carry on shootin' if you like, but you'll maybe want to take a look-see this way, learn what's what."

There was a pause of perhaps half a minute, then the front door opened. Radiant Cobb stepped out, rifle raised and aiming.

"There she is," said Ottoline Beavertail. "I can see where you don't get your good looks from, Jayne."

"Let my boys go," said Radiant icily.

"Not gonna happen, lady. I'm holding all the aces. You ain't got no alternative but to fold."

"This here rifle says otherwise. One squeeze of the trigger, and you don't got no head anymore and the Beavertail Gang don't got no leader."

"Maybe, but then my people'll shoot back and you'll be dead too. And the little entertainment we've got planned goes ahead anyway."

"Mama," said Jayne. "Put the gun down. I've got this. I'm gonna make sure you and Matty are okay." To Ottoline Beavertail he said, "You know I'm the one you really want to make pay. This is all down to me. Matty and my mother, they were only doing what I told 'em to."

Matty stirred. "No, Jayne," he said groggily. "We... We were all..."

"Pay him no mind," Jayne said. "Him and my mama, they were all for giving in to you and your gang. I'm the one convinced 'em stand up to you. So I'm the one you need to punish."

"I'd never have pegged you for the self-sacrificing type," said Ottoline Beavertail. "Just shows how wrong you can be about folks. Guess all it takes is the right incentive."

"Jayne..." said Radiant Cobb.

"Mama, I said I've got this."

"Yeah, 'Mama,'" said Ottoline Beavertail. "Butt out."

"You keep up that kinda talk," Radiant warned, "it's just gonna earn you a hole in the head all the sooner, you one-eyed witch."

"Oh, for—!" Ottoline Beavertail swung around, slickly drawing a pistol at the same time. She cracked off a shot before Radiant could even react. Radiant let out a yell and crumpled to the porch floorboards, her rifle tumbling from her hands.

"Mama!" Jayne cried.

"Ah, she's fine," said Ottoline Beavertail. "I only winged her. Somebody go and pick her up and haul her sorry, wrinkled ass over here."

Two gang members hurried off to do as requested. They lugged Radiant off the porch, dragging her to where everyone else was standing.

They deposited her in front of Ottoline Beavertail, on her knees.

"Mama, you okay?" Jayne said. He could see she was bleeding from one bicep. It was far from a fatal wound but it was clearly giving her grief.

"I've been better," an ashen-faced Radiant replied, gritting her teeth against the pain. "Also been worse."

Jayne rounded on Ottoline Beavertail. "Betcha feel proud of yourself," he rumbled, "shootin' an old lady."

"She ain't much older'n me," the gang leader replied, "and you wouldn't have cared, if it'd been the other way round."

"That'd've been different. I ain't close kin to you."

"Fact is, she's alive, the way I want her. Way I want you too. And now that we have our audience all lined up and ready, let's get on with the show."

"One last time," Jayne said. "I'm beggin' you. Not Matty. Me."

"Nuh-uh." Ottoline Beavertail produced a bone-handled pocketknife. "No can do. Only one way this is gonna work, and that's this way."

"Bitch!" Jayne roared, and lunged for her. He almost managed to break free from the two gang members who were holding his arms. One of them gave him a hefty kick to the back of the knee. Jayne's leg buckled under him, numbed from the calf down. Now he, too, was kneeling, like his mother.

Ottoline Beavertail held up the pocketknife, which Jayne recognized as the type known as a stockman knife. She opened out the largest of its three blades. The other two smaller blades had specific functions, one a blunt-tipped sheepsfoot blade, useful for levering stones out of hooves, the other a hooked spey blade for skinning. The four-inch master blade was all-purpose, designed for cutting, whittling, gutting, and anything else you could imagine.

"I'd tell you I was gonna make this quick," she said, "but then I'd be lyin'."

She strolled over to the suspended Matty. He saw her coming and moaned.

"Matty," Jayne said. "Look at me. Look at me, Matty. Eyes on mine. Look at me!"

Matty raised his head. Their gazes locked. Jayne tried to transmit to his brother every emotion he was feeling: compassion, pity, fury, sorrow, regret. He wanted the last thing Matty ever saw to be his face. He wanted him to know that he was loved, loved fiercely, and that nothing would ever change that.

"Just for the record," Jayne said to Ottoline Beavertail, not taking his eyes off Matty, "you'd better not leave me alive after this, woman. Elsewise there'll be a reckoning. You have my word on that."

"Oh, like I'd be so stupid as to let any of you hillbillies live," she replied. "The trouble you've put me to? The loss of so many of my gang? You're all three gonna die today, not a shred of doubt about it. But it's gonna be the most fun makin' you two watch as Matty here gets his."

She tore Matty's shirt open, exposing his bare torso. She held the knife, point upwards, beneath him.

"You wouldn't give me your cattle, Matty," she said, "so it's kind of fitting that I treat you like cattle. And you know what happens to all cattle eventually? They get carved up."

She slashed him across the abdomen.

Matty screamed.

She slashed again, parallel to her first cut.

She kept going, both parallel and crosswise, making incisions just deeper than the skin.

Matty bucked and writhed in agony. His face was puce, the veins puffing out on his temples. His breaths came in strangulated gasps.

"Matty!" Jayne ordered, his voice hoarse. "Keep looking at me. Come on."

Radiant Cobb, meanwhile, murmured a prayer for her younger

son's soul, committing him to the Good Lord's safekeeping.

Ottoline Beavertail continued to slice away at Matty's belly. Little by little she was degrading the integrity of his abdominal muscles, like unpicking the threads of a tapestry.

Matty's eyes remained fixed on Jayne's but they were now glazed and vacant. Jayne hoped that his brother was in a place beyond the pain, already halfway to the next life.

The ragged bloody ruin that was Matty's belly bulged downwards. All at once, his abdominal muscles could no longer hold. The damage inflicted by Ottoline Beavertail was too great.

Jayne shut his eyes, but could not close his ears to the hideous wet *sloosh* of Matty's entrails spilling out in lumps onto the ground.

41

As her fellow crewmembers' dreams turned into horror shows, River was there with them like an unseen phantom, bearing witness.

She ran breathlessly with Mal as he and his family fled into the forest in the hope of escaping the oncoming Reavers.

She felt the shock and dismay Kaylee felt when the charismatic Caleb Dahl revealed himself to be a ruthless people-trafficker.

She knew exactly how filled with dread Zoë was upon meeting the Butcher of Beylix, a.k.a. Derrial Book.

She writhed in despair just as Wash writhed in despair from the double blow of Blue Sun annexing Pteranodon Inc. and his wife's betrayal. She was with Simon as he dodged bullets fired at him by his nearest and dearest, family members he had trusted.

She looked on, alongside Jayne, while Matty was slaughtered in front of him, in the most callous and brutal manner imaginable.

All around her, she sensed that the crew's bodies were registering the effects of acute stress. Their adrenal glands were secreting excessive quantities of catecholamine hormone. Their heart rates and respiratory rates were rapidly rising. Their blood vessels were constricting while at the same time, behind their eyelids, their pupils were dilating. Their livers were releasing higher than normal amounts of glucose in order to fuel the fight-or-flight response.

Jayne, in the infirmary, groaned. Wash, in the pilot's chair on the bridge, was frenziedly shaking his head from side to side. Down in the cargo bay, Mal's legs twitched and a little bit of drool leaked from the corner of his mouth. Up in the galley, Zoë was curled in a ball, fetus-like, rocking slightly. In the engine room, Kaylee lay on the floor, digging at her face with her fingernails. Simon, in his bunk, was raking the air with his hands as though fending off an invisible attacker.

River knew that their individual agonies were only going to get worse. Each was nearing breaking point, both physiologically and psychically. They were at risk of cardiac arrhythmia and aneurysm. The traumas they were undergoing seemed so real to them that, even if they survived, their minds might be left permanently scarred.

There was something else, too.

River's slumbering consciousness expanded outward, spreading beyond the people aboard *Serenity* to encompass the ship herself.

Serenity was sailing blithely through space at three-quarter burn. In his dream, Wash had engaged autopilot on the Seraphim he imagined he was piloting. In reality, he had not done the same with the ship he was *actually* piloting. His hand hadn't gone anywhere near the correct button on the control console, instead merely making a minor adjustment to the onboard climate settings. *Serenity*'s current heading was taking her away from Canterbury, but as River extrapolated the ship's trajectory, she saw that it was taking her *towards* one of the planet's moons. Not the larger and further away of the two, known locally as Luna Major, but its smaller, nearer counterpart, Luna Minor.

How *Serenity* had not yet drawn the attention of the Alliance ships in the area was some kind of miracle. River could only assume it was the directness with which she was flying. She wasn't skulking around furtively; she was moving with apparent boldness. It was much the same as if you were a thief leaving the scene of a robbery and wanted to throw off suspicion. If you strode along with a breezy, confident air, not hunching down or checking over your shoulder all the time, nobody would look twice at you.

River rechecked her calculations. In her mind's eye, a straight line arrowed out across the void from *Serenity*'s bow in the direction of travel. Its endpoint lay on the rugged, roughly dumbbell-shaped lump of lifeless rock that was Luna Minor. Close enough to the moon's center to be called a bullseye.

A more sophisticated spaceship had automated systems that would take over in the event of an imminent collision and steer the vessel out of harm's way without the need for human intervention—the so-called "suicide brake," a piece of software that was almost impossible to disable.

The adjective "sophisticated," however, did not apply to *Serenity*.

At present speed, the ship would reach Luna Minor in slightly under half an hour. The moon had no atmosphere to impede her progress. *Serenity* would pile-drive into its surface doing several thousand miles an hour. After that, there wouldn't be a ship to speak of. There would be millions of tiny fragments scattered over a vast debris field, and a brand-new impact crater.

In other words, if the crew's nightmares didn't kill them, the imminent crash-landing would.

Proximity warnings hadn't yet begun sounding. *Serenity* remained oblivious to the danger she was in. But even when the alarms went off, would it be enough to rouse anyone from the torpor induced by the siren? River thought not.

There was nothing for it. Somehow she had to wake herself up.

She tried. She fought against the anesthetizing embrace of the sedative Simon had given her. It was like trying to swim up through glacially cold water to reach the air above. She could get near the surface but was unable to break through. Every time, she came tantalizingly close. Every time, she failed and sank back down into the depths. The depths where it was dark and calm. Where she could, if she wanted to, just float. No struggle. No fear. Numb.

No!

River all but screamed the word to herself.

Something else. There had to be something else she could do. Otherwise everyone on the ship was going to die.

She thought hard. If she couldn't beat the sedative and wake herself up…

Wake up the crew.

But which of them first?

Him. It would have to be him.

42

Wash spent his days moping around the mansion. He neither went out nor received callers. He left the running of Pteranodon Inc. to Zoë. She, in turn, circulated a brief internal memo among the corporation's upper echelons, the CEOs of its subsidiary companies, and a select handful of shareholders saying that her husband was taking a sabbatical and was not to be contacted. She informed her underlings that all decisions were to be referred to her, and her alone.

Wash let his hair grow shaggy. He became unshaven. He didn't shower or change his clothes nearly as often as he ought.

Several times, in private, Zoë chided him. She said he should clean himself up, stop being such a sore loser, get out there and show his face. He was acting like a spoiled child.

His answer, each time, ran along the same lines. She was his wife in name only. She didn't have the right to criticize or cajole him. What he would really prefer her to do right now was go away and leave him be. Of course, he phrased it somewhat more vividly than that.

"You stay bitter like this, Wash," Zoë said one time, "it's going to eat you up alive. A sensible man would pick himself up, dust himself off, and get on with it."

"A sensible man," he replied, "would never have gotten hitched to a deceitful harpy like you in the first place. In fact, a sensible man would shoot you dead where you stand."

"Oh no," Zoë said in a voice filled with casual menace. "A sensible man wouldn't even think of trying to kill me."

"Because Blue Sun would come down on him like a ton of bricks?"

"Blue Sun nothing. Because I'd break every gorramn bone in his body."

Judging by her tone, Wash didn't doubt it. He was beginning to understand that the Zoë he'd courted and married was gone. In truth, she had probably never existed. The real Zoë was the one he was living with now: cool, no-nonsense, ruthlessly businesslike. That other Zoë—the perfect wife, mother, and helpmeet—was just an illusion she had concocted. Bait in a trap.

He remained in a profound funk for well over a month. His self-neglect got to the point where he was hardly eating. His main source of caloric intake was booze.

One day, in a fit of rage, he went around the house chucking out every item manufactured by Blue Sun or one of its subsidiary companies. It left the kitchen cupboards more or less bare, most of his clothes gone, and quite a bit of the newtech gone too. He heaped everything in a great big pile on the lawn, which he poured gasoline over and set alight. The pyre burned all afternoon.

Zoë came outside briefly to watch. "You know I'm just going to rebuy every single thing you've trashed," she said.

"Eh," said Wash. "Worth it just to see this lot go up in flames."

As evening fell, the pyre began dying down. Wash sat in a deckchair, working on his sixth beer of the day.

That was when the girl appeared.

She was sitting cross-legged on the grass beside him, a slip of a thing, dark-haired, big-eyed, wearing a long dress and large, clumpy boots.

Wash would have been more startled had he been less drunk.

"Where'd you come from?" he said.

"Your head," she replied. "And mine. It's complicated."

"Sounds like it."

"Don't you recognize me?"

Wash eyed her up and down. She did look familiar, but he was damned if he could place her.

"You… work for me?" he ventured. "Like, one of the household staff?" He knew most of his domestic servants, but new ones came along from time to time.

For answer, there was only silence. The girl had vanished.

Wash looked at his beer bottle, then at where the girl had been, then back at his beer bottle, and finally shrugged and took another swig.

"Sorry."

Beer spluttered from Wash's mouth.

The girl was back again.

"This is harder than I thought it'd be," she said. "But I believe I'm getting the hang of it now."

"It's funny," Wash said. "For a moment there, you'd gone."

"I know. I'm aligning my consciousness with yours. It's like synchronizing two grandfather clocks, getting them to tick and tock together. Takes precision."

"I'll have to take your word for it, being as I have no idea what you're talking about."

"Understandable. I'm River, by the way."

"Nice name. Hi, River. I'm Wash. Want a beer?"

"Sure."

He handed her one from the cooler by his side.

She uncapped the bottle with a casual flick of one finger.

"Neat trick," he said.

"I'm full of them," she said, taking a sip. "You sure you don't know who I am?"

He shook his head. "Got this feeling you're someone I *should* know, but I'm darned if I can think how or why."

River tilted her chin contemplatively, then nodded to herself. "Yes. We haven't met. In your dream, that is. You've led a completely different life. No *Serenity*."

"Serenity," said Wash. "I *wish* I had serenity. Been a long time since I ever felt anything close to serene."

"But that's the thing, Wash. *Serenity* is where you're at. All this, the big house, the grounds, this fire, that deckchair you're sitting in…" She pointed out each item in this inventory with the neck of the beer bottle. "None of it exists. At the moment, you aren't here. You're on the bridge of a Firefly called *Serenity* that's on a collision course with a moon."

"Sure I am."

"You have to open your eyes. You have to see the truth."

Wash thought he would humor her. He opened his eyes as wide as they would go and peered around owlishly.

"Nope," he said. "All I see is the fire, the moon rising, fireflies glowing in that patch of shrubbery over there."

"Those aren't the kind of firefly I mean," River said. "That isn't the moon I mean, either. You need to wake up, Wash, otherwise we're all going to die."

"Wake up. Sure."

"You sense it, don't you? Deep down. You know me and you know you should believe me when I tell you we're in danger. Here's what I want you to do. Set down that beer and reach out in front of you. Go on. Put out your hands."

Obligingly, Wash groped the air in front of him.

"Do you feel something?"

"The heat from the fire."

"Anything else?"

"No, just thin air."

"Nothing solid?"

"No. There's nothing there, River. There's only…"

Wash frowned. His fingertips had brushed against a cool, hard surface. He felt for it again and rested his hand on it. He couldn't see it but he could definitely touch it. It was smooth. Inclined at a shallow angle. His hand explored further. There were... switches? Buttons?

"A ship's control console," River said. "One you know so well, you could be blindfolded and still find exactly where everything is on it."

"I... I must be even drunker than I thought."

"Or," she said, "you aren't drunk at all and what you're touching is real. Concentrate, Wash. Really focus. Do you think you're genuinely a plutocrat?"

"I don't know what a plutocrat is."

"A very rich businessman."

"Oh. Then yeah, that's me. Sure."

"Is it? Does any of this feel right to you? Do you like having so much money? Do you like the responsibility that comes with it? Because the Wash I know, he's a guy with a simple outlook. He likes to fly. He likes bad shirts and toy dinosaurs. He loves his wife and she loves him. He's always ready with a wisecrack. This? It's a distortion. It's what you thought you wanted, but what the heart desires isn't the same as what the heart needs. And now it's all gone wrong, doesn't that somehow feel *better*? Like it ought to be? Don't you want to just burn everything, like you're burning these material possessions here? Get rid of it all, because it's all false?"

Wash was studying her speculatively, his hands still caressing the invisible control console.

"All you have to do now," River went on, "is take the final step. Reject it completely. Remember who you really are. Look, Wash. Open your eyes and truly *look*."

Wash stared into the remnants of the fire. The shimmering embers swam in his vision. The darting fireflies likewise, and the rising moon. They danced, swirled, coalesced into a new configuration.

All at once he was looking at the lights of *Serenity*'s control console. He was in the pilot's seat. He felt its upholstery beneath his back and his butt, the padding that had conformed to his body's contours over thousands of hours of occupancy.

This was him. This was where he belonged.

His head was pounding. It was as though he had gone from getting drunk to being hungover without anything in between. His heart was racing, his pulse like thunder in his ears.

He hated this. Where he had been just moments earlier, out back of his mansion on Persephone with a bonfire of Blue Sun products smoldering in front of him, might not have been perfect. It was preferable to this, though, surely.

He looked around him. The girl, River, was gone again.

He looked ahead. In the forward view ports, Canterbury's Luna Minor hovered centrally, a pitted mass of rock like a big gray potato, of no great consequence.

Wash wished to be happy again. He wished to be somewhere where his head didn't hurt and his body didn't feel like it was rebelling against him.

Where was he at his happiest?

Piloting.

But not piloting a clapped-out Firefly like this one. That was how the illustrious Hoban Washburne had started out, flying hunk-of-junk spaceships on cargo runs. Before Pteranodon Inc. Before Zoë. Back when he was a nobody.

Nowadays a Seraphim was more his style.

And he owned a Seraphim, right?

Wash took a breath, closed his eyes, reopened them, and lo and behold, he was at the yoke of his Seraphim, just as he'd hoped. The gorgeous Paradise-class cruiser was gliding through the Black.

Better. Much better.

"I see," said a voice beside him.

River had reappeared. She looked dismayed.

"You again?" said Wash.

"I thought I'd woken you up," she said.

"From what? I wasn't asleep."

"Well, you are, as a matter of fact. And now you've hit reset. Oh well. I guess I'm going to have to get a bit more proactive."

So saying, she lunged for the controls and started thumping clusters of buttons at random.

The Seraphim whirled and cavorted giddily.

Wash shoved River aside and fought to regain control of the ship. "What the hell's gotten into you?" he barked as the Seraphim settled, steady once more. "You don't treat a fine piece of astroengineering like this like that."

"I'm trying to shake you up, Wash. I don't want to hit you, so I'm doing the next best thing."

"You're nuts."

"So I've been told."

"Nuttier'n squirrel poop."

"I've not been told *that* before."

River made a bid to wrest the yoke from Wash's clutches.

Suddenly two hands seized her by the shoulders and yanked her away. The same two hands tossed her mercilessly to one side, so that she fetched up in a corner of the Seraphim's bridge.

"Wash," said Zoë. "Is this girl the reason we're Crazy Ivan-ing all over the place?"

"It so happens she is," Wash said, pleased to see his wife.

"Let me deal with her."

"Be my guest."

Zoë stalked towards River intimidatingly. "Now see here, you *bù huǐ hèn de pō fù*. My kids are on this ship, and you're scaring them by making it veer about every which way. I'm not fond of people scaring my kids. Anyone does that, quickly learns not to do it twice."

43

"Which are you?" River said, as Zoë loomed over her. "Badass-warrior Zoë? Blue-Sun-stooge Zoë? Or is it both at once? I'm confused."

"*You're* confused?" said Zoë. "Aren't you River Tam, who can barely string a coherent sentence together? Yet you're talking like a normal person."

"Huh." River pondered it. "So I am. I guess this is the me who isn't all the other me's, the me underneath that muddled mess of Rivers the doctors at the Academy created. The real me. Only in dreams. Of course, Blue-Sun-stooge Zoë isn't supposed to know how I normally am. But then we aren't supposed to be on the bridge of a Seraphim, either. Wash and I are both dreaming at once. I'm in his dream but also in mine. The two are overlapping. The intersecting region in a Venn diagram. This is going to take a little getting used to."

"How about I simplify it for you?" Zoë reached down and grabbed River by the hair. She hauled her upright and started dragging her towards the door connecting the bridge to the rest of the ship. "You don't belong here. Out you go."

River's response was to push off the floor with both feet and perform a perfectly executed backflip. She swung herself over Zoë's head, landing astride her shoulders. Her own head stayed low, her hair still in Zoë's grasp.

She could do this sort of thing in dreams. She could do it in real life, too, for that matter. She just hadn't had cause to yet.

Scissoring her legs around Zoë's neck, she began to squeeze. Zoë let go of her hair and seized ahold of her thighs with both hands in order to pry them apart. River simply squeezed tighter.

Wash, meanwhile, was blithely flying the Seraphim. Either he was unaware of the fight going on right behind him or he didn't care.

Zoë threw herself backwards, sending both her and River crashing into a wall. She was attempting to dislodge River, but River clung on.

River kept having to tell herself this wasn't the real Zoë, this was just a dream construct. She admired the real Zoë hugely for her cool-headedness under pressure, her skills as a strategist, the way she acted unhesitatingly. This Zoë was not *that* Zoë. Still it felt bad trying to throttle her into submission.

Now Zoë began pummeling River's knees in hopes of breaking her hold that way.

Dream pain still hurts, River thought, but she grinned and bore it.

Gradually Zoë's efforts weakened. River was cutting off the supply of air to her lungs and blood to her brain. She should pass out at any moment.

The punches faltered. Zoë tottered. She sagged to the floor.

River relaxed her grip.

Quick as lightning, Zoë was back up on her feet.

"So easily hoodwinked," she snarled, and delivered three astonishingly swift blows to River's face.

Reeling, River felt herself being hustled out of the bridge through the doorway. She tried to resist, but in vain. Zoë hurled her to the floor in the corridor outside.

"And stay out!" she said, hitting the switch that closed the door.

River sprang up, trying to get to the door before it slammed shut. Too late.

A message lit up in red on the status panel beside the door: LOCK ENGAGED. NO ENTRY.

"*Zhēn dǎo méi,*" River hissed.

She hammered on the door a few times with her fists. Nothing from the other side but derisive laughter.

She perceived quite clearly that she had been shut out of Wash's dream-state. The door symbolized that. And even if she did manage to break in again, Zoë had become Wash's appointed gatekeeper, there to guard against further incursion. She would defy River every step of the way.

River had had the one chance with Wash and it hadn't worked out. He was now fully resistant to any attempt she made to wake him.

That left her no choice.

She was going to have to wake one of the others.

But which one?

44

Strapped to a chair, buck naked, Zoë screamed.

She hated herself for screaming. She was desperate not to show weakness before this man.

But the pain was so acute, so all-consuming, that screaming was the only thing she could do.

Derrial Book, the Butcher of Beylix, stepped back from her. The drill-like tool in his hand was akin to something a surgeon or a dentist might use. It was doubtful, however, that a medical professional would use it the way he was. Blood dripped from its cylindrical steel bit, whose rotations had slowed to a standstill. Blood, little shreds of flesh, and even the odd tiny bone fragment.

Zoë's breath came in short, hissing gasps. She fought to get it under control. Cold perspiration coated her face. She hurt in about a dozen places at once. She couldn't tell which was the freshest source of pain, couldn't even look down at herself to see her wounds. Her head was held rigidly in place by a band attached to the chair back. She could look only at Book.

"Now then," he said. "That was just the warm-up. A few exploratory probings, to see what you're made of. I can tell you're a tough woman, Miz Alleyne. You're going to last as long as any of your colleagues ever did. Longer, perhaps. But that's only to your disadvantage, and my advantage."

"*Bèn tiān sheng de yī duī ròu*," Zoë spat.

"Stupid inbred sack of meat I may be," Book said placidly, "but I am not the one being tortured. Nor am I the one who has been relentlessly pursuing Alliance officers to the ends of the 'verse and either dragging them off to face a kangaroo court or summarily executing them. That sort of behavior cannot stand, Miz Alleyne. Those men and women are heroes. Heroes in a war we ought to have won. And you are treating them as villains. The real villains here are your paymasters on Londinium, the so-called Accord. That motley assemblage of former Browncoat bigwigs. Do you think *they* weren't guilty of deeds just as bad? Do you honestly believe your side's hands are any less bloodstained than ours?"

"We tried to fight clean," Zoë said. "If it happened we did wrong now and then, it was in the name of right."

"Ah, the old 'the end justifies the means' argument. But turn that on its head. What if you'd lost? Then the end wouldn't have been worth any of the steps you took to get there. Until Serenity Valley, the Unification War was poised on a knife-edge. That it tipped in the Independents' favor is just a quirk of fate. If it had tipped in ours—well, you and I would not be having this fascinating conversation, for one."

"And wouldn't that be a pity."

Book smiled, and Zoë was struck by the weirdest feeling. She felt that, under other circumstances, she might have liked this man. She might even have considered him a friend.

Or was that just one of his torturer tactics? Coming across as nice and kind and reasonable, even when he was doing vile things you? Didn't that just make the whole situation worse? When pain was being inflicted by someone so seemingly likable, that made it that much more intense and humiliating.

"A pity indeed, Zoë," Book said. "May I call you Zoë? 'Miz

Alleyne' feels so formal, and we seem to have got to know each other rather well already, despite it being such a short acquaintance."

"You can call me Zoë, long as I can keep calling you *bèn tiān sheng de yī duī ròu.*"

This time Book simply brushed the insult aside. "The fact is, Zoë, we who served in the Alliance armed forces can't have you and others like you hunting us down. We don't deserve such shabby treatment. We were simply carrying out our orders, doing what we could to end the war as swiftly as possible."

"Yeah. Right. So noble. And I suppose your interrogations were all part of that."

"They certainly were," Book said. "A military, if it is to succeed, needs intelligence about the enemy, and one of the fastest and simplest ways of obtaining said intelligence is extracting it from enemy troops. I did my best to be efficient and cause the minimal amount of suffering to my subjects. Sometimes, alas, in order to do that, I had to cause the maximum amount of suffering in the shortest duration. That's just the way it goes. With you, it's a little bit different. There is no purpose to what I am doing, you see, other than to hurt you and debase you. You don't have any information I need. All I am hoping to achieve is to make your last hours of existence as excruciating and miserable as they can be. Speaking of which..."

Book turned to a workbench that, through no coincidence, sat just within Zoë's field of vision. On it were laid out all manner of sharp objects: sawtoothed things, bladed things, long pointed things, things with little inbuilt motors, things that retracted, things that expanded. All bore the patina of age but looked well cared for. She imagined these utensils traveled with Book wherever he went. She pictured him poring over them in private, recalling with relish the howls and shrieks each would elicit from his victims and dreaming up new ways of using them.

"You must understand," the Butcher of Beylix said, "that from here onward your life is going to be measured solely in pain. Time is going to lose all meaning for you. There will simply be periods of torment with intervals for recovery in between. Those will be your day and night. You will weep. You will cry for your mother. You will void your bladder and perhaps also your bowels, although, please, you mustn't be embarrassed about that—I'm used to it. At several points you will long for death. You will beg me to kill you. But my purpose is not to kill you. Quite the opposite. It is to keep you alive as long as possible.

"Nor," he continued, "will there be any last-minute reprieve, in case you were holding out that hope. No one knows where you are, not even your erstwhile brother-in-arms, Malcolm Reynolds. No one has any idea where this building is save the Alliance loyalists who brought you here, the same men who stripped you of your weapons and more recently your clothing and fastened you to that chair. The same men, moreover, who are stationed in the hallway outside this room, listening to you suffer. They are probably having a nice smoke. They are almost certainly laughing as they hear you scream. They may even be making bawdy jokes about your undeniable sexual allure and what they would like to have done to you if they'd had their druthers. They will not feel the same way about you, however, when I am through with you. I may indeed invite them in to look at you in your final moments. The revulsion on their faces will tell you all you need to know."

He selected one of the implements on the workbench, something like a cross between a switchblade and an egg-whisk with an on-off button and a sliding lever embedded in the handle.

"I'll make sure you will be able to see them," he said. "But to do that, you only need the use of *one* of your eyes."

As he approached the chair, Zoë braced herself. There was nothing else she could do. She had flung abuse at Book, and if any of it had hit home, that would have been some small compensation;

but instead it had just bounced off him. She doubted he had a better nature she could try appealing to. She was all out of options.

Except delaying him. Postponing the evil moment as long as possible.

"What made you like this?" she said.

Book paused with the egg-whisk-like implement just inches from her face. "Funny thing," he said. "I always thought I was destined for holy orders. As a boy and even as a young man, I could imagine nothing better than becoming a Shepherd. I felt God moving strongly within me. I was all about doing good works, and was keen to share my religious certainties with others."

"And this is how you wound up. I'd say God wasn't your boss anymore. You're working for the other guy."

Book laughed hollowly. "The war soon taught me that God is an irrelevance. A just deity would never have allowed the 'verse to tear itself apart the way it did. He would never have pitched brother against brother, neighbor against neighbor, friend against friend. If I'd still harbored any religious inclinations after the war started, they were dispelled by the sight of people in the same predicament you are in, praying to the Lord to deliver them from my ministrations. Needless to say, their prayers were never answered."

He looked somber for a second, almost mournful.

"And that's enough procrastinating, Zoë," he said. "I've enjoyed chatting with you, and I imagine there'll be more opportunities to do so, further down the line. It's good to pause every now and then, so that we can each regroup and get our strength back."

At the periphery of her vision, Zoë glimpsed a thin, pale girl in a long, floaty dress. She was standing in a corner of the room. She hadn't been there a moment earlier. She had just sort of *flickered* into view.

"Who—?" she began, and then the implement in the Butcher of Beylix's hands started to whine and whirr, and there was blinding agony.

Literally blinding.

45

For several seconds, River was too appalled to act. The sight of Zoë in that chair was horrific. Not just her injuries but her *helplessness*. It wasn't the real Zoë, of course. River knew that. Just a dream Zoë. But even so, she was repelled by what she was seeing.

The fact that Zoë's torturer was Shepherd Book only made it worse. When, a while earlier, River had seen him introduce himself to Zoë as the Butcher of Beylix, it had been like a punch to the gut. The shock had made her reel inwardly.

More shocking still was watching him ply his trade now. The calm adroitness with which he delved his cutting implement into Zoë's eye socket. His indifference to the piteous wail that escaped her throat and the frantic flexing of her body against its restraints. The slight flaring of his upper lip as he expertly torqued and tugged. The practiced ease of it all.

Book straightened up, and Zoë's struggles subsided, her whole body going limp. Within the bulbous end of the egg-whisk thing there was a bloodied ball of jelly. In Zoë's face there was a hollow, dripping gouge where that ball of jelly belonged.

Book turned to the workbench and laid the torture implement down.

That was when he noticed River.

"Ah," he said. "It appears we have a witness. Just wait there, young lady. I'll come to you in due course."

"You don't scare me," River said. "You did once, when your hair was big and frizzy. It's all close-cropped now. But even if it wasn't, I can handle you."

"Can you?" Book picked up a knife fashioned from a single piece of stainless steel with a wickedly curved blade. He moved towards River. "I believe you know me as a good man." He jerked a thumb towards Zoë, who had passed out from her ordeal. "Not the person Zoë there has met, but someone else. You would never expect me to harm you. But I think, River, you always intuited that beneath my Shepherdly exterior lies something darker. I think Zoë—the real Zoë—was aware of it too. During my time aboard *Serenity* there were several occasions when hints of my dubious past revealed themselves. Hence Zoë has envisaged me as this fictitious character called the Butcher of Beylix. For I am her worst fears realized. I am the turncoat comrade. I am the sternly smiling face of the Alliance. I am the deep-seated sense shared by all those who come through a war unscathed, that they didn't deserve to. I am—"

"Someone who talks too much."

River darted at Book, driving an elbow into his midriff and at the same time batting his knife hand aside with her other arm. Book stumbled back against his workbench, which rocked with the impact. Several of his torture devices slid off and fell to the floor with a clatter.

River pressed home the attack. Still warding off Book's knife hand, she battered his ribs, sternum, and gut with a flurry of vicious short-range jabs. The blows landed thick and fast. She was determined not to give him a moment's respite.

She became aware of laughter—a low, genial chuckling. She looked up to see Book grinning twinkly-eyed at her and shaking his head.

"You can't hurt me, River," he said. "You can't because deep down you don't want to. To you, I am still wise, winsome Shepherd

Book. You can't get over that, and it makes me impervious to your assault. Do your worst. I can take it."

River stepped back, panting. He was right. She had liked the real Book. He had always exuded a sense of peace and dependability. This Book wasn't that Book, but he was similar enough. Her fondness for him was working against her. It encased him in a kind of armor.

Dream logic really sucked sometimes.

The knife flashed through the air. River barely saw the thrust coming. She ducked aside, the blade missing her by mere millimeters.

She aimed a retaliatory heel-kick at Book's leg. The move ought to have dislocated his kneecap. Book just smiled.

Again the knife came towards her, its blade a shimmering arc. She shot up both hands to catch Book's wrist. The knife stalled in midair.

But Book planted his foot against her hip and shoved her away hard. River lost her grip on his wrist and went flailing backwards, slamming into the wall. The wind was knocked out of her.

Book was on her in an instant, plunging the knife towards her face. She twisted to one side. The knifepoint glanced off the brickwork exactly where River's head had been a split second earlier.

River hit Book in the armpit with a straight-fingered jab, directly over the axillary nerve. Under normal circumstances, the blow ought not only to have hurt severely but to have rendered Book's arm numb from the shoulder down.

But these were not normal circumstances, and Book was immune. He swung his fist backwards, fetching her a hefty clout with the blunt end of the knife.

River staggered, falling to her hands and knees.

Her gaze fell on Zoë, who was still insensible in the chair, her intact eye closed.

She hated to leave Zoë like this, but she had no choice. She wasn't going to win against the Butcher of Beylix. He was like some unstoppable robot. He would just keep on coming at her, shrugging off everything she threw at him.

River needed to enter another crewmember's dream.

Who did she think she could successfully awaken? Who, out of the four she hadn't yet merged dreamscapes with, would be keenest to be extricated from their nightmare?

46

Jayne didn't even try to fight back the tears. He let them come flooding down his cheeks. Choking sobs made his chest heave.

Matty had beaten damplung, only to suffer a quicker but no less cruel death. And Jayne had been powerless to do anything but look on.

The Beavertail Gang slid the corpse off the pole, onto the ground. Matty lay atop the heap of his own intestines, still hogtied, his blood soaking the dirt in a puddle a couple of yards in diameter.

Radiant Cobb wept too. But her tears, unlike Jayne's, came silently. They rolled from eyes that were fixed on Ottoline Beavertail with a ferocious intensity, burning like fire.

All at once, she was on her feet. She snapped her head backwards, the rear of her skull smashing the nose of the gang member behind her. As he fell to the ground with a yelp, she dived for his sidearm.

Nobody had been expecting her to move. Nor had anybody been expecting a sixty-something woman—one with a bullet lodged in her arm, no less—to be able to move so fast.

Radiant whipped around, thumb-cocking the pistol, and fired at Ottoline Beavertail.

The gang leader doubled over. The bullet had struck her just above the waistband of her jeans. She teetered but caught herself before she could fall.

Radiant fired again, but one of the gang football-tackled her just as she squeezed the trigger. Her arm flew up and the shot went wild. She and the gang member crashed to the ground.

At the same moment, Jayne reared up from his kneeling position. His mother had at least not had her hands tied behind her back. Jayne did. But he was determined this wouldn't hinder him. He was going to cause the most damage he could to these bastards, given the limitations. He was as good as dead, but he wasn't going down without taking a few of them with him.

He headbutted the gang member nearest him. Another, he kicked between the legs. She might have been a woman, but a steel-reinforced toecap in the crotch was still a steel-reinforced toecap in the crotch, and she sank down with a sickly moan, hands clasping her groin. Then Jayne ran headlong at a third gang member, pile-diving his shoulder into the man's solar plexus. All the air shot out of the man's lungs with an almighty "Whooooof!"

There was pandemonium. The last thing the Beavertail Gang had anticipated was the two Cobbs still left alive turning the tables on them. Several were under the impression that Ottoline Beavertail had been killed. All of a sudden, it looked as if they were no longer as in control of the situation as they had thought. There was shouting, consternation, confusion.

Then one voice rose above the hubbub. It was their leader's. Ottoline Beavertail bellowed at her gang to get their act together, stop messing about. "There's just the gorramn two of them! Why're y'all hangin' around with your peckers in your hands? Get in there and grab 'em!"

Several of the gang piled in on Radiant Cobb where she lay on the ground. One of them wrestled the pistol from her hand. Radiant punched and kicked and even bit, a veritable hellcat, but eventually they were able to subdue her.

Jayne, they were more circumspect about. He was charging to and fro in their midst like a raging bull, and although several of the gang drew their guns, they were reluctant to shoot, for fear of missing him and hitting a comrade. A couple of intrepid souls picked up makeshift weapons—a fencepost, a length of rebar—and moved in to belabor him with them. Soon enough, they had battered him into submission. Jayne ended up facedown in the dust, bruised and groaning. He was dragged by the feet over to where his mother lay pinned beneath a couple of the gang's heaviest members.

Ottoline Beavertail walked stiffly up to the two Cobbs, clutching her side. "Damn," she said with a hiss of pain. "Forgot how ruttin' much it hurts, getting shot. Still, looks like a through-and-through. Missed the vitals. So there's that."

"You got lucky, bitch," Radiant Cobb grumbled. "I was shootin' left-handed. If it weren't for my gun arm being out of action, I'd have drilled you straight through the heart."

"Well then, let me return the favor." Ottoline Beavertail lined up her pistol with Radiant's chest. "Or should I make it so quick? Nah." She shifted her aim to the top of Radiant's leg.

Bang!

Radiant shrieked.

"Mama!" Jayne cried.

Blood began pulsing out of the bullet wound.

"Ooh, now will you look at that?" Ottoline Beavertail said. "Think I may have nicked the artery. What are the odds? That's gonna be a slow death. Ten minutes, fifteen tops." She addressed her gang. "Guys? How's about we run a sweepstake? Someone start a stopwatch going. My money's on twelve minutes."

A gunshot rang out.

One of the gang keeled over, stone dead.

All faces turned towards the house. By the front door there stood a girl. She was holding the rifle Radiant Cobb had dropped. She worked the lever action, chambering the next round.

"There's another of 'em?" said Ottoline Beavertail.

The girl fired again, dropping a second gang member.

Jayne blinked. Dust had got in his eyes. He wasn't sure he was seeing what he was seeing.

"River?" he said.

The girl fired a third time, by which point Ottoline Beavertail had overcome her surprise.

"What the hell are you all waiting for, you useless *wáng bā dàn*?" she yelled at her cronies. "Get her!"

47

It wasn't the easiest trick to pull off, jumping from one crewmember's dream to another's.

It had been different when River was simply transplanting her consciousness into their heads and viewing events from their perspectives. That had been like drifting between rooms in a house, inhabiting each in turn for a while, peering out the window to see what lay outside.

Now, she was having to be present within the person's dream, projecting herself bodily into the narrative and influencing how things played out. She was no longer a passive observer but an active participant. Her dreaming and the other's had to become one, a fusion of selves. That took concentration and effort.

And the dreams fought back. Each dreamer seemed to regard her as an interloper, a threat to the structured artifice of their hallucination.

Wash had resisted her intrusion by means of Zoë.

Zoë had resisted her intrusion by means of Book.

Here, with Jayne, it was the Beavertail Gang who were going to do their best to oust her. There was a score of them still standing, and they were marshaling themselves to shoot back. Radiant Cobb's rifle had an eight-round capacity. Assuming Jayne's mother had reloaded fully before coming out of the house, that left five rounds after the three River had fired.

She had better make them count.

Her next target was Ottoline Beavertail herself. River figured that with the gang's leader out of the picture, she could that much more readily rout the rest.

She moved to one side slightly, to line up a clear shot.

But Ottoline Beavertail proved aggravatingly difficult to kill. The first round River loosed off, which should have been bang on the mark, ended up nailing a gang member who inadvertently got in the way. Her second attempt had the same result: someone strayed into the bullet's path. Ottoline Beavertail seemed to have as many lives as a gorramn cat.

Then came the return fire. A blizzard of bullets. River scooted into the doorway while ricochets and splinters of wood flew all around her.

She reeled off a last three shots with the rifle, then dropped it and scurried across the main room of the house to where Jayne had left Vera.

Gang members swarmed towards the front door. River scooped up Vera. The gun was as heavy as it looked. She lodged the butt against her shoulder and began firing. The recoil was phenomenal, a mule kick.

She shot through the doorway at first, and then, when the attackers scattered to either side, through the walls. At this range, with a gun of Vera's caliber, it didn't make much difference if there was a piece of timber between you and your target. Each round blasted a fist-sized hole in the wall. From outside there came gasps, screams, and oaths.

The magazine ran dry. River swiftly slotted in the rounds that were open-stored on the stock.

She reloaded just in time to kill a gang member who courageously, or perhaps foolishly, rushed in through the doorway. She took out another who was attempting to shoot her through one of the broken, boarded-up windows.

"Jayne!" she yelled. "I can't do this on my own. You have to help me."

She was making an appeal not only to the man out in the farmyard but to the man who was dreaming. Somehow, at either level or both, Jayne had to be able to assist her. The conditions here weren't the same as they'd been with Wash and Zoë. In their dreams they had both lived lives in which they had never met River Tam. When she'd turned up, she'd been more or less a stranger to them.

Jayne's dream, on the other hand, was taking place after he had spent time on *Serenity*. He knew who she was and thus had a greater incentive to side with her.

"Jayne!" she called out again, as gang members poured in through the doorway, guns blazing.

"River…"

She barely heard his reply over the din of gunfire. His voice sounded forlorn. Hopeless.

She held off the gang with Vera's few remaining rounds. Then she was out of ammo and weapons.

She scrambled over to a front window and peeked out.

Jayne had his hands on his mother's leg. He was pressing down on the bullet wound, desperately trying to stem the bleeding. Radiant Cobb lay still.

"River, you gotta get help," Jayne said, looking towards the house. "She's dyin'. My mama's dyin'."

He didn't notice Ottoline Beavertail limping up behind him. She was still clutching her side with one hand. In the other hand she had a pistol, and it was aimed at Jayne.

As she pressed the muzzle of the gun to the back of his head, Jayne stiffened. Then, with a determined grimace, he focused his attention on his mother again. He was going to prevent her dying if it was the last thing he did.

"He ain't comin' to your rescue, little girl," Ottoline Beavertail said to River. "And you ain't comin' to his. It's over."

"Dammit, Jayne," River said resignedly. "I honestly thought you'd be the one I could rouse."

Members of the Beavertail Gang surrounded her, their guns leveled.

"You really are a shabby bunch of *niào shǐ de dǔ guǐ*," she said to them.

The nearest to her grinned like a weasel in a henhouse. His skin was pockmarked, his teeth uneven and incomplete.

Eagerly, he thumbed back the hammer on his six-shooter.

But River was gone.

48

"Simon!" said Kaylee.

Simon and Kaylee had gone half a mile into the woods. They were running full tilt, and Simon was getting short of breath, his lungs starting to heave. Behind him he could hear his father, Bryce, and Uncle Holden charging through the undergrowth in pursuit. Every now and then they would call to one another. Their voices were distant but not, Simon thought, distant enough.

Bryce was the one shouting the least. Out of the three of them, he was the most experienced hunter. He knew you should try not to give your position away to your quarry. Bryce would also, Simon had no doubt, be able to follow the trail he and Kaylee were leaving. They would have stood a reasonable chance of getting away if it had been just the other two. With Bryce on their tail, the odds were stacked against them.

"Simon!" Kaylee said again, more urgently. They had just arrived at a small clearing, some twenty feet from end to end. Trees stood all around it like whispering sentinels. Their shed leaves made a thick carpet.

"Don't stop," Simon panted. "We have to keep going."

"I can't."

Kaylee staggered to a halt.

Simon turned, ready to protest.

She looked deathly pale, and she was hugging her waist with one arm.

Blood seeped between her fingers.

"Oh my God," Simon said.

Kaylee crumpled to her knees. Simon caught her before she fell over completely.

He lowered her to the ground, setting aside the sheath knife.

"Take your hand away," he said. "Show me."

Kaylee lifted her hand to reveal an exit wound in the left side of her abdomen, just below the ribcage.

"Must've been when we started running," she said. "All the bullets flying around us. I sorta felt it go in, but everything was so crazy. Just didn't really register. It hurts, Simon."

Simon rolled up her shirt to get a better look at the wound.

"What's the diagnosis, Doc?"

"It doesn't look so bad. You're going to be fine."

"Know what? You're a terrible liar. Remind me to play Tall Card for money with you sometime."

"No, really."

"It's written all over your face, Simon. Come on, be honest."

Simon took a deep breath. "Okay. I think you have a duodenal perforation. There may well be trauma to other peritoneal organs too."

"English?"

"The bullet's gone through your bowel, and maybe shrapnel from it has hit your liver and spleen as well." Simon began removing his jacket.

Kaylee braved a smile. "Getting undressed? Now's not the time for that, lover boy."

"I'm making a compress." He folded the jacket up tightly and laid it over the wound. "Have to keep pressure on it. How are you feeling?"

"You mean other than the big hole in me that feels like a red-hot poker?"

"Dizzy? Nauseous? Faint?"

"Little of all three."

"Okay. You've probably got delayed shock. The adrenaline surge was keeping it at bay, but not anymore. Try and keep from passing out if you can."

"I'll do my best." A dreamy smile appeared on her face. "You're so good-looking, you know that? You could have had any girl in the county. Any girl in the 'verse, even. Why me?"

"We need to get you help."

"Well done for ducking the question."

"I'm going to yell to my father."

"You think that's a good idea?"

"It's our only hope."

"He wanted you to kill me. Him and both them other two."

"Maybe he'll have a change of heart. I'll beg him. I'm still his son."

"No. It ain't gonna happen that way, and you know it."

"We have to get you to a hospital, Kaylee!" Simon said, his voice cracking. "I can't save you here, out in the woods. I can if I have an operating theater. We'll get you back to the lodge. There's a first aid kit there. I can stabilize you, then we'll call in an airborne medevac unit and…"

"Sweetie." Kaylee patted his arm weakly. "They got me, simple as that. They have what they wanted now. Simon's 'unsuitable' girlfriend isn't going to pose a risk no more. The Tam family bloodline won't get polluted."

"No." It was more a sob than a word.

She gazed up at him lovingly from her bed of fallen leaves. "It's okay, Simon. It just wasn't meant to be. Maybe in another life, another world, we'll be together forever. In this one, all we had was that little time. But it was good while it lasted, wasn't it?"

Heavy footfalls crashed nearby. Simon's relatives were getting closer.

"Will you kiss me?" Kaylee said. "One last time?"

He bent and kissed her. Her lips felt cold beneath his.

Bryce lurched into view. A moment later, Gabriel Tam appeared in the clearing, closely followed by his brother-in-law, Holden.

"Well, well, well," Bryce crowed. "Look at that. I could have sworn I'd hit the little minx. Seems I did."

Simon's head whipped round. "*Qù nǐ de!*"

"That's no way to talk to your uncle, Simon," his father said. "Show some respect."

"I don't respect him," Simon snarled. "I don't think I ever did. I don't gorramn respect you either, not anymore."

"Son, you're upset. I get that. But in time you'll come to see that we've done you a tremendous favor."

Simon turned back to look at Kaylee. He refused to talk to any of them from now on. He would simply ignore them, pretend they didn't exist.

"Kaylee," he said.

Her eyes struggled to gain focus. She was fading fast. He had seen the signs often enough to recognize them.

"I love you, Kaylee."

Whether she could hear him or not, he couldn't tell. His jacket was now soaked through with her blood. There wasn't much point holding it in place, but he continued doing so anyway. Just to keep her here, with him, that little bit longer.

She reached a hand up. She stroked his cheek. She was telling him to let go. Let *her* go.

He could barely see her face now through the tears blurring his vision.

"Kaylee…"

It was then that a sixth person entered the clearing.

49

River knew, as soon as she stepped into Simon's dream, that she should have got there earlier.

In the middle of a forest clearing, Simon was bent over the supine form of Kaylee, whose eyes had lost all their usual luster and whose chest was rising and falling erratically as her lungs took their last few desperate sips of air.

Watching over the pair were River's father and two uncles, hunting rifles in hand. The three older men were blank-faced, as though they had switched off every emotion. All River could detect in them was a kind of grim satisfaction, the sense of a difficult job accomplished.

As River looked on, Kaylee's chest went still.

In that moment, Simon was broken. He bowed his head. His shoulders heaved, and a series of deep, guttural cries escaped his throat—a sound so raw, so primal, it was barely human.

River longed to rush over and comfort him, even though she was well aware that Kaylee was not dead in the real world. Not yet, at least. With *Serenity* hurtling towards Luna Minor, it was only a matter of time.

Instead, she addressed the others. They were her first priority. Potential opposition.

"Dad," she said. "Bryce. Uncle Holden."

Her father scowled. "River? Honey, this is a surprise. Didn't expect to see you here."

"I need you to leave, all three of you. I want to speak with Simon, alone."

"Leave?" said Bryce. "Now why should we do that?"

"Because you're only going to try and stop me waking Simon up. I'd much rather you just walked away and didn't make things difficult for me."

"Difficult? I've no idea what you're implying."

"I think you do, Bryce. Your goofy playboy act serves you well, but underneath it you're sharper than you let on."

"The girl has something of an attitude, doesn't she?" said Uncle Holden. "I've always said you and Regan give her far too much leeway, Gabriel. Isabelle and I are much stricter about what the twins do and say, and they're all the better for it."

"With all due respect, Holden," said Gabriel Tam, "Cordelia and Flavia aren't geniuses. River is."

"Even so. River's success in life has come at a price. I certainly wouldn't let my daughters be quite so pert as yours has just been."

"You know what, Holden?" Gabriel nodded. "Actually, you make a good point. River, apologize to Bryce."

"Or what?" River said. "You'll shoot me, like you did Kaylee?"

As if on cue, all three men raised their rifles.

River had been hoping not to antagonize them. That hadn't been the plan at all. It was hard not to resent them, however. They might not be her real father and uncles. They might be just warped versions of the genuine Gabriel Tam, Bryce Tam, and Holden Buckingham, twisted out of true by the effects of the siren on Simon's psyche. But how they had behaved, what they had done, was still unforgivable. They had just murdered one of the kindest-hearted people River had ever met. They had tried to murder Simon too. How could she keep herself from hating them for that?

"Last chance, River," her father said. "Apologize, or you'll go the same way the mechanic girl did."

Simon's dream was doing its best to reject her, just as Wash's, Zoë's, and Jayne's had.

But time was running short. River had to get *someone* on the ship to wake up, and if there was any person she could get through to, it was surely her brother. Assuming, that was, Simon's grief over Kaylee hadn't utterly destroyed him. Which it may well have.

Another, similar trauma might just do the trick.

River wondered how this was going to feel. Would it hurt? Probably would.

She squared her jaw, balled her fists, and broke into a run.

As one, the three rifles zeroed in on her.

As one, the rifles fired.

50

"River!"

Simon was in his bunk, sprawled half on, half off the bed.

He gaped around him in alarm.

River. Where was River? He had watched them shoot her—his father and his uncles. Maybe they had just winged her. No, unlikely. Three shots. High-velocity hunting rifles at point-blank range. He had seen her body hurtle backwards, limbs flailing, as though she'd been suddenly yanked by a rope. That wasn't "winged."

But there was still a chance she was okay. He had failed to save Kaylee, but if River was only wounded, he could save *her*.

It took him several moments to realize he wasn't in the forest clearing not far from the family hunting lodge. He was aboard *Serenity*.

He was also feeling like death warmed up.

He began to analyze his physical condition. Rapid heartrate. Pain between the temples. Difficulty focusing his eyes. A twinge in his chest.

All symptoms of excessively elevated blood pressure.

He put index and middle fingers to his wrist, finding his pulse. He concentrated on slowing his breathing, reducing the excess carbon dioxide in his cardiovascular system. He wasn't ill. This was a panic attack.

Hardly surprising, given that he'd just seen both Kaylee and River get shot.

But neither of them was here with him now, in his bunk.

A dream.

Must have been.

Some kind of appallingly vivid dream.

The breath-control exercise worked. Simon's pulse began to steady. His head began to clear.

He got to his feet.

And promptly keeled over, flat on his face.

51

Riding in Caleb Dahl's chauffeur-driven limousine along the highway that traced the curve of Clearcrest Bay, Kaylee seethed with self-recrimination. How could she not have seen this coming? The mansion on Harmsworth Avenue. The dim sum and mint juleps. The overpayments. The man's sleek magnetism. Even this gorramn limo. It was all too perfect. *Of course* there had to be a catch.

The catch, in this case, being that Caleb Dahl was an out-and-out crook.

They sat together now, Dahl with his gun trained on her, and he was smiling as silkily as a well-fed lion. When he caught her looking at him sidelong, all he did was arch an eyebrow, as if to say, *This is your fault, Kaylee. You should have known better.*

"Who are they?" she asked eventually.

"Who?" he replied. "Those folks back at the spaceport? Nobodies."

"They're somebodies to you. Else why would they be in chains? Must have a value if you don't want 'em getting away."

"If you must know, they are the dregs of the 'verse," Dahl said. "Some of the worst the Border planets have to offer. A concatenation of scoundrels and wastrels, drifters and druggies, hoboes and vagabonds. People no one wants in their neighborhood. In a way,

I'm performing a useful service. I'm kind of a cleaning operation, like the plumber who comes to unclog the sink."

"They can't all be scoundrels and wastrels and whatever else you just said. I saw children on that Firefly. Kids not even in their teens."

"Even scoundrels and wastrels have families. Sometimes you get one fella, he comes with dependents. A job lot, you might say."

"But what do you want them for?" Kaylee said. "Do you sell them off as slaves? Forced labor? What?"

"Now that there would be a poor business model indeed. Trying to convince people to purchase as employees those who are congenitally not predisposed towards working? To shift the shiftless?" Dahl chuckled at his own wordplay. "I would be a pauper within weeks."

"Prostitution, then."

"Do I look like some glorified whoremonger?"

"Don't know. Never met one, glorified or otherwise."

"No, Kaylee, the raggedy-ass assortment on that ship—and all the others I've smuggled onto New Virginia before them—have but one thing to offer. By simple virtue of their being born with the parts common to all us humans, they can make themselves very lucrative."

It took Kaylee a moment to fathom the meaning of this.

"Their organs," she said. "You're an organ peddler."

"I prefer to think of it as 'dealer in pre-mortality donations,'" Dahl said. "You know how it works in the normal course of events. You have an organ that's failing, you put yourself on the waiting list for a replacement. Assuming you get lucky and a match is found, it costs you a small fortune in hospital bills for the transplant op. If you have insurance, your premiums skyrocket to the very limits of exorbitancy and beyond. Me, I cut through all that. I offer a range of organs, in all tissue types, fresh as they come. Well, maybe not *wholly* fresh. Some of the donors have a history of abusing their bodies. I can't guarantee that the organ you're getting will be in pristine condition. But at least you'll be getting one and, providing you can scrape together the dough, at a relatively affordable price."

"It costs someone else's life. That's not my definition of affordable."

"Not necessarily their life. A single kidney, for instance. We can harvest one of those, and the donor won't die."

Kaylee thought through the ramifications. "You're saying you keep your so-called donors alive?"

"As long as they can continue to provide viable parts, yes. Plus, I own several properties around town where I furnish them with accommodation, food and water, round-the-clock medical care, a few creature comforts—likely more than they could ever lay claim to beforehand, during their previous unproductive existences."

"They're your prisoners and you gradually dismantle them piece by piece until they've got nothing left to offer."

"When you put it like that, it sounds as though I'm cannibalizing them for parts, like you yourself would with an old wreck from the junkyard," said Dahl. "And now that I think about it, it's a fairly accurate comparison. Just a mite reductive for my tastes."

"You're inhuman."

"I've been called worse."

Kaylee could scarcely bring herself to ask what she asked next. "And me? What are you intending to do with me? Am I going to become another of your 'pre-mortality donors'?"

Dahl chewed his lip. "See, I am in a quandary over you, Kaylee. You know too much now. That's plain. I can't really let you go free. You're the type that would run straight to the Feds and blab. But I've grown more'n a smidge fond of you. There's my dilemma. I wouldn't want to have to do away with you. Apart from anything else it would be a shame to lose such a talented mechanic. And one who is honest, good-natured, and easy on the eye as well. Which, mechanic-wise, makes you pretty much a unicorn. No, I am most conflicted here, so I'm taking you home until I can figure things out."

At least she wasn't going to die imminently. That was some

comfort to Kaylee. Unlike poor Gerard the spaceport security guard, whom Dahl had killed on the spot without batting an eyelid.

In the interim, however, while Dahl pondered her fate, she was presumably going to be his captive. Detained at his mansion like the proverbial bird in a gilded cage.

The limousine pulled up outside the mansion gates. They opened automatically, and the car glided through and continued on towards the house, its headlamps illuminating its route between the cypresses that lined the crushed-shell driveway.

As soon as the limo drew to a halt, Dahl climbed out, beckoning Kaylee to follow him with a wave of his gun. A sea breeze wafted her face as she stood. Distant breakers rumbled and sighed. She looked towards the gates, which were just beginning to swing shut. Too far to make a run for it. She would never reach them before they closed, and, anyway, if she did attempt a bid for freedom, Dahl would probably decide he had no choice but to shoot her. She would be making his mind up for him.

At that moment, a vehicle parked a short way down Harmsworth Avenue, in the shadowy margin between two streetlamps, revved into life. Tires screeched as it accelerated from a standing start and made for the narrowing gap between the closing gates. It scraped through with inches to spare and came careering up the driveway, continuing to gain speed.

Dahl didn't hesitate. He loosed off a couple of rounds at the approaching vehicle. Whoever was behind the wheel clearly meant him no good.

At the same time, Dahl's chauffeur stepped out of the limousine, drawing his own gun. He leaned on the limo's roof and got off a couple of shots of his own.

The bullets sparked off the oncoming vehicle's bodywork. It was now close enough that Kaylee could identify it as a tow truck. She had a sneaking suspicion she knew *whose* tow truck it was too.

Dahl steadied himself, lining up a shot at the truck's windshield. Kaylee flung herself at him, ramming an elbow into his arm and throwing off his aim.

Next instant, the tow truck went barreling front-fender-first into the side of the limousine. Kaylee and Dahl were both standing to the rear of the car, out of harm's way. The same could not be said for Dahl's chauffeur, who was on the other side of the limo. The crunching, rending impact shunted the limousine sideways towards the house, taking the chauffeur with it. His legs were caught beneath the chassis and he went under. His scream was abruptly cut off.

The tow truck and the limo it had T-boned came to rest against the mansion's front steps. Neither vehicle had benefited from the crash. One side of the limousine was caved in. The tow truck's front end had concertinaed inward and fluids were spattering out from under its engine block. Both, it would be safe to say, were write-offs.

Caleb Dahl looked aghast. No, Kaylee thought, he looked *affronted*. As though he couldn't believe anyone would have the nerve to do what the driver of the tow truck had just done.

"Now, who in tarnation would—?" he began.

She cut him off. "My father, that's who."

The driver's door of the tow truck—upon which the words ALOYSIUS FRYE AND DAUGHTER, MECHANICAL REPAIRS were stenciled—squealed open. A determined-looking Aloysius Frye emerged, a double-barreled shotgun in his hands.

"Drop it," he said, leveling the shotgun at Dahl.

Dahl leveled his pistol at Aloysius Frye in return. "You drop yours."

"Don't reckon I can do that, Mr. Dahl, being as that's my daughter you have there. Her safety is my one and only concern, and until such time as it is guaranteed, this shotgun of mine ain't gonna budge."

"But Aloysius," said Dahl, regaining some of his customary suaveness, "is this any way to treat your benefactor?"

"Benefactor? Hah! Is that what you call it? I call it what it was:

289

a transaction. Even at the time, I knew it was a devil's bargain, but I made the deal anyway, 'cause I had no choice. I guess I should've foreseen it would come back to bite me in the ass. Devil's bargains have a way of doing that."

"Pop?" said Kaylee. "What are you talking about?"

"Never you mind, pumpkin. Just step on over here, by my side, and together we'll take our leave of this place—unhurt." The last word was directed at Dahl, with heavy emphasis. "Explanations can wait for later."

"You never told her," Dahl said, mildly amused. "Of course. That'll be why she didn't put two and two together just now, after she discovered the line of work I'm in."

"There's a reason I forbade you from associating with this man," Aloysius Frye said to Kaylee. "I didn't want you knowing what it was, because I'm rightly none too proud of it."

"He's a criminal," she said, thinking this alone was reason enough.

"He's that and more. Took me until tonight to figure out you'd disregarded my instruction. I'd had my suspicions for a while about those two names that kept turning up in our books: Mr. Calabash, Mrs. Darlington. Not to mention the way you got squirrelly whenever I asked about them and the jobs you were carrying out for them. It was kind of an obvious code, in hindsight. I oughtta've cracked it sooner. Then you didn't come home this evening when you said you would, so I decided to stake out Dahl's house. Moment I saw you step out of that limo, him holding you at gunpoint, I knew my worst fears had come true."

"And I'm glad you came, Pop, really I am. But you have to tell me how you and he already know each other."

"Like I said. Later."

"No, Aloysius, tell her now," said Dahl. "Or rather, allow me. It's really quite straightforward, Kaylee. Your father needed a new heart. When was this, about ten months ago? Is that right, Aloysius? His old one was giving out on him. But business wasn't so great. He couldn't afford the hospital fees, and as for health insurance, being a self-employed person his coverage was as basic as it gets. So he came to me. You can work out the rest."

"All my savings," Aloysius Frye said. "Every last scrap of platinum I had. And even then it wasn't enough. I'm paying him off the rest of what I owe monthly, at an extortionate rate of interest."

"I think it's quite a fair rate myself," said Dahl. "And you should feel honored. I don't extend credit to just anyone."

"But you said you'd had your heart fixed," said Kaylee to her father. "I took that to mean…"

"You took it to mean what I wanted you to, pumpkin. That it was a minor ailment and the docs were able to correct it. I'm sorry I wasn't honest. I didn't want you to worry. More to the point, I didn't want you to know I was in hock to this bastard."

"But you must realize where your replacement heart came from."

Aloysius Frye gave a sorrowful shake of the head. "I try not to think about it. Sometimes it keeps me up at night. Often, in fact. But we had a pact, didn't we, Mr. Dahl? I asked you never to call round my place of work, as a condition of our deal, so's I'd never have to see your face again and be reminded of what I'd done. You agreed to it. Then you broke it."

"I had mechanic work I needed doing, so I went to the best in town," said Dahl. "It just so happened you weren't in that day, but your delightful daughter was, and she has proved every bit your equal on the engineering front."

"I've no notion what you did to squirm your way into her trust. All I can say is *yān guò de hún dàn* like you should be strangled at birth."

"So I'm the bad guy?" said Dahl, mock-offended. "Am I the one with a dead stranger's heart illegally installed in his body?"

"No, but you're the guy who enabled it, which in my book makes you worse."

"Oh well, in that case…" Dahl swung his gun around to point at Kaylee's head. "Since I'm the *worse* guy, Aloysius, it won't hardly come as a surprise if I kill your only child right in front of you."

52

It wasn't easy, dying. Even in a dream.

It wasn't easy, moreover, when your killers were the spitting images of your father and your two uncles.

The shock of rifle rounds hitting her catapulted River out of Simon's head, into a kind of limbo. She lay on her back, with the clear impression that three jacketed-lead projectiles had thumped into her torso more or less simultaneously, sending her flying backwards and causing irrevocable internal damage. The pain was sudden and immense and crushing.

Around her the forest faded, the air paling as though a mist was setting in. She sensed she was sinking into a profounder layer of sleep, as dark and deadening as ocean depths. The pain began to ebb. So did light. If she let this happen, if she succumbed, there would be nothing to worry about. Oblivion was nothing to be scared of.

No.

No!

She could not give in. She had to fight on. Her life depended on it. So did the lives of everyone else aboard *Serenity*.

She thrashed upwards, shaking off the cold comfort of nothingness.

Had it worked? Was Simon awake now?

Whether he was or not, River couldn't take any chances. She had to carry on.

Kaylee next.

She cast about, searching for Kaylee's dream world. She gained fleeting glimpses of everything Kaylee had undergone lately. Kidnap by Caleb Dahl. The clifftop mansion. The dramatic arrival of Aloysius Frye in his tow truck. The standoff between the two men, each pointing a gun at the other.

She homed in on these impressions, letting them draw her like a moth to a porch light. She pushed through the barrier separating Kaylee's consciousness from her own. It was a thick membrane. She shoved and clawed until she had created an aperture large enough to slip through.

She stood on the driveway of Dahl's house, feeling vertiginous and short of breath. It was becoming harder and harder to inject herself into the others' dreams. She was growing tired. Her chest still felt tender from the bullet wounds. How much longer could she keep this up?

As long as she had to. That was what she told herself. She would soldier on until she got as many of the crew as she could to wake up and stop the ship.

Kaylee could do it. Kaylee's sleeping body was down in the engine room. All she had to do was disable the engine somehow.

That was assuming River could wrench her out of her dream and back into wakefulness…

She looked at the tableau a few yards in front of her. The crashed tow truck. The limousine bent like a boomerang. And beside the vehicles, Kaylee's father aiming his shotgun at Caleb Dahl, who in turn was aiming his gun at Kaylee's head.

"Don't," said Aloysius Frye plaintively. "Don't shoot her."

Dahl's pistol didn't waver. "Yes, I thought that's how it might be," he said in that slow, syrupy way of his. "I may not have kids of my own but I understand full well how they're a parent's weak spot. This girl is as dear to you as life itself. So I expect you now to place your weapon down on the ground, meek as a lamb, or else that heart of yours—which I deem still my property—will have itself plenty to ache about."

"Pop," said Kaylee. "Don't do it. Soon as you do, he'll kill you."

"That's as may be, pumpkin," her father said, "but I don't reckon as I have a choice. If it's me that has to die, rather than you, I'm content with that."

"He'll shoot us both anyway. That's the kind of man he is."

"How about this?" said Dahl. "You comply with my request, Aloysius, and I swear I will let Kaylee go free."

"No. Don't trust him, Pop."

"I vow it, on my mother's grave."

"He's a liar. He's tricking you."

Aloysius Frye looked as though he was weighing the matter up. In the end, however, there really was no alternative. He set the shotgun down.

In his position, River would have done the same. Dahl would not have hesitated to shoot Kaylee. Aloysius Frye could then have shot Dahl in return, and that might have been satisfying as revenge but it wouldn't change the fact that his daughter was dead.

"So what now?" Aloysius Frye said, straightening up.

"Now," said Dahl, "I think you have something which technically belongs to me and which therefore is mine to dispose of as I see fit. Namely your heart."

He was just training the gun back on Kaylee's father when River made her move. Nobody was aware of her presence yet. The three had been concentrating on one another, to the exclusion of all else.

She propelled herself forward, fast as she could go. There couldn't be a split second's hesitation. The dream would bite back unless she defanged it first.

She went into a roll, snatched up the shotgun and blasted Dahl with one barrel. He was knocked off his feet and went slithering across the crushed-shell driveway, dead as a doornail.

River wheeled around.

"Kaylee," she said, "I'm so sorry about this. Forgive me."

Still crouching, she gave Aloysius Frye the second barrel. Kaylee's father went down with a gaping hole in his belly.

Kaylee's hands flew to her face in horror. "River! What…? Why…?"

"Listen to me," River said, tossing the smoking shotgun aside and going over to Kaylee. "You're asleep. This is all a bad dream. Your father was dead already. You know this. Everything that's happened to you over the past few weeks, it isn't real. You are Kaywinnet Lee Frye and you are currently lying in *Serenity*'s engine room and we are in terrible danger. The ship is on a collision course with Canterbury's Luna Minor. If you don't wake up and do something to prevent it, we are going to crash into the moon and we are all going to die. Nod if you understand."

Kaylee was numb with shock. Her breath was coming in rapid, stuttering hiccups. "No. No. No," she said.

"Kaylee. Please. You may be our only hope."

"You… You shot my daddy."

And mine shot me, River thought. *But who's counting?*

She said, "Like I told you, he wasn't your father. I had to take him out of the equation, Dahl also, because otherwise they'd have done their best to kill me."

"No. Not Pop. He wouldn't hurt you. He—he's a good man."

"He *was*," River said. "I never met him but he must have been, to have raised such a good person as you. I know how much you miss him. You wanted him alive again, and this dream gave you that. But it is only your imagination, Kaylee. You've become trapped in it and I need you—we all need you—to free yourself."

Kaylee's tear-brimming eyes fixed their focus on River. "Are…
Are *you* real?"

"I am. I'm River. The River you know. The River you're friends
with."

"If that's the case, what are you doing here?"

"I came to rescue you."

Kaylee's expression was hardening. "And why don't you act
like River? You're not even speaking like her. Your eyes—they don't
look lost. They look sharp. If, like you say, I dreamed my dad alive
again, maybe I'm dreaming you too. You as I'd like you to be."

"We can discuss this another time," River said. "I really need you
awake now. You aren't in Tankerton. You are in *Serenity*'s engine
room. I want you to feel the deck plates under you. I want you to hear
the engine churning. When you wake up, you need to fix it so the
ship won't hit Luna Minor. If anyone can do that, you can."

"No," said Kaylee. "No. My father. I can't leave him."

"You already did. You told me how you buried him in the
cemetery at the church your mother helped out at. How Shepherd
Driscoll conducted the ceremony. How it rained all day right up
until the coffin went into the ground, then the clouds cleared away
and there was a rainbow and you took that as a sign. A sign that
everything was going to be all right. Do you remember that?"

Kaylee frowned. "I… remember that."

"And if you remember that, it can't be your dad lying over there.
How can it?"

Kaylee looked at her father's bloodied corpse. "But he…"

"And why would I kill him anyway? That would be crazy.
Unless I had a good reason to, and that reason is, he doesn't exist.
He never did."

"This… This doesn't make any sense."

"Deep down you know it does, Kaylee. But I can't wait for you
to work out the ramifications all the way through. We don't have that

luxury. I'm sorry about what I'm going to do next."

"What are you—?"

River slapped Kaylee as hard as she could.

"Oww!" Kaylee cried, clutching her cheek.

"Wake up, Kaylee," River said. "You have to wake up."

Kaylee glared at her—wounded, betrayed.

River steeled herself and slapped her again. It was tough. Kaylee was a dear friend.

"Wake up," she insisted, slapping her a third time. "Wake up and save *Serenity*."

53

Wake up and save Serenity.

The words resounded in Kaylee's mind as she came round on the floor of the engine room.

During her first few seconds of consciousness, Kaylee had only the vaguest recollection what they meant. *Serenity* was in trouble. Something about Canterbury's Luna Minor. *Serenity* on a collision course.

She saw River standing in front of her outside Caleb Dahl's house. River behaving in a way she had never known River to behave before—alert and coherent. River saying, "If you don't wake up and do something to prevent it, we are going to crash into the moon and we are all going to die."

Then other images came flooding in. Her father, dead on the ground. Slain with his own shotgun. By River.

And immediately after that, a terrific, gut-churning sense of panic. Nothing felt right. Everything was out of kilter. Kaylee had been in Tankerton. Now she was here on *Serenity*. But she had returned to Tankerton after a spell aboard *Serenity*. So how could she be back on the ship?

The panic intensified, deepening into dread. Was she going

mad? Her heart was racing. The engine room felt claustrophobic, like a prison cell. Normally this was her safe place, where she felt happiest, most in control. Now its walls were closing in on her. Even the steady thrum of the engine was not the comforting sound she was accustomed to; it seemed more like the growl of some wild carnivorous beast.

She was exhausted. She just wanted to sleep. In sleep, she could surely find refuge from the unreality of the waking world.

Her eyelids drooped.

Wake up and save Serenity.

She snapped back into consciousness. Dammit! River had been insistent. Kaylee had to do something to prevent the ship hitting Luna Minor.

Why me? Why not Wash? He's the gorramn pilot.

Kaylee didn't know why River had chosen her, out of all the crewmembers. Maybe the others were out of commission for some reason. That would account for the collision course. Wash would never have let that happen if there'd been something he could do about it. Same went for Mal.

She forced herself to get up off the floor. She managed to push herself onto all fours. She felt sick. The engine room was spinning around her. She grasped her rainbow hammock—the one she napped in from time to time—and used it to haul herself to a standing position.

Fear was like a knife in the belly. Stabbing, stabbing.

She couldn't do this. She could barely stay on her feet.

Come on, Kaylee, she told herself. *Your father would be ashamed of you if he could see you now. Fussing and fretting like an old biddy. Be strong.*

"Kaylee?"

Her father was right there, beside the accelerator core. His hands hung limply by his sides. The shotgun wound in his abdomen was large and foul.

"Why'd your friend shoot me?" he said. "I gave her no cause to do me harm."

"Pop..."

No. He could not be here. Not on *Serenity*. It was impossible. He had died not long after Kaylee signed on as Mal's new engineer.

Died from heart failure, not from a cartridge-load of buckshot.

"Kaylee," Aloysius Frye implored.

"No," Kaylee said. "You ain't real, Pop."

He staggered towards her, his arms out as though to embrace her. Blood poured from his wound, and inside his intestines coiled and glistened like huge fat worms.

Kaylee cringed and squinched her eyes tight shut.

He wasn't real, he wasn't real, he wasn't real...

When she opened them, her father was gone.

Kaylee fought to steady her breathing. The fog in her head was beginning to lift, at least somewhat. Her nausea had eased off a fraction.

Wake up and save Serenity.

If the ship was on a collision course, the easiest way of diverting her was going up to the bridge and inputting a new route. But the way Kaylee was feeling right now, she doubted she could manage the trip to the bridge. There was no guarantee she would reach it without passing out.

Powering down the engine wouldn't make any difference. Inertia would keep *Serenity* going at the exact same speed.

There was some staggeringly obvious solution to the problem, she was sure of it. She just needed a moment's calm to figure it out.

It came to her in a flash.

Of course!

Kaylee let go of the hammock and took a tentative, tottering step towards the engine.

All at once her head seemed to empty out, like water rushing down a drain. Everything grayed. She sank to her knees.

The engine was only a few feet away.
She could make it.
She had to.
She tried to stand.
Again, that sensation of emptying.
Again, she sank to her knees.
She wasn't going to make it.

54

The Serra-Reynoldses had been running uphill for almost half an hour.

Mal could feel himself starting to flag. Master DaSilva was a dead weight on his shoulder. The slim little tutor couldn't have been more than a hundred and twenty pounds soaking wet. To Mal, he felt like twice that now, and getting heavier by the second.

Ahead, Inara had picked up Samadhi and was carrying her clasped to her chest. Jackson, just behind his mother, was managing to keep pace, and in spite of everything Mal allowed himself a twinge of pride. The boy was terrified but uncomplaining. He was probably at the limits of his endurance, but he was determined not to be the one to let the family down.

They were following an old deer trail. The forest itself was too dense to run through easily. There were gnarly tree roots everywhere, ready to trip up the unwary, and low-hanging branches to duck under. The trail allowed for faster movement.

But it also made things simpler for the pursuing Reavers. They could be in no doubt which way their prey had gone.

Their utter confidence was apparent in the noises they were making. They bayed and whooped triumphantly to one another, sounding more like wolves than anything.

Every once in a while, Mal would steal a glance behind him. Sometimes he would glimpse a figure—a hulking, shaggy-haired creature armed with a bladed weapon such as an ax or a machete— and he would urge his tired legs to work that little bit harder.

All at once the family emerged above the tree line. Open ground lay before them, without cover, without anything that resembled a place of refuge, just a grassy slope strewn with rocks.

"Mal..." said Inara.

"Up to that ridge," Mal panted. "Gotta be something beyond— somewhere we can hole up."

Mal knew the countryside around here pretty well but he hadn't ventured this high up very often. He had a feeling there was a cave in the vicinity—one of the locals had told him about it once—but he couldn't rightly recollect if it lay at the top of the deer trail or on a different patch of mountainside altogether.

As they crested the ridge, he stumbled. His aching legs just wouldn't carry him a step further. He fell down, Master DaSilva spilling from his grasp.

"*Tī wŏ de pì gŭ!*" he exclaimed.

"Mommy, Daddy swore," said Samadhi.

"I know, honey," said Inara. "But I think, in the situation, it's allowed."

Mal wanted to get back up straight away, but Inara laid a hand on his shoulder.

"We need a break," she said. "We can't go on like this without resting."

"A minute," Mal stated. "No more."

Peering towards the trees, Jackson said, "Where are the bad men? I don't see 'em."

"They're there." Wiping sweat from his eyes, Mal scanned right and left. "You can't see them 'cause they're hiding and don't want to be seen."

"Can they see *us*?"

"You can count on it. They're figuring out the best way of headin' us off."

"What's that mean?"

"It means they're cunning and they're goin' to do whatever it takes to catch us."

"What happens when the bad men catch us?" Samadhi asked.

"They won't, dear," Inara said.

"But if they do?"

"It's going to be fine."

"Don't lie to her, Inara," Mal said.

"Oh, and you want I should tell her the truth?"

"She needs to be scared."

"She's plenty scared already. We all are."

"What *happens*?" Samadhi insisted.

"They kill us," Jackson said authoritatively. "That's what Reavers do. I read about it on the Cortex. They like killing people."

"I don't want to be killed."

"And you ain't gonna be, honey," Mal said. "Not if I can help it."

What he was thinking was that, if it came down to it, the Reavers would not kill his children. He himself would. Anything to spare them the abominations the Reavers would inflict on them.

Just then, Master DaSilva began to stir.

"My head," he groaned, blinking around him. "Did you—did you *hit* me, Mr. Reynolds?"

"May have. It was for your own good."

"Of all the—!"

"Think you can stand?" Mal said.

"I'm not sure. Maybe."

"Good. Up you get. Everyone? We've had our minute. We gotta move."

Mal himself was so fatigued, he could hardly go another step.

The ridge might be a good spot to make a stand against the Reavers. High ground and all. He doubted he'd be able to hold them off for long, however, just him and his Liberty Hammer.

And he had the sense that they were dividing their forces, one group to make a frontal approach from the tree line, another to come around at the family from the side, along the ridge itself. Reavers might not be what you'd consider human anymore, but neither were they brainless. They could ambush. They could strategize. Certainly splitting up was what Mal would do if he was them, and fighting them on two fronts was a battle he simply wouldn't win.

The family and Master DaSilva set off down the other side of the ridge, into a gully. The rocks underfoot grew more numerous, impeding their progress. The going got even more treacherous the further they descended, the rocks giving way to scree and loose shale. Everyone slithered and slipped, and Master DaSilva lost his footing and fell several times.

"This really is intolerable, Mr. Reynolds," he declared at one point. "I don't even think we're being chased any longer. I think our pursuers have given up."

"If you think that, then you ain't anywhere near as smart as you're cracked up to be," Mal replied. "Reavers don't give up, not until they've gotten what they're after."

After his sixth or seventh tumble, Master DaSilva simply stopped.

"I am not going an inch further," he said. "Bad enough you hit me. I could sue you for that. I shall certainly report you to the Sihnon Union for Private Tuition Professionals. Look at me. My jacket sleeve is torn. My pants are ruined. My shoes too. These are patent leather. I refuse to continue with this ridiculousness. I am turning back."

"Do that," Mal said.

"I shall."

"Mal," said Inara. "You can't be serious."

"He's holding us up," Mal said with a shrug. "He says he wants to turn back, I say let him."

"But—"

"He ain't my family, Inara. You and the kids, you're all I care about. DaSilva's welcome to go his own way. I don't advise it, but he's a grown man. It's his lookout."

"Quite," said DaSilva. He executed a smart about-turn and trudged upslope.

"Mal," Inara said. "Stop him."

"Nope. Kids? We keep going downhill. Got that?"

"Will Master DaSilva be okay?" Samadhi asked.

"He'll be fine," Inara said, with a guilty backward glance at the tutor. "I'm certain he will."

It wasn't five minutes later that they heard the screaming.

The hideous, pain-wracked screaming that echoed over the mountainside and lasted for a small eternity before it subsided into brief, gasping shouts. Pleas for mercy. Prayers to God. And finally, one last semi-demented howl before a blessed silence fell again.

"Was that Master…?" Jackson began, but Mal just grimly ushered him onwards.

A short while afterwards, they came to the cave.

Mal had been starting to think that they would never find it; that it might not even exist.

But there it was, burrowing into the side of the gully. Its mouth was roughly triangular, ten feet tall at its apex. Daylight did not penetrate far inside, only a few yards, but the cave clearly ran deeper than that.

"In there," Mal said to his family. He was feeling the first faint stirrings of hope. A dangerous luxury, hope, but there it was. Maybe, just maybe, they were going to survive this.

"Are you sure?" said Inara. "If this entrance is the only way in and out, we'll be trapping ourselves."

"It's a defensible position. Anyone comin' in after us will have to come in single file. Then I can pick 'em off one by one."

"Are there bears inside?" said Samadhi, squinting into the cave worriedly.

Mal would have taken an angry grizzly over a Reaver any day. "No, Samadhi. No bears."

"It's dark," said Jackson.

"That way the bad men won't see us. We're the ones hiding from them now. Come on, in you go."

Inara led the way, Jackson and Samadhi following. Mal entered last, having taken a final quick look around beforehand. No sign of the Reavers, but they must be close. He didn't think they would pass by the cavemouth and not investigate. He didn't think the family would get that lucky.

The interior of the cave smelled musty and dank. The ceiling quickly lowered as Mal ventured further in, until he was having to stoop so as not to bang his head. Then it rose again, and the tunnel broadened out somewhat.

"Inara, kids," he said, "no need to go too far. As long as we're out of immediate sight."

Their three dim forms halted ahead.

"Here?" Inara said.

"That'll do. Everyone, hunker down. Find a rock to hide behind, or a crevice to squeeze into, if you can."

"Okay, Daddy," said Samadhi. "What are you going to do?"

"I'm going to stay right here."

Mal was still within sight of the cavemouth but just past the narrowest part of the tunnel. A perfect pinch point.

He drew his gun and dropped to a crouch, facing the entrance.

"Now listen up, all of you," he said. "Especially you, kids. I may have to start shooting, and when I do, I want you to cover your ears. Got that? Jackson? Samadhi? Because it's gonna get very loud in this enclosed space and it'll hurt your hearing."

"Got it," said Samadhi.

"Yeah," said Jackson.

"And if you can shut your eyes, too, that would be a good thing."

Mal fetched out his box of spare ammo, laid it within easy reach, and then waited, his every nerve taut.

With all the loose rock outside, it would be hard for the Reavers to approach the cave soundlessly. By the same token, crazed and depraved as they were, they might not trouble with stealth and just come rushing in.

What if they had another RPG? They could just blast the ceiling of the cave and trap the family inside it forever.

But that wasn't the Reaver way. Up-close-and-personal killing, that was their way. They liked to see their victims writhe. Hear them scream. Savor their terror.

Mal's main concern was making every bullet count. If he missed or even only winged one of the Reavers, he probably wouldn't get the chance to make up for it. The savage would reach him and that would be the end of that. Each shot had to kill outright.

After several minutes, Inara sidled up behind him. "Where are they?" she whispered.

"Damned if I know," Mal said, still staring towards the cave entrance, "but I ain't movin' from this spot until every last one of them's dead."

"About Master DaSilva..."

"Now ain't the time to berate me about that. I did what I did 'cause I had to. I don't regret my decision none, and neither should you."

"No, I just wanted to tell you, it was the right thing. I hate myself for even thinking it, but if you hadn't left him, if you'd stopped to argue with him, we might not be alive now. He should have realized his only chance of safety lay with you. But Mal... If you can't hold off the Reavers... If they get to us..."

"You already know what I'm going to do in that eventuality, Inara. And if I'm in no fit state to, you're gonna have to take this gun and do it your own self. Just make sure you leave a bullet in the cylinder for you."

She looked at him with love, faith, and the utmost sorrow.

Then Samadhi let out a whimper.

"Daddy…" she said fearfully.

Mal spun around. It took his vision a moment to adjust to the gloom deeper in the cave. He could make out Samadhi and Jackson, both of them huddled down on the damp floor. And behind them…

Behind them were humanoid shapes.

With bladed handweapons.

And gloating grins.

And disfigured faces.

Mal felt a sudden clenching in the pit of his stomach, a stab of pure anguish.

Unbeknownst to the family, the Reavers had overtaken them.

They had got to the cave first and been lying in wait all along.

55

"**M**al!" River yelled as she charged into the cave.
    Mal pivoted around.

"I've got this," she said, drawing level with him.

"River?" he said, perplexed.

"River?" said Inara, in much the same manner.

As River darted past, she launched herself off the cave floor with one foot. Her other foot kicked off the wall. The move sent her bounding over the heads of Jackson and Samadhi, right into the Reavers' midst.

She was weaponless. The Reavers were not.

She was alone. They were several.

But it was close quarters, with little elbowroom. In order to swing ax, machete, or sword effectively, you needed space. The Reavers, clustered together like this, had negated their one main advantage.

River would make sure their oversight cost them.

A throat strike to the nearest of them crushed the man's larynx. The stimulants the Reavers were on might harden them against pain, but if you couldn't breathe, you couldn't breathe. The man—his face was a raw red ruin, lacking any skin whatsoever—went down choking and gasping.

Without pausing, River aimed a roundhouse kick at the next nearest Reaver. She registered that the woman's nose was missing and that a replacement nose, someone else's, had been stapled on in its stead. River's boot sole connected with the back of the woman's neck, shattering two of her cervical vertebrae. The Reaver fell stiffly, like a toppled tree.

A third Reaver jabbed his knife at River. She elbowed the blade aside, stepped closer to the man, and delivered a palm-heel strike to his sternum. Not only did bone shatter beneath her hand but the blunt-force trauma stopped his heart.

She snatched up his weapon. It was a kind of double-ended dagger whose curved blades formed a crescent. It looked crudely constructed but was well balanced and razor-sharp.

A Reaver lunged at her and River thrust the dagger upwards under his chin, through the roof of his mouth into his brain. She yanked the weapon out and, without even looking round, rammed it backwards, planting the other blade between the ribs of yet another Reaver.

The inarticulate snarls and growls the Reavers had been making gave way to uncomprehending grunts and even mutters of alarm. This girl—this tiny slip of a thing—was decimating their ranks. To them it seemed inconceivable.

Yet the remaining Reavers, four in all, were not going to back down. If anything, they became more dogged than ever in their determination to kill their foe.

River sliced. She slashed. Blood sprayed in arcs. One after another, Reavers staggered and jerked and fell.

In the end, a single Reaver remained.

And he had Jackson in his clutches.

The boy was too frightened even to scream. The Reaver, clad in ragged leather with matted hair hanging over his face, had an arm around Jackson's neck. In his other hand was a knife.

"Fllll…" he said, struggling to form coherent words. "Fllllaaa… Flllayyyy himmm."

His grin showed an array of additional teeth inset into his gums— other people's teeth.

River shook her head.

Then she moved, lightning-swift. Her dagger had cut through the meat of the Reaver's upper arm, severing all the major tendons and nerves, before the Reaver even realized. His knife slipped from suddenly flaccid fingers.

River rear-thrust the dagger hilt deep into his back.

The Reaver's dying gasp was a mix of agony and ecstasy.

She stood, panting, dripping with other people's blood. Jackson was beside her, trembling from head to toe. A little way off, Samadhi was slack-jawed with astonishment. Further off, Mal and Inara were too stunned to react.

"Mal," River said. "I'll make this quick. There is a thing in Jayne's bunk, beneath the floor. I tried to point it out to you but you must have not been able to find it. Some kind of machine but I don't know what it is. I call the noise it's emitting the siren. It's leaking through the case and it's making everybody on *Serenity* dream. Hallucinate, in fact. Including you. *Serenity* is in trouble. She's going to crash. I think—I hope—Kaylee can stop that happening. But you can help."

"What in the name of—?" Mal began, but she cut him off.

"You need to go to Jayne's bunk and break the machine. That should end the hallucinations. If you don't, Kaylee may not be able to shake off the siren's effects. If she doesn't turn the ship, we all die. Got that?"

"River, don't think I'm not happy to see you or thankful to you for saving us from those Reavers," Mal said, "but all I'm hearing now is *fēng le* talk. Machine? Siren? I don't even own *Serenity* no more. Sold her years ago. Been on Sihnon ever since."

"Jayne's bunk," River stressed. "The machine. Find it. Break it. Tell me you'll do that."

"I won't do what I can't do."

"You're going to have to, and I'm going to get you to *Serenity* so you can."

It had occurred to River that there was one surefire method of getting someone to wake up from their dream: visiting violence on them. Slapping Kaylee seemed to have worked. In Mal's case, however, given how deeply he was invested in his fantasy of marriage and fatherhood and domestic bliss, something stronger was called for.

When River's relatives had shot her, it had acted like an ejector seat, propelling her straight out of Simon's dream.

Death was the answer.

She flung the dagger.

56

"Whoa!"

In *Serenity*'s cargo bay, Mal abruptly awoke.

He was lying on a packing crate. His back ached. His head was throbbing. He was aware of his surroundings, but nothing made sense. A moment earlier he had been in a mountainside cave with Inara and their kids. River had just rescued them from a marauding band of Reavers. Then...

Then she had thrown a dagger at him.

Straight into him.

He had felt it enter his chest.

Felt it penetrate his heart.

Felt everything just *stop*.

Now this.

He tried to get up. Accomplished the feat on the third attempt.

He knew there was something he had to do. Knew it was urgent.

But he knew, too, that he should be with Inara, Jackson, and Samadhi on Sihnon.

Yet he was aboard *Serenity*. He was in the exact same spot he had been when he had sat down on this crate for a rest, shortly after liftoff from Canterbury.

How could both things be true at once?

Answer was, they couldn't. One or other of them was a falsehood.

He rapped the crate with a knuckle. It was solid. Real.

But the cave on Sihnon had likewise felt solid and real.

He pinched himself. Literally pinched himself.

The pain was real.

But so had been the panic, the dread, the desperation he had experienced when fleeing from the Reavers.

Jayne's bunk.

River had said something about Jayne's bunk. Something Mal had to do there.

Mal was a pragmatic man. He wasn't on Sihnon now. He was on his ship. He should deal with what was to hand.

Briefly he closed his eyes.

Once again, he was in the cave. There was Inara. There were Jackson and Samadhi. There were the Reavers' heaped bodies.

No River.

But his wife and children were looking at him eagerly, lovingly. Their terror was giving way to relief. They knew the crisis was past.

"PROXIMITY ALERT. PROXIMITY ALERT."

Mal's eyes snapped open. A recorded voice—female, emotionless, loud—was making an announcement over *Serenity*'s intercom system.

"PROXIMITY ALERT. PROXIMITY ALERT. EVASIVE MANEUVER REQUIRED."

Amber emergency lights started revolving inside their plastic bubbles.

Serenity *is in trouble*, River had said in the cave. *She's going to crash.*

It seemed she had been correct.

She had also told Mal that Kaylee was addressing the problem. But he needed to help.

Jayne's bunk.

Mal set off up the staircase towards the crew's sleeping quarters.

As he arrived on the catwalk, he heard a rasping, sinister snigger. A black figure flitted before him.

Reaver.

No. River had killed the Reavers. They had been back on Sihnon. There were none on *Serenity*.

Mal shook his head defiantly. He looked again. No Reaver in sight.

"PROXIMITY ALERT."

Cautious, he traversed the catwalk and entered the fore passage. At the far end, the door to the bridge was shut. The door to Jayne's bunk lay to his right, nearer.

You need to go to Jayne's bunk and break the machine, River had told him.

But wouldn't it be better if he went to the bridge first and steered *Serenity* out of danger?

Ahead, between him and the bridge, a pair of Reavers loomed into view. Mal recoiled instinctively, his hand going to his gun.

The Reavers trod towards him, exuding pure menace.

A noise behind Mal caught his attention.

Two more Reavers were stalking towards him from the catwalk.

There were no Reavers on *Serenity*.

Mal told himself this, even as he prepared to fight them.

57

"PROXIMITY ALERT. PROXIMITY ALERT. PROXIMITY ALERT."

The automated warning resounded through Kaylee's head. The phrase was exactly the same each time, delivered in a dispassionate monotone. Yet somehow, through sheer repetition, it began to sound frantic.

"PROXIMITY ALERT. PROXIMITY ALERT. EVASIVE MANEUVER REQUIRED."

She picked herself up off the floor. She didn't know how long she had until *Serenity* hit Luna Minor. There might not be enough time left for her idea to work.

Still, she had to try.

"Kaylee…"

"Simon?"

Simon was standing in the engine room doorway. He looked as awful as Kaylee felt.

"What's going on?" he said. "Are we crashing?"

"Not if I can help it. Simon, are you real?"

Strangely enough, he didn't seem surprised by the question. Kaylee could only assume that whatever she had just been through,

Simon had had a similar experience.

"I couldn't feel this bad and *not* be real," he said. "Are you?"

"Real? Yeah. Pretty sure."

"Oh God, Kaylee. I saw you... I saw..."

"Not now, Simon," she said. "Right now, you're going to just have to do as I tell you. It's a good thing you showed up. What I'm planning is tricky for one. It'll be a darn sight easier with two."

"Okay. What do you need?"

Time was precious, and it would have taken too long to explain. Instead, Kaylee simply pointed.

"See that lever over there on your left?"

Simon gestured vaguely.

"No, your other left. *That's* the one. You're gonna throw it. Not yet! When I tell you."

As Simon grasped the lever handle, Kaylee walked groggily over to the main interface console. She felt thick-headed, operating at about a tenth of capacity. Just putting one foot in front of the other took every ounce of concentration.

She was going to initiate a forced shutdown of the master piloting system. That would free *Serenity* from the autopilot for approximately five seconds before a failsafe kicked in and the autopilot reassumed control, as it was programmed to. During that brief interval the ship's energy matrix would be governable from right here in the engine room. Throwing the distribution lever would divert power away from one thruster, rerouting it to the other thruster. This would veer *Serenity* to one side.

Question was, would the ship change course soon enough, and sharply enough, to avoid plunging into Luna Minor?

Kaylee began logging into *Serenity*'s mainframe. Her fingers prodded the screen clumsily. She just wanted to sleep.

Her father was beside her, looking over her shoulder.

"Sure this is what you want to do, pumpkin?" he said. "Wouldn't you rather come home to New Virginia with me? We've dealt with Caleb Dahl. He won't be botherin' nobody no more."

Out of the corner of her eye Kaylee saw the shotgun wound in his belly.

She refocused her attention on the screen. She had accessed the mainframe, the ship's nervous system. Her fingers bounced over the screen as she keyed in the shutdown command.

"PROXIMITY ALERT. COLLISION IMMINENT IN SIXTY SECONDS. EVASIVE MANEUVER URGENTLY REQUIRED."

"Sixty seconds," said Aloysius Frye. "That ain't long at all."

"Please," Kaylee said. "Would you pipe down just for a moment?"

Shutdown ready to commence, the screen prompted. *Are you sure?*

"You bet your sweet ass I'm sure," Kaylee said, and hit Enter.

"Now," she said to Simon. "Throw the lever."

Simon's head was hanging, his stare vacant.

"Simon, I said throw the gorramn lever!" Kaylee yelled in a voice so strident, she scarcely recognized it as her own. "Do it now!"

He snapped to attention. He tightened his grip on the lever handle. He pulled.

Just in time.

Kaylee heard the shift in the tone from both of the actual thrusters. Through the soles of her feet she felt the output differential between the starboard one and the port one.

An instant later, the autopilot re-engaged. Kaylee knew there was a good possibility that her plan would fail. *Serenity* would register the power rerouting as an inappropriate action and would correct this apparent error by resuming their previous course.

Then...

"EVASIVE MANEUVER INITIATED," said the automated voice.

"Smart girl," Kaylee said softly. "I knew you'd get it."

"Did it work?" Simon asked.

"I think so."

"COLLISION IMMINENT IN FORTY-FIVE SECONDS."

"Then why are we still going to crash?"

"Because we're dangerously near the surface of Luna Minor," Kaylee said. "But she's trying. I know she is. *Serenity*'s trying hard as she can to get us out of this."

The ship's hull was groaning under the sudden, violent strain of the turn. A low vibration ran through her from bow to aft, increasing in intensity.

"Come on, come on," Kaylee murmured under her breath.

"COLLISION IMMINENT IN THIRTY SECONDS. TWENTY-FIVE SECONDS. TWENTY SECONDS."

The vibration deepened. Shipboard artificial gravity insulated those inside from sensations of pitching, yawing, and rolling, but nonetheless Kaylee had a clear impression of *Serenity* slewing sideways, to starboard. It was the spaceship equivalent of a handbrake turn. She pictured *Serenity*'s underside flaring above Luna Minor's surface. The ship laboring to bring herself about, away from the moon. Her nose gradually, gradually lifting, striving for the stars.

"FIFTEEN SECONDS. BRACING FOR POSSIBLE IMPACT IS RECOMMENDED."

Kaylee looked across at Simon. He looked at her.

Her father was gone—not that he had been there in the first place. It was just her and Simon in the engine room, and the ship reorienting herself, battling her own momentum.

Just Kaylee and Simon, their gazes locked, and *Serenity* valiantly endeavoring to save herself and all those on board.

58

"EVASIVE MANEUVER INITIATED. COLLISION IMMINENT IN FORTY-FIVE SECONDS."

No sooner did Mal hear this message than he understood that Kaylee had succeeded. He could feel *Serenity* shuddering. The ship was turning.

The Reavers closed in on him, fore and aft.

The door to Jayne's bunk lay just a couple of yards away. Mal dived for it. He plunged through. Clinging to the ladder, he slammed the door shut and pounded the switch to engage the lock.

As he shinned down to the floor, the Reavers began hammering on the door.

Mal crossed the room. Vera was still in the corner, like before.

"COLLISION IMMINENT IN THIRTY SECONDS."

It was getting harder and harder for him to recall River's instructions. He dimly remembered her saying that the thing he was looking for, the machine, was beneath the floor.

Was that true? Did Jayne have a secret hiding place under the deck plates?

Who was he kidding? This was Jayne. Of course he did.

Mal scanned the floor. Nothing looked out of the ordinary.

"COLLISION IMMINENT IN TWENTY-FIVE SECONDS."

Then his eye fell on one deck plate whose screws all showed signs of having been worked on more often than the others. Their cross-head drive slots had fresh, shiny scratches.

Mal searched around for a screwdriver. The Reavers kept hammering on the door.

"COLLISION IMMINENT IN TWENTY SECONDS."

Jayne's chest of drawers yielded a screwdriver. Mal set to work.

"COLLISION IMMINENT IN FIFTEEN SECONDS. PREPARATION FOR POSSIBLE IMPACT IS RECOMMENDED."

It sounded as though the Reavers were about to break in. Mal couldn't think about that. He couldn't think about the collision warning either.

"Ignore 'em," he said to himself, gritting his teeth. Every instinct he had was screaming at him to protect himself, his crew, his ship. "Ain't real. The Ghost Machine. River's 'siren.' *That's* real."

He worked fast.

The first screw came out. He started on the second.

"COLLISION IMMINENT IN TEN SECONDS. NINE. EIGHT. SEVEN."

The second screw was out.

"SIX. FIVE. FOUR."

The warning voice fell silent.

Mal couldn't help but hold his breath and count down the last three seconds anyway, in his head.

When nothing happened—no impact—he exhaled the breath and started on the third screw.

The door was giving way under the force of the Reavers' assault. Mal didn't have to look at it to know this. He could hear it creaking as it began to bend away from its frame.

The third screw was tricky. It didn't seem to want to come out. Mal's palms were slippery on the screwdriver handle. He wiped the sweat off on his pants and resumed his efforts.

The screw popped free.

Mal dug his fingertips beneath the deck plate. He levered up the edge and heaved the plate to one side, using the last remaining screw as a hinge to swivel it around.

In the crawlspace below sat the flightcase. The very same gorramn Blue Sun flightcase they had been supposed to transport for Badger. The one Mal thought Jayne had abandoned somewhere out in the badlands of Canterbury.

"Jayne, you *fèi fèi de pì yan*," he murmured.

He didn't know the code number for the flightcase, but he already owned a key that could open most locks.

He drew his Liberty Hammer, shielded his face against debris with his free hand, and shot the lock three times until its clasp sprang open.

Lifting the lid of the flightcase, he found a device nestled within.

The Ghost Machine.

It sat snugly cocooned in its purpose-cut foam insert. It was a matt-black cube, featureless apart from the Blue Sun logo embossed on top and a green operating light that glowed steadily. From it came a buzzing like a swarm of angry hornets.

Mal could not immediately see an on-off switch. He hoisted the Ghost Machine out of the flightcase. It vibrated in his hands.

The Reavers were nearly through the door.

There, on the side. A simple power switch. All he had to do was flick it.

He did.

The operating light continued to glow. The Ghost Machine continued to buzz.

He flicked the switch back and forth a couple more times. No dice.

"Of course it wouldn't be that easy," Mal sighed.

Some kind of glitch inside the machine. A short circuit, a bust contact, rendering the power switch irrelevant.

The bunk door broke loose. The Reavers were coming in.

Just as Mal's gun could open locks, it could also stop machinery. He emptied the rest of its cylinder into the Ghost Machine.

The final bullet did the job. The light winked out. The buzz was hushed.

Mal threw a glance over his shoulder. He fully expected to see Reavers piling into the room. At the same time, he knew he would not. The notion all at once seemed preposterous. More so when he looked at the door and saw that it was still in place. There were no Reavers on board. Never had been.

Mal sat back on his haunches, closing his eyes.

He caught a flash of a memory that was not a memory. Inara. Their children. Life on Sihnon. It was like a phantom of happiness haunting his brain. He tried to hold on to it. Cling to it. This impossible fantasy. Just a moment more.

It slipped through his fingers. Vanishing. Gone, leaving no trace except a faint, yearning ache.

He sat like that for several minutes, feeling wrung out and almost inexpressibly sad.

Then Wash's voice sounded over the intercom.

"Ahem. Everyone. This is your pilot speaking. It appears we… we've narrowly avoided front-ending ourselves against a moon." Wash was trying to sound upbeat, but on this occasion it wasn't coming naturally. "I, ah, I have reassumed full control. I'm not saying it was a close-run thing. All I'll say is, if spaceships wore underwear, *Serenity*'d be needing a clean pair of panties right now."

59

Mal had words with Jayne in the infirmary. They were not all of them very nice words. Some, indeed, were downright unpretty.

Zoë and Simon were present at the altercation, and for a time they just let Mal rant and rave. So did Jayne, although he put in the occasional protest when he could.

"I realize you're mighty peeved, Mal," he said, "but when we get down to it, it weren't my fault. I didn't turn the gorramn thing on. I'd've knowed if I had."

"You brought it onto my ship," Mal said.

"Well, wasn't that what we came to Canterbury to do?"

"Originally. But then I changed my mind."

"Even so, you said I was allowed to bring the flightcase aboard if I wanted to badly enough."

"That… That was just talk. I never for one moment thought you'd actually manage it."

"Obviously you underestimated me."

"Still doesn't change the fact that you sneaked the flightcase on board and stashed it in your bunk without my knowing."

Jayne's smile was smug. "You didn't want what was in it.

Why shouldn't someone else have it?"

"We nearly died, Jayne," Zoë felt moved to point out. "That device—that Ghost Machine, as Mal says it's called—it had us in its clutches and it ended up almost killing us."

"And I keep tellin' you, weren't my fault."

"You're sure you didn't turn it on?" Mal said.

"How the hell could I? I couldn't even open the ruttin' flightcase. And what would've been the point anyway, turning it on? I've no idea how that happened."

Mal mused for a moment, before deciding to come clean. "When I waved Badger, he did mention something…"

"Something…?" Simon prompted.

"About not dropping or jarring the flightcase."

"But didn't you do just that, sir?" said Zoë. "When you shot the float-sled it was on?"

"That is indeed true, Zoë. Thank you for pointing that out and saving me the trouble of saying it."

"And when it was dropped…"

"I guess somehow the mechanism was tripped. Badger said it was delicate. A spark jumped a gap in a circuit, most likely, and the Ghost Machine started up. It would've done its job much more quickly if it hadn't been in the flightcase. That was like putting mufflers on a horse's hooves to dampen the clip-clop."

"Hah!" Jayne snorted. "So it was *your* fault, Mal!"

Mal tipped his head to one side, doing all he could to hide his chagrin. "Let's agree to call it an unfortunate chain of events, and leave it at that."

"What you mean is I'm off the hook because you're letting yourself off the hook too."

"That's about the size of it."

Jayne deliberated. "Guess I can live with that."

"And speaking of 'off the hook,'" said Simon, "your vitals

are fine, Jayne. I don't need to keep you for observation anymore. You're free to go."

"Like I needed you to tell me that," Jayne muttered, sliding off the med couch. "I'm going to my bunk, to wave home. Anyone needs me—don't bother."

As Jayne left the room, Mal caught Zoë looking at him. There was something in her expression, an unfamiliar suspiciousness. It was almost as though she was wary of him. As though he had done something to earn her mistrust.

"Zoë? Anything you'd like to share?"

She glanced away, looked back. The suspiciousness was gone. Buried.

"Not a thing, sir."

"We all had those hallucinations, didn't we? The Ghost Machine makin' us imagine stuff."

"That's right."

"Care to talk about what yours was like?"

"Can't hardly remember," Zoë said.

"Simon?"

Simon shook his head. "Me either."

They were both telling the truth, Mal was sure. He himself could no longer recall the specifics of the imaginary life in which he had been embroiled by the Ghost Machine. But he had a strong sense of its overall shape. Outline not detail, like an object seen through frosted glass.

Zoë and Simon, Jayne too, had been lost in worlds of their own. Whatever had happened to them there, it was over, gone—but it lingered. Mal wondered if they were glad to be back to reality or if, like him, they still felt a vague pang of loss.

60

Mal was still asking himself that question later, as the crew gathered around the dining table for lunch. On their faces he saw fleeting shadows of confusion, as if they were still adjusting to things as they were rather than as they weren't.

He noticed that Simon was being more than customarily solicitous towards Kaylee. She, in turn, seemed in a melancholy mood, not the bright, talkative Kaylee everyone was used to.

Wash was snuggled up to Zoë, hugging her with one arm as though he would never let her go. Jayne, meanwhile, munched his food more contemplatively than was his habit—in the normal course of events, he was more a wolfer than a chewer. Mal asked him if there was any news from his mother and brother on Sycorax. All the big mercenary would say was that everything was fine, although there'd been no improvement in Matty's condition. After that, he clammed up altogether.

It was River who was acting no differently, and for some reason, to Mal, this seemed anomalous. Solemn, big-eyed, she shunted her food around her plate, making patterns out of it and occasionally eating. She kept directing looks at the other crewmembers, too, as if expecting them to ask her a question.

Nothing untypical about any of that. This was often how River behaved.

However, Mal could not shake the feeling that she was seeking acknowledgment for something.

And that she deserved it, as well, although he couldn't rightly think why.

He canvassed opinion from the others regarding what to do with the bullet-wrecked remains of the Ghost Machine. Zoë proposed tossing it out of the airlock. The move was enthusiastically seconded by Wash, and a show of hands made it unanimous.

"Glad we've all agreed on that," Mal said, "'cause it so happens I jettisoned the gorramn thing already. It's so much space trash now."

"Then why put it to the vote?" Simon asked.

"Gotta give the impression I care what the rest of you think," Mal replied with a grin.

After the meal was over and the dishes cleared away, Mal drew River aside for a private chat.

"River. Everything fine and dandy with you?"

"A-okay," she said unconvincingly.

"Only, you seem kinda glum."

She thought for a moment, then said, "Our revels now are ended. These our actors, as I foretold you, were all spirits, and are melted into air, into thin air. And like the baseless fabric of this vision, the cloud-capped towers, the gorgeous palaces, the solemn temples, the great globe itself, yea, all which it inherit, shall dissolve, and, like this insubstantial pageant faded, leave not a rack behind. We are such stuff as dreams are made on; and our little life is rounded with a sleep."

Mal did a double take. "That's a pretty-soundin' piece of speechifying. Poetry?"

"Shakespeare. *The Tempest*."

"Nice. And is there any particular cause to be quoting Shakespeare?"

"Not really. Just felt like it."

"All right, then."

Well, I tried, Mal thought and turned to go.

River plucked at his sleeve. "Mal?"

"Yeah?"

"The Ghost Machine."

"What about it?"

"At table, you told us Badger said it was 'a device for situational control.'"

"I did and he did."

"Do you think there are more of them out there? More Ghost Machines?"

"Can't say. It's likely. I could ask Badger, I guess, but I doubt I'd get a straight answer. Man's so crooked, he could swallow nails and spit out corkscrews."

"I saw someone do that once," River said. "But he was a stage conjuror. He also made doves out of fire, or fire out of doves, one or the other." She leaned in closer. "Blue Sun."

"Yeah," Mal said. "It's them fine folk that built the device."

"For the Alliance to use to manipulate people."

"In some way or other, yes."

"How?"

"Brainwash them, maybe," Mal said. "Tranquilize them. Seems the sort of thing the Alliance might do. Gotta keep the masses subjugated somehow, to prevent them from gettin' uppity. If you can't shoot 'em, sedate 'em."

River nodded darkly. "If ever we come across another of those machines, or anything like it, promise me we do all we can to stop it hurting people."

"Well, sure."

"Promise. Cross your heart."

Mal crossed his heart, and River skipped away, noticeably lighter-spirited for having had this conversation.

Mal was pleased with himself. He couldn't foresee a circumstance in which he would have to follow through on the pledge he had just made, but if River had taken comfort in what he had just said, so be it.

"We are such stuff as dreams are made on," he echoed under his breath, "and our little life is rounded with a sleep." He shrugged. "That Shakespeare fella sure had a way with words."

Serenity was flying.

Time to find another job.

ABOUT THE AUTHOR

James Lovegrove is the *New York Times* bestselling author of *The Age of Odin*. He was short-listed for the Arthur C. Clarke Award in 1998 and for the John W. Campbell Memorial Award in 2004, and also reviews fiction for the *Financial Times*. He is the author of *Firefly: Big Damn Hero* with Nancy Holder and *Firefly: The Magnificent Nine*, and several Sherlock Holmes novels for Titan Books. He lives in south-east England.

For more fantastic fiction, author events,
exclusive excerpts, competitions, limited editions and more

VISIT OUR WEBSITE
titanbooks.com

LIKE US ON FACEBOOK
facebook.com/titanbooks

FOLLOW US ON TWITTER AND INSTAGRAM
@TitanBooks

EMAIL US
readerfeedback@titanemail.com